CH00841765

Acknowledgements

My first shout out is and will always be to my family - both immediate and extended. You are the people who love me unconditionally and for that I am eternally grateful. To my beautiful husband Jim who lifts me up when I'm falling and helps me to soar amongst the clouds. Aaron, Josiah and Nathan I promise to try and stop being that annoying parent, but I can't guarantee it! Thanks for putting up with the ' in a minute' or 'give me a second' moments that have littered our conversations along the way to completing Forbidden Colours. Oh and let's not forget the naughty Spaniel Poppy who's walks have see-sawed between sporadic and fleeting to lengthily and thought provoking!

To friend and fellow author Chris Roberts for being the best editor a girl could have and for telling it as it is, I truly value your feedback and support. To James at GoOnWrite.com for another outstanding cover.

The support I have received from fellow writers and readers on this journey has been immense - thank you, thank you, thank you. Writing can be a lonely pursuit. I am greatly encouraged by the online communities on Twitter, Facebook and through my writers group Authors Helping Authors. Their words of encouragement and sheer helpfulness has been much needed and is gratefully received - You guys are amazing!

To all of the readers - I hope you enjoy Forbidden Colours as much as I've enjoyed writing it. I shall leave you with the question that started this whole process...... What If?

1

Present Day....

Katzuko Yates eyed her daughter thoughtfully. A sense of apprehension gripped her. Those years in Japan were long ago; she wondered if she could be clear with her explanation. Even though buried, her memories continued to breathe under the mountain of life she'd lived. Dare she even speak of them? Could she speak of them? Their place of residence had become an unmarked grave in her history. Her family had a right to know, after everything that had happened. His world was dark and full of shadows; where would she begin? For over 25 years she had told no one. Now she was being drawn back into his world. It was a time she wanted to forget. The tie that had been bound to her so tightly was about to be broken.

Staring from the window, she hoped to find the words she needed. The right words to explain, at least in part. Autumn was coming. The leaves on the trees were now in full transition. A kaleidoscope of seasonal colours danced outside the window. A procession of translucent red and orange flares, delicately framed, melted in and out of the landscape across Central Park. The last drops of sunlight polished the trees before becoming woven into a tapestry of cyclical splendour. Autumn was a special time. A nip in the air followed by a sharp intake of breath, that's how she had found those first few autumns in England. A long time had passed since then. The season would bring about change. She needed both right now. It had been Autumn when she had met him and it had been Autumn when she'd escaped. It was Autumn once again. Now it was time to explain.

One Year Earlier....

Midori Yates had graduated from Kings College London with a 2:1 in Biomedical Science. What had seemed an all-consuming three years was now over. She could finally get her life back - but back to what? She had absolutely no idea what to do now. Pretty soon she would have to leave her digs. Moving back home didn't really sing 'career woman'. If she didn't find a job quickly she'd be out of options. She had concentrated more on completing her dissertation than finding one. Sitting with a coffee in her hand, she scanned the web. She wasn't fussy, any job (well almost any job) would do. She uploaded, amended and hit send to any advertisement with the word 'graduate' in the title. Living in London was not cheap and she was running out of reserves fast. Three years at Uni and still no bloody job, she thought. The future was definitely not bright but may well end up being Orange, she scolded herself. At this rate I really will end up working in a phone shop. How could life already be this hard? She was 23 and felt as if she was carrying a basket of bricks towards the edge of a cliff, with no way back. She had stopped counting after application number fifteen. No point beating myself up, she thought. Her personal statement now shone brighter than silverware in Tiffany's, thanks to her university tutor. It resembled an entry for the Nobel Prize, minus the all-important medal and prize money. Two cups of coffee and an almond croissant later she was ready to embark on another soul destroying round of "pick me".

Weeks of silence followed. Of those courteous enough to respond, their rejection spiel gave no real insights into why she did not get the job. From what she could garn, it boiled down to probability. 'Due to large volume of applications' or 'overwhelming response'. No one said 'your application is rubbish', or 'you don't have the right skill set'. Maybe the bright orange phone shop back home in Somerset was as good as it was going to get.

She would give it until Friday. After Friday all bets were off and she would accept defeat. Midori listened to the rain hammering at the window. The continual beating of the large drops against the panes summed up her mood perfectly. She felt foolish, dejected and almost beaten. She had given little thought to her future. Her rose-tinted spectacles had stayed firmly in place over the previous three years. Optimism to the point of blindness, her mother called it. Her mother's observations stung - she knew she was right. She had been so focused on getting her degree, the job bit had got caught up in the washing and was now going round and round in circles, hidden in with the sheets. The analogy of the one odd sock that no one claims said it all. Each day as she waited for the post, a sense of anticipation rose within her. Her spirits lifted to the 'what ifs' and 'maybe todays.'

As she sat quietly staring at the computer, the familiar thud of the post landing softly but resolutely onto the door mat signalled its arrival. It was a sound she greeted cautiously. Flicking through the takeaway menus and double glazing leaflets, she spied two plain typed envelopes that spoke of rejection. Rejection letters had their own special air about them. Without a ripped envelope between them they managed to convey their contents. Maybe it was the uniformity of the typeface or the blasé air of 'open us or don't open us, we don't really care' that she subconsciously breathed in. If nothing else she was becoming adept at guessing the contents. She wondered if she would be able to do the same with luggage? Now there was a job that did exist! A large manila envelope caught her eye. She had almost placed it in the rejection pile but something about it differed from the rest. It was bright and sharp, and for manila that's a pretty difficult feat to achieve.

Dear Miss Yates,

Thank you for your application. We would like to invite you to attend an assessment centre on Thursday October 8th at 11am. Please bring with you 1 form of photo ID and your national insurance number. A map giving directions is enclosed. We look forward to meeting you on the 8th.

Yours Sincerely

M Day

HR Director

KLD Pharmaceuticals

She wasn't even sure for what or when she had applied. In fact she wasn't sure she had applied at all. Anyway, what did she care, she needed a job and she would do her absolute best to get one. The lease on the flat was due to end in three weeks. Right now preparing for her interview with KLD would get her undivided attention.

Midori didn't know too much about the workings of drug companies but judging by their offices they were doing well, despite the recession. Sitting in the corridor alongside five other hopefuls she felt small and inferior. Floor to ceiling glass coupled with ultra-white walls made her feel as if she had entered a space age waiting room. KLD's Buckinghamshire offices were sited on the Green Shoots business park. Green Shoots was the equivalent of Monaco in the business park world. You had to be a certain kind of wealthy to even rent space. To be able to afford state of the art office space was one thing, but KLD had a state of the art research facility tagged on to boot. Everything shouted out 'new' and 'au courant.'

The elevators had amused her the most. There were no buttons, only a symbol that, despite her best efforts, she struggled to understand. She stood confused for an age until she realised the symbol represented a listening ear. It was as simple as saying the floor number you wanted and then, as if by magic, you were transported to the correct level. She had to admit she was impressed. If the technology was cutting edge in the elevators what did that say about the serious stuff?

The interview had been tougher than she had anticipated. On reflection, she could have answered the questions set by the panel more fully but, overall she was happy. She was still not sure what the job was. It would have been downright rude and inappropriate to ask during the interview: no, she would cross that bridge as and when.

The assessment had consisted of three parts – an interview panel of three, who had nodded in the right places, a written test akin to an twister for the mind (an aptitude test by any other name), and a scientific paper to assess and summarise. Who turns up for an interview not knowing what to prepare? She was kicking herself. The more she saw of KLD the more she wanted the job – whatever it was! Not for the first time in her life, she was winging it. The stakes were higher than ever. Midori had searched through all of her applications the night before and drawn a blank. Not surprising really, usually she deleted applications after a month of not hearing back, too depressing to keep. A panel of three would now decide her fate. All that was left was to enjoy that elevator one more time. I may never get another chance, she thought.

'Ground floor', she said rather too loudly.

2

The last of her worldly goods had made their way into the boot of her dad's VW Golf. At least the rain had held off, that was one consolation. The journey down to Langport, Somerset would take about 4 hours. The number calling her mobile was coming up as unknown. She ignored it, probably PPI. It rang again. It was Maggie Day from KLD. They wanted to offer her the job of Medical Sales Representative for KLD Pharmaceuticals. She hung up. A beaming smile threatened to overtake her face. Her dad eyed her curiously.

'So?'

'So..... I have now joined the great British work force. I've been offered a job as medical sales representative', she said proudly.

'That's great news love. What's a medical sales representative when it's at home?'

'I really don't know dad, but it's a job'.

'So do you want me to unload your things then? I suppose you'll be staying in London?'

'No, that's the best bit dad. They want me to be based in Somerset, so it's perfect really'.

She had a job, a real job. She had not thought to ask what the job entailed, but judging by the type of company KLD were she would enjoy it regardless. The fact that she could be based in Somerset too was the icing on the cake. She had longed to move closer to her family. The good news was she wouldn't have to move back in with her parents (well not for long). She would be able to afford a place of her own soon. Life was finally moving on.

An initial training course of a month and numerous exams at KLD's headquarters had her head spinning. She had been tested and evaluated to within an inch of her life and she had loved every second of it. It was the start, she thought, the start of my career path. In some ways it was like university, only she was getting paid! She would do her best. Putting in anything less than 100% had never been an option. Mark and Katzuko Yates had nurtured that trait. Growing up in rural England had thrown up many challenges for her and her brother, but using circumstance to justify your decisions had always been a no-no. Her mum would give her 'the look' and that would be that. 'You are in charge of your own choices Midori, there will always be a choice no matter what'. Her mum was definitely the wise owl of the Yates clan.

A major Dutch pharmaceutical company, Klein Lowry Davies specialised in neurological therapies. For a company with a limited heritage of five years they had made impressive headway on the global stage. They had built a portfolio of products which were the envy of the healthcare industry. Its reclusive owners Mary Klein, Kaas Lowry and Dirk Davies had seemingly come from nowhere. Their astute business sense and entrepreneurial leadership had taken the company from national to global success almost overnight. They had a reputation for being ahead of the curve. They had invested heavily in research long before the company was formed. Now a strong pipeline of products kept the company in a strong financial position. KLD's portfolio included everything from anti emetic drugs (anti sickness) to triptans for migraine right through to more specialist niche drugs such as peptide nanoparticles for hard-to-treat brain infections. The strategic director had outlined the proposed trajectory for the company's growth and direction over the next three years. KLD was looking to further align its business to tackle the unmet need within brain diseases. More and more treatments for conditions such as multiple sclerosis and Alzheimer's were planned for the coming years. Midori stood in wonder. If pharmaceuticals could be considered sexy then this is what it looked like, she thought. Their approach to business seemed to mirror her ideas of what 21st century medicine should be. She felt she was one lucky lady.

Her training course was much like the interview, all-encompassing and exhilarating but at the same time as nerve-wracking as hell. Of the twenty or so candidates who had been successfully recruited, most had previous pharmaceutical industry experience. A nagging thread of doubt had pulled and begun to fray. She brushed it off, not wanting to entertain the thought that her perfect bubble may not be quite so perfect. She wanted a career, to make her mark. She could do that in any industry, but pharma was the one that had come through for her, she told herself. How important was it for her to like the pharma world? From what she had discerned KLD were different, they were game-changers. Her new colleagues told tales of past lives, where redundancy ruled. It was a numbers game, they told her. The stakes were high because of the costs involved in drug development. It appeared redundancy was an ever-present concern no matter who you worked for. All it took was for a drug to not perform well and savings would have to be made. Staff were the easiest resource to change quickly. Companies could hire and fire with ease. Market forces and shareholders held the keys. Very few employees complained because ex gratia pay-outs were generous.

'Never ever believe you are indispensable and never believe that anyone in this industry cares about you Midori'. Ellen had been made redundant four times in three years. 'That's why they pay well, it's the chance you take working in Pharma. If a drug doesn't get approved or accepted nationally you may as well kiss your job good bye', she said philosophically. Her outlook seemed a little jaded and cynical to Midori.

'Why doesn't the company get all the approvals they need up front and then launch a drug and employ staff? Surely that makes more sense? It's like buying a shop and paying for staff when you've got nothing yet to sell, who does that?'

'Yes, that would make sense if you were talking soap powder or ice cream, but companies invest millions in bringing their wonder drug to market, it has to work, there is no plan B. They have gone past the point of no return. Prior to the launch of a new drug there are safety trials, feasibility studies, clinical trials. It's taken years of development. They cannot afford to fail'. Ellen's words like filamentous achenes from dandelion clocks attached themselves to Midori and hung heavy. She repeated Ellen's words.

'No, you're right. I suppose they cannot afford to fail'.

Centoria was to be her focus. It was KLD's latest drug and had been licenced for the treatment of amnesia. Centoria was a nanoparticle that had been discovered by accident during trials looking at treatments for meningitis. In drug terms, Centoria was revolutionary. It treated both psychogenic and organic amnesia. Sat in the boardroom at KLD, Midori tried to absorb as much as she could. Cassandra, KLD's medic, explained: 'Psychogenic amnesia is thought to have a trigger; stress or trauma for instance. It is characterised by retrograde memory loss autobiographical in nature - such as loss of identity, who you are, knowledge of relationships, family history etc. It can last from hours to years. Psychogenic memory loss differs from organic memory loss in that there appears to be no brain structure involved or damaged during the period of 'loss'.

Organic amnesia on the other hand can be due to trauma to the brain, substance abuse or epilepsy. It is thought to result from direct damage to areas of the brain'.

OK, she was with her so far, two types of loss, one triggered by emotion of some sort, no structural involvement, the other due to trauma with structural involvement. She was just about to silently high five herself when Cassandra continued.

'The fact that Centoria works across both types of amnesia makes it unique, there is absolutely nothing that compares'. Midori raised her hand

'So how does it work, if the loss that's incurred has two completely different origins and causes?'

Facts were her thing. She loved the minutiae of detail, she liked explanation. If she could pull facts apart and then put them back together again mentally then everything made sense. No wonder she loved science so much. Oh and puzzles, she loved puzzles.

Cassandra stared at her for what seemed like an age. Maybe that's her thinking face, Midori reasoned.

'We are not... that's to say we...we do not know the exact mode of action, but, we do know that

RBap48 proteins within the hippocampus and its sub regions are activated, producing a proposed cascade that seems to restore functionality'. Cassandra looked up at the blank faces staring back at her.

'Are you saying you don't know how it works?' asked one of the other employees.

'Those of you who are experienced within drug development will know this is not uncommon. The mode of action of many drugs is only theorised and speculated. Most general anaesthetics' mode of action, for example, is unknown. We at KLD will continue our trials post marketing. It is an exciting time for all of us'. Her voice strained to sound reassuring. She didn't want questions, she just wants to deliver what needed to be said and then go back to her lab, thought Midori. Cassandra reminded her of some of her not so engaging university tutors who seemed to be stuck in the wrong jobs. Anaesthetics, now that was a surprise. Yep, she still had a lot to learn, she told herself.

After a bit of research, Midori understood. The fact that KLD did not understand how Centoria worked was not news. Many drug companies brought drugs to market without knowing the intricacies of how they worked.

After a short coffee break, Cassandra had continued. She presented positive trial upon positive trial, data set upon data set – it was indeed impressive. Forthcoming trials were to be in the field of Alzheimer's. If they proved positive it would be a complete game-changer for the company. It could change the face of medicine, thought Midori excitedly. These trials had not yet begun: it would be at least ten to fifteen years even if things went well before it could be brought to market. Cassandra had likened it to the launch of anti-cholesterol tablets in the late 1980s. This is why I'm here, she thought, forget what Ellen said: I can make a difference, and companies do care.

3

She had found a small new build apartment not far outside Langport. It was far enough away from mum and dad, but close enough if she needed them. Dad had already got to work putting up some shelves and mum was regularly delivering frozen dishes of loveliness. Somerset was her home and she had missed it. It was good to be back. The smell of wood smoke hung heavy in the air. Happy memories of crisp autumn days and bright woodland walks flooded in. She had got used to the stares that she and her brother Raiden would get as children as they ran through the woods upsetting the Sunday morning dog walkers. They would stand there on bright cold days, not being able to feel their fingers as their parents, speaking softly and with reverence, tried to describe the privilege of living in such a beautiful place. Their mother would describe how Somerset was a million miles away from her homeland of Japan. How Japan would always hold onto her soul but her heart now belonged in

England. Midori at the time had not really understood. But now she had a sense of what her mother had tried to convey.

Here was home. The light was powerful and magical. She had forgotten just how much it enhanced the beauty of the landscape, especially at this time of year. She had driven out to her favourite spot near Cheddar Gorge. Looking upwards, she felt as if the sky was within her grasp as the clouds, fragile and ethereal, drifted low above her head. Looking down was like receiving your favourite gift over and over again. The force majeure that was Cheddar gorge, a testament to the power of nature. She watched as the sun dipped in and out of the delicate clouds, changing the landscape below. Sketches of burnt orange light cast shadows across the limestone. Great hunks of rock, a backdrop for the dance of seasonal light, as it pirouetted across the sky. Seared gingers fused with golden ambers and vied for position amongst the weathered crags. She caught sight of the feral Soay sheep, like moving dots of cotton wool, on distant pinnacles. She felt at her most connected high up here. As she looked down upon the Somerset levels below, memories of home cooked puddings tickled her taste buds. Autumn meant homemade apple crumble with Mochi balls. Yes, apple crumble and Mochi balls definitely signalled autumn in the Yates household. Her parents had been the bedrock of fusion long before it had become a 'thing.' She did not know if she could ever move away from here again. It was part of her DNA. She wondered if Raiden had ever felt this way. Two years her senior, Raiden had always been her tower of strength. With him in her corner she could take on the world and stand a fair chance of winning.

She noticed the depth of colour change around her. The day had moved from fair and fine to dark and grey. Midori looked skywards, noticing how the clouds were rolling in fast overhead. The wind had picked up, the grey clouds blackened as she made her way back to the car. She would stop by mum and dad's on the way home and see if there was any crumble going spare.

On paper, her job seemed simple. She was to visit specialist neurologists in Somerset and discuss the benefits of Centoria. As a relatively new drug, clinicians may not yet have heard of it despite the positive trial data appearing in some leading journals. For the majority she would be their first point of contact.

She had never sold anything in her life. Why they thought she would be any good at this job she didn't know, but if passion played a part then she would be like a duck to water. Her manager was an experienced 'pro' with twenty years' pharma experience under his belt. Rick Clunie had been one of the three on the interview panel. His questions had been the easiest to answer and he had made her feel at ease. He had been supportive and encouraging from the start. She felt the most confident she had ever been.

She believed in Centoria. It had the power to change lives and that was something she could take pride in. The information prepared by KLD had been carefully crafted to show the drug at its best. She noted that only the best trials had been printed on the information sheets. They were displayed in a way that would draw your eye to the most appealing data set. She believed in what she was doing: it was the job of marketing to present the best case possible, she told herself. If this drug could have a positive impact on just one person's life then she would feel she was making a difference.

As first days go, hers was a baptism of fire. She had been told to 'spec' the consultant neurologists at Queens University Hospital in Somerset. 'Spec' was industry talk for speculative. She was to turn up at the hospital and see if any of the clinicians would see her or make future appointments.

Queens was a fine example of an old Victorian hospital with 21st century fittings. Its big draughty corridors and ill-fitting windows imparted a sense of times past. A time capsule for 18th century medicine. How anyone ever made a full recovery in somewhere so grim was a mystery, she thought. The wind had picked up and was whistling through the corridors, creating a most unearthly sound.

The hospital in some ways was as traditional as they came. That was until you hit the 1970s additional extension. Bouncy false floors coupled with awful pastel shades gave a sense that Mr Wolf would definitely be able to blow this house down. The old and the new wings had been metaphorically 'sticky-taped' together. The 70s were not really a time for great design or attention to detail; she was surprised the 'new' wing had lasted this long.

Queens was the neurological tertiary centre for the whole of the South West. It had made some recent high profile breakthroughs in Parkinson's and more recently Huntingdon's disease. Anyone who was anyone in the neuro field would bite your arm off to work at Queens, despite its quirky appearance. Its neurology department was made up of twenty four healthcare professionals, making it one of the largest in the country. It had eight full time neurologists, plus specialist nurses in the fields of epilepsy and Parkinson's. Queens took a holistic approach to the management and care of its patients. A plethora of physiotherapists, dieticians, acupuncturists and a whole host of dedicated nurses and care assistants were all part of the patient's journey. Its consultants were some of the most highly skilled in the world and had built their reputations on pioneering works they'd carried out. Whilst also dealing with the needs of the local population, Queens was renowned for successfully undertaking some of the more complex and unusual surgical procedures anywhere in the UK.

Midori strode confidently into the hospital in search of the neurology department secretaries. These were the gatekeepers for the consultants' diaries and time. Rick had advised her to try and see consultant neurologist Justin Rees-Hughes or Professor Franklin. Both may be interested in Centoria, he'd instructed. The secretaries' offices were buried deep in the basement of the new building. Pastel walls had given way to faded cream but the bouncy floor was still intact. It must make pushing a wheelchair fun, she thought. The words Department of Neurology Secretaries leapt boldly from the tan brown door. Midori gave a gentle knock and waited. Nothing. She knocked again, louder. A gruff female voice shouted.

'For God's sake come in'.

Alarm pricked her senses. This was not what she'd expected. A woman who she surmised must be a secretary gave her a filthy look. She half wondered if she had done something to upset or offend her. Impossible, I've just walked in.

'Hello my name is Midori Yates. I am a medical representative from KLD and wanted to see if either Dr Rees-Hughes or Professor Franklin would be available to see me please?' Midori had softened her voice and wore her expectant face.

'They don't see reps', snarled the overweight, underdressed woman who briefly peered up from her computer. She had looked her up and down and carried on typing. She could not have been more disinterested or unhelpful. All she had to do was be polite, Midori thought, wanting to scream straight back into the rude woman's face.

Why did this awful woman think it was OK to talk to someone like that? She had been polite and had even smiled at the toady-faced secretary. She took a deep breath. It was all she could do to not punch her.

'Would you be so kind as to tell me how they find out about new treatments that may benefit their patients please?' Midori could feel her face flushing a light shade of pink. She would kill toady-face with kindness - that would do it.

Toady-face did not even glance up from her computer this time.

'I don't know, but I know they won't see you'. No eye contact, nothing. Rude, rude, rude. The word rattled around Midori's head to the point of almost making it out of her mouth. No, this was not the day to lose it. Oh God, this was horrid and it was only day one, she reminded herself.

'Can I leave my card and this piece of infor-mation please?' said Midori, her voice taking on a firm but not rude tone. It was a 'you know what, I may have to take this shit from you but I dare you to be rude to me again' voice.

'Sure, I'll pop it in their tray', said toady-face, taking the information from her and leaving it on the side of her desk. Still no eye contact, no acknowledgement of Midori. She couldn't imagine how it could have gone any worse.

'Can I take one for Mr Campbell please?'

Midori turned to see a small, waif-like, older woman sitting at a desk behind the door. She could easily have missed her had she not spoken up.

'Mr Campbell likes hearing about new treatments. I'm Penny, Dr Campbell's secretary', she said smiling. Midori was stunned – someone was actually being nice to her.

'Yes, yes of course, here I'll leave you my card just in case they have any further questions. Thank you so much', said Midori, returning the smile. 'I had hoped to see one of them today but...'

'They all have theatre lists today. Mondays usually is not good', Penny offered. 'But I will make sure he gets the information. If he wants to know more then he will usually contact you direct'. Penny's smile was genuine and engaging.

'Thank you, I appreciate it'. Some of her faith in humanity had been restored. Nodding in toady-face's general direction she turned and left. By now her face was a deep shade of crimson. She had got so angry with that stupid woman that she felt as if her face was on fire. If she didn't know differently she'd be convinced steam was escaping through the top of her head. Penny had been nice though, she reasoned. She had been warned the secretaries and receptionists were like pit bulls. What she hadn't anticipated was the level of venom that had been directed at her. She had been made to feel as if all of the problems in the world were the result of Midori Yates. She contrasted that first response to the one received from Penny. Penny had treated her like a human being. How she worked with such a witch was beyond her.

Rudeness notwithstanding, it was depressing to once again realise that it was still only day one of her great job. The rest of her morning lent itself to more of the same. She walked from one department to another and was greeted with a stream of insolence. There appeared to be at least three toady-faces to every Penny. By 12.30 she was ready to hang up her boots. If I'm allowing myself to get riled so easily, then maybe this job isn't for me after all, she reflected. She needed a coffee and fast. The restaurant was on level 3, wherever that was. She navigated her way towards it deep in thought. She was only trying to do her job, a job that was starting to look harder and more depressing than she had initially thought. Why were there so many unhappy people out there whose sole purpose appeared to be dragging others into their despondency? Surely life's too short for such unpleasantness. Her mother would not have been impressed. She could hear her mother's accented tones ringing in her ears. 'There is never any excuse for rudeness, Midori, never'. She needed to model herself more on her mother, she thought wistfully. Mum would have death-stared her into an apology. No one messed with Katzuko Yates. Her mother was artful in using nonverbal cues to elicit the responses she wanted. Quite how she managed it Midori didn't know. She had seen her in action many times and had looked on in awe at how skilfully she had handled rudeness. Depressingly it was a skill she definitely had not passed down to Midori.

She ordered a flat white and found an empty table. It was almost lunchtime, but the vast restaurant seemed lifeless. She had developed a banging headache which now sat across her forehead. Her teeth were clenched tight. She wondered how long had she been doing that. Bloody hell, her day could not have gone any worse. She had not seen one person about Centoria. It's ironic; drugs companies invest hundreds of millions of pounds trying to find cures for all manner of things but clinicians have very limited ways of finding out about them, especially if they have bloody-minded minions, oh it is so infuriating. Midori popped two paracetamol onto her tongue and washed them down with her coffee. Picking up her phone, she called Rick.

'To be honest Rick I'm not sure I'm cut out for this. I've had to put up with so much stick from the secretaries and admin staff, I haven't even seen a consultant yet', she moaned.

Manager Rick Clunie was the best kind of boss. He was someone who had sat in Midori's shoes, albeit years before. He had worked his way up from sales rep to his position of senior business manager and had a well-rounded view of both sides of the business. Through hard work and determination he had made a steady climb into management. He was tall with red hair and freckles and Midori had instantly liked him. He was comfortable to be around. He didn't say much but what he did say was measured and insightful. He was the type of man who had been born serious. She wondered what it would take to make him smile. She tried to picture Rick smiling, which in turn brought a generous smile to her face.

Rick had seen the industry change and had been carried along with it. He was one of life's passengers. There had been a seismic shift in how the pharmaceutical industry was currently viewed. Its standing had changed. Doctors welcoming discussions with medical representatives about new products was the exception rather than the rule. The working environment of a medical rep had become pretty hostile. Some of this was due to the pompous view clinicians held of themselves. The rest could be lain firmly at the door of the industry itself. It had not always been the most honest or ethical. Past interactions had been dubious to say the least. No, the industry had not done itself any favours. But there were always two sides. The NHS was now on its knees through lack of funding and increased bureaucracy. Why did successive governments feel the need to mess with the system? OK it wasn't perfect, but it had worked well enough before becoming a political football. Now clinicians spent more time filling out paperwork than actual time with patients. They no longer had time for patients, let along to talk to pharmaceutical companies.

No, Rick thought, I would not want to be starting my career now. He was glad he had his holiday home in France. His retirement plan got a step closer each day. Most clinicians refused to see any representatives for fear of what colleagues and peers would think. They did not want to be seen to be influenced by pharmaceutical companies. Quite happy to take our money and get taken to congresses though eh? There was a value in having open dialogue and good levels of communication. Other industries managed it, why not ours? Rick was lucky, his relationships with leading clinicians had been formed back in the day. Professor Franklin was a trusted friend and ally, so what if he turned a blind eye every now and again? He played the game just like everyone else.

'The first few months are going to be hard, Midori, we spoke about this', said Rick, his voice calm and collected. 'All you can do is your best. You know it's not you that has the problem here, it's them. As long as you are professional and honest, you can stand tall with your head held high. I've every faith in you, just keep trying'. He tried to sound encouraging.

'OK but I just don't get why they won't see me. I've a brand new treatment that could really help patients suffering from amnesia, it's had a fantastic write-up in various respected journals, and

I'm not even going to get a chance to tell them about it. At least they could make an informed choice if they knew it even existed'. She sounded exasperated.

Rick chuckled; she had an enviable fire in her belly - that was for sure. He was glad he'd listened to Franklin and employed her. What Franklin had to do with the girl was none of his business. He'd paid him handsomely for employing her too.

'Midori - just keep going, the harder you work the luckier you'll get. You'll get there I promise'.

'Why are you laughing?' her tone a bit sharp.

'It's just that you are so passionate, I hear it in your voice. It reminds me of myself a few years back, that's all. Trust me Midori, I know you want to make a difference, and that will take you far, it means a lot. Call me later, I'm sure your day will get better, bye for now'. And with that he hung up.

Midori noticed the man on the next table had been staring at her for quite some time. Maybe she had been a bit too passionate or a bit too loud, or both. Maybe he had clocked that she was a pharma rep and was giving her 'the evils' as her brother would say. He was a funny looking man, handsome in a dishevelled sort of way. But it was his eyes that unsettled her. They held her gaze and bored down into her. A chill ran down her spine and an attack of goose-bumps signalled a warning. OK, time to stop trying to analyse the crazy man. You're in a hospital, for goodness' sake. She tore her eyes away and gathered her things. I have to accept its going to be hard. Rick has confidence in me so I need to have confidence in me too, she thought. She still had a few more departments left on her list to visit before finally throwing in the towel. She would keep trying.

Rejection gave way to despondency, as she schlepped through the various hospital departments. She received the same response from the neuro intensive care secretaries and the emergency department. She smiled, gave her business card and information about Centoria and left. She would have to suck it up. She just wasn't sure for how long she could keep smiling in the face of such mounting apathy.

As she headed down to car park B the wind was whipping up a storm. Leaves were flustering and clustering across her path. She pulled her coat closer to her body; a touch of frost was not far away, she reckoned. The oak trees had been forced to bid farewell to their honeyed leaves, laying out a golden carpet under foot. The change of seasons felt tangible and inevitable. Out with the old, onto the bonfire with the lot of it. She stood by her company car and smiled. She had been given a pillar box red Audi A3 company car. She had an expense account, a company iPhone and an iPad. These were the 'perks' that helped to make the job more bearable. Think of your salary, she told herself. She was being paid to do the job to the best of her ability. Sadly her performance today meant she should pay them. This is not what good looks like, she whispered. Yet she had given it her best shot and that was all she could do. They had employed her, they must believe in her. She was out doing her job and for now, that would have to do.

'Excuse me', said a lilting deep voice, in an accent she couldn't quite place.

Startled, Midori turned to see a tall, dark, very handsome indeed, 30-something man standing towards the back of her Audi A3. She could not take her eyes off him. She was aware she was staring but she was struggling to avert her gaze. An invisible magnet had glued her to the spot and all she could do was observe him. Her mouth was drifting further south with each passing moment.

'Sorry, I didn't mean to make you jump. Let me introduce myself - I'm Nick Campbell, consultant neurologist here... here... at Queens', he said, pointing to the hospital, as if trying to gain endorsement from the bricks and mortar beyond. He held out his hand. Midori carried on staring. It was all she could do to move her head slightly. The poor man had been holding out his hand for too long now, the moment for handshakes had passed. She had left him hanging. Oh God, I'm embarrassed and mute, what next? She was still staring; a slight tingle on her face signalled a rising blush. Nick, unperturbed by her apparent inability to communicate, held up a Centoria leaflet.

'My secretary gave me this leaflet'. He pointed to it, as if to confirm he was telling the truth. Still Midori didn't respond.

'And this business card – you are Midori Yates from KLD aren't you?'

He looked down at the business card, then back at her. Maybe he'd got it wrong; the girl was still staring at him blankly. He now doubted he had the right person. Penny had pointed her out very clearly as they had walked across the car park together. He stood expectantly, staring at Midori, her long jet black hair blowing fiercely in the wind. Penny had not told him how incredibly beautiful this girl was. Thankfully he'd started talking before his brain had registered just how stunning she was. Now he was completely tongue tied. The two of them stood gazing at one another for what seemed like an age.

She would have to say something, even if it was just to say her name, but before she could answer, he continued.

'It's just that Penny, that's my secretary...' he pointed at a distant figure heading for the main entrance. 'You had left this information for me this morning and ...' Why on earth was he talking so fast? One minute nothing, now three hundred words a second. This beautiful girl had disarmed him without saying a single word, he thought. Now, here he was, feeling a bit foolish - she may not even be the right girl! God, maybe Penny had got it wrong, maybe this wasn't her. Maybe she didn't speak English. Shit, he had just assumed. He continued slowly, talking loudly and in phonics.

'CEN–TOR-IA? YES? NO?'

Midori laughed nervously. The spell was broken; she had finally managed to disengage from his gorgeous eyes. The talking to her like a tourist thing had done it. It had been a touch of pure comic genius, she thought. Many things had happened to her whilst growing up in Somerset but being mistaken for a tourist was not one of them. Never before had she felt so embarrassed. She had reduced a rather handsome consultant to talking to her as if she were in kindergarten and she had not even opened her mouth. Thankfully Nick was laughing too, although his laugh was more anxious in nature.

'I'm so sorry, so sorry. I was... you see... never mind. I was miles away and well... anyway. Yes you do have the right person, yes, I am Midori Yates'. Her laughter now under control, she stretched out her hand and widened her smile. Please take my hand, she willed. His handshake was firm. A small tingle of excitement danced up her arm.

'You had me worried there for a minute. I only speak English and even that's a struggle'. His voice was light, and that lilt, where on earth was it from? He took her hand and shook it gently. It was surprisingly soft. His lengthily fingers had completed enveloped her hand. She realised she was now staring at his hand. Really Midori, get a grip, it's as though you've never seen a man before. The little annoying voice inside her head was still giving up its blindingly obvious advice, she thought.

'I'm sorry I didn't mean to make you feel uncomfortable, I really was miles away. So, CEN-TOR-IA', Midori attempted to copy his syllabic pronunciation and they both laughed comfortably.

'Well I'm just thankful you are the real Midori Yates'. Now it was his turn to stare. His lopsided smile gave him an endearing cheeky chappie quality she thought. Nick cleared his throat.

'Yes, Centoria is something I would like to know more about, I've got a spare hour before my outpatients clinic starts so I hoped I could catch you to have a chat? His eyes questioned, desperately looking for reassurance.

Midori was curious. Here was a really rather good-looking man, wanting to talk science with her. It was as though all her Christmases had come at once. He looks incredibly young for a consultant, she thought and where on earth is that accent from it's gorgeous...

'Of course, yes that would be great. I'd love to have a chat.... about Centoria'. Midori wanted to kick herself, why did she have to add that bit in, why? Why wasn't her mouth or her brain working properly? She was so stupid when it came to small talk, especially, it would seem, with Nick Campbell. Thankfully, either he hadn't noticed her embarrassment, or was very gentlemanly and had ignored it.

'Great, my office is in Block H, I have some rather disgusting coffee or some equally dire tea if you'd prefer?'

OK, so this is not exactly how I'd predicted my day would pan out, but I'll go with it, life can be full of surprises, she mused. She could feel the nervous tension rising in her stomach. If she didn't know better she'd have thought she'd swallowed some jumping beans, which now seemed to be congo-ing around her intestines. The opportunity to talk to a consultant, especially one with an interest in amnesia, was too tempting. The fact that he had found her in car park B had sparked her interest - that and his oh so handsome features. She tried to steer a few covert sideways glances in his direction. He must be at least 6ft 2; his tightly curled ebony hair was close cropped and luxuriant. His shoulders were broad, but not in a menacing way. He reminded her more of a rugby player than a weight lifter.

'Coffee sounds great, lead the way'. The tonality in her voice was unmistakably upbeat. Yes of course she would talk to him about Centoria, but it was Nick Campbell she wanted to get to know better. He had somehow quietly slipped under her skin and was aggravating her senses. Microscopic missiles of curiosity were firing off from the top of her head to the tips of her toes. She fell into step beside him as he led the way through the complex hallways and rat runs of the hospital. He was a large framed man, with a very large gait; at times Midori struggled to keep up. No need to go to the gym tonight, a day walking the wards with Nick Campbell was all she needed. She really did need to do more exercise, she told herself. Panting was not a good look.

Thankfully Nick did most of the talking. He was now an easy conversationalist. He had only been at Queens since January. He had met Professor Franklin, neurology clinical lead at a convention a few years back. Professor Franklin had recently moved from the Brain and Spine Institute in Paris to Queens in Taunton, Somerset. He had a remit to build a new specialist team to develop research into Alzheimer's. He'd managed to persuade Nick to move thousands of miles from Washington State USA to the UK, a place he had only ever read about in neurology journals.

'I'm originally from the Bahamas, but there is very little work there, especially if you want to do research. I did most of my studying and clinical practice in Washington but Professor Franklin's offer was too good to refuse', he explained. Midori panted slightly as they made their way up a sixth flight of stairs. Midori made a mental note to get booked back into a weekly Kendo class.

'Professor Franklin has just received permission from the ethics committee to start his own clinical trials into Alzheimer's. That's what really drew me here. It's a real passion for him. Sadly his wife died from early onset Alzheimer's a few years back. It's an interest of mine, something I did a bit of research on back in Washington'. He had stopped by a bank of elevators and turned to face her. She could so easily get lost in his eyes. They were the colour of sable and conveyed a depth that was rich and comforting. She deliberately bit the inside of her cheek. It was a technique she'd learnt when practicing Kendo. It would immediately bring her back to where she should be, not to where she wanted to be. As he cocked his head off to the side slightly, his half-smile told her he was waiting for her to respond.

'Sorry, did you say something?'

'Stairs or elevator?'

'Oh, er, stairs'. Goodness, she must have been away with those intoxicating eyes; she had not even heard him. He hadn't even broken a sweat and was still managing to walk and talk. Midori couldn't even stay on the same planet. Keep it real, Midori, keep it real.

'It's like a dream come true working with the Professor. He is one of only a handful of neurologists across the world who are looking at protein blocking, you know?' He was not really asking a question but she nodded knowingly just in case.

'It is hypothesised that protein blocking could be a way of slowing down or stopping the build-up of protein plaques in dementia patients. Current treatments are mainly focused on increasing levels of Cholinesterase not on protein blocking'.... Nick's enthusiasm was infectious. He had become animated and larger than life and was carrying Midori along with him. 'It's an absolute honour that he asked me to join his team, I really am very lucky you know.'

No one could beam more brightly than Nick Campbell right now; his passion is so overwhelmingly obvious she thought. 'Not much further', he said, holding the swing doors open. A further expanse of corridors appeared before them.

'I think I may need a Sat Nav to find my way out again', laughed Midori. She had given up trying to remember her way back after the three left turns followed by the two rights.

They were now in the old wing of the hospital and it showed. It had an air of age about it. The thick white brick walls had recently been painted and smelled vaguely fresh. It was late October and not full blown winter yet, but the overwhelming chill in the corridor made her shiver. 'I bet this place can be a bit creepy at night', she said.

'Yeah definitely, it used to be an old Victorian lunatic asylum. I'm sure one of the porters told me it's haunted', he said pressing forward through another set of heavy wooden doors. Midori made a mental note never to be in the hospital when it was dark. The dark made her feel uneasy at the best of times. Throw in a couple of Victorian ghosts as well and that was her recipe for hell. Randomly she thought of that TV show, now what was it called, Ghost Hunters. Raiden had made her watch it once when she was about fourteen. She had still been awake at 2am and had finally gone to sleep with the light on and her Bruno Mars album on continual repeat.

'Here we are'. Relief flooded in. Yep definitely need to up the exercise regime, she told herself.

A small brass sign saying Faculty of Advanced Neuroscience hanging on another set of double doors was the only indication they had reached their destination. Pushing open the doors revealed the end of a corridor flanked by three doors on each side with a fire exit highlighted at the end. Nick's office was last on the right, almost next to the fire escape.

'Come in, come in', he said, heading towards what seemed to be a desk. At least she thought it was a desk. It was hard to tell what might be buried under the mound of paper that seemed to cover it. The room was dimly lit and the only light emanated from the open door. A small square window shaded by a large oak tree outside did little in the way of adding any natural daylight. Mr Campbell flicked on the lamp on what she now clearly identified as the desk. Midori eyed the room. So this is what's it's like inside a neurologist's mind, she thought. You can tell a lot from how people are, how their minds worked, by looking at their desks. There were piles and piles of paper everywhere. Some looked like medical notes for patients whilst others looked like a combination of clinical papers and journals. There was a faint whiff of furniture polish, which was reassuring. Not bad enough to call in the hazmat team just yet, she thought. Despite the chaos, the room was homely. There was something comforting about it. What this room said about Nick Campbell she wasn't sure, but she had been pleased to note the absence of any 'family' type memorabilia. A framed photo of a group of smiling med students and a cork pin board with a variety of postcards of the Bahamas mixed in with pizza and Chinese takeaway menus was as 'family' as it seemed to get. Oh yes, Mr Nick Campbell definitely had her full attention now.

'I have to say Mr Campbell, your office is not quite what I was expecting', said Midori, eyeing the Professor type cuddly owl perched rather precariously on the edge of the desk.

'Please call me Nick. I know it's a bit of a mess, sorry, just so much to do', he said, climbing over two rather large storage boxes. Nick cleared a space on the desk and leant against it, the owl wobbled rather comically. He gestured for Midori to take the black swivel office chair directly opposite. His brow furrowed, making him look incredibly serious. She regarded his features once again. Small facial changes had cleverly set the tone. She was sure he was not even aware of it. His face really was incredibly expressive.

'Right, first things first. Coffee - instant only I'm afraid? I have yet to find the box which contains my trusted coffee machine. I brought it with me from the States, that's how attached we are!' It was Midori's turn to look serious. Nick laughed. 'I am joking, not about bringing it with me, but about being attached to it.'

'Oh, I'm glad you're not attached'. Did I really just say that? Did I?

'To the coffee machine...not...' her voice trailed away. I'll just keep digging shall I; I'll dig my way right out of the door. Midori could feel her face turning from amber to red. She had never been one for blushing, but today, well today she was going for an Olympic gold! Nick was either too gracious to make a thing of it or too embarrassed by her - which one she hadn't yet worked out.

'If there is one thing I cannot stand it's instant coffee, so apologies because that is all I seem to be able to offer at the moment', he said.

'That's OK, instant will be fine', answered Midori, also now perched a bit like the cuddly owl rather uncomfortably on the edge on the chair. Thankfully she hadn't started to wobble, not yet anyway. One false move and I'll be on the floor, she thought. Quite why she felt the need to perch she wasn't sure, the chair at first glance had not appeared that stable - perhaps that was it.

In the corner of the room on top of the grey steel filing cabinet sat the kettle. It was almost as if Nick had read her thoughts.

'I fill it up first thing when I get in around 8, then I only need to refill it at about 4pm, there's a water fountain just down the corridor, I use that...' he offered by way of an explanation. The kettle grumbled as if awoken from a deep sleep. 'I pinch these little milk sachets from the canteen', he said, holding up little round milk pods, the kind you get in hotels. He looked very pleased with himself. 'My naughty little secret'. He winked at her and laughed.

'Now it's your secret too' he jested.

Midori was beside herself. Not only had he winked but she surely had not misread his flirting with her? Had she? Nick continued putting a spoon of instant into each cup.

'Once I have things straightened up a bit I'm going to invest in a mini fridge... ah the joys of working in the NHS'.

'How do you ever find anything?'

'Organised chaos', he said. 'That and magic Penny, I don't know how things would be if she didn't keep me slightly organised'. His voice elevated over the whirr of the kettle. Reaching a crescendo of sound akin to the take-off of a 747, the kettle clicked off.

She lifted the coffee towards her nose and inhaled deeply. He was right about the coffee, it was awful. A consultant's salary was not too shabby yet here she was drinking the worst coffee she had had in a long time. She loved her coffee; she didn't really know anything about it but she knew what she liked and this most certainly was not it. With her first pay cheque she had indulged herself and invested in a beautiful cafetiere from Whitards of Chelsea. As painful as it was she now felt obliged to cautiously sip the foul tasting liquid that was masquerading as coffee. Settling back onto his precarious perch Nick smiled. Did he have any idea how bad it was? She noted he had not touched his yet.

'So, tell me about Centoria, I've read the latest paper in the New England Medical Journal and it sounds very interesting. I can think of a patient who may benefit from trying it, but I really need to know more'. He was staring directly into her eyes. Those eyes, so bright and open, he was obviously very keen. Her heart swelled. See, there are people out there who want to help patients, she thought. OK it was time to put into practice what she had learnt.

'Centoria is a compound derived from the stamen of the acacia flavescens tree, more commonly known as the yellow wattle tree. It's found mainly in Eastern Australia'.

Taking another sip of the foul brew, she swallowed hard and continued.

'Already known for its psychoactive properties, trials of Centoria were initially focused towards levels of brain activity within meningitis. However, it soon became apparent that Centoria was up regulating the RBap48 proteins within the hippocampus and its sub regions'.

She eyed him cautiously. He appeared attentive and completely focused.

'That's when the trial focus was switched - it was hypothesised that an up regulation of RBap-48 may enhance memory loss'. Nick was nodding thoughtfully. 'The amazing thing about Centoria is the way it looks after and expands areas of the brain such as the hippocampus. It appears to increase its size. New neural pathways are formed, which seem to have a transformative effect. Before and after CT scans confirm the increase in size and an increase in neural pathway development of patients treated with Centoria, compared to those treated with other drugs'.

Nick Campbell appeared transfixed; it was as if she had just told him the secret of the universe. She felt good. Speaking clinically to a consultant who really was interested, and who wanted to have a good conversation, had brightened her day in more ways than one. Maybe this job wasn't so bad after all.

'Wow that is very impressive; Prof Franklin and I have been doing some theoretical studies ourselves looking into RBap-48 in relation to Alzheimer's disease. So by up regulating RBap-48 I assume it restores the memories contained within the hippocampus, is that what you're saying? Tell me Midori, how is the drug delivered?' he questioned.

'It is all hypothetical at this stage, Mr Campbell. We are not really sure but it does seem to be the down to the RBap-48 protein. It appears to restore the patient's memories to before the amnesial event. I think of it like restoring the factory settings on your phone. Initially a loading dose via IV is given with subsequent doses via oral capsules. The course of treatment ranges from 2 weeks to 2 months dependent on response. Nanotechnology is used to stabilise the active ingredient within polymer capsules using patented solid lipid nanotechnology. Trials have shown 3 times more Centoria gets delivered to the brain via the polymer nano capsules than traditional methods'.

She smiled; she had delivered her pitch perfectly, exactly as she'd been taught. The training department would be proud.

'Centoria's licence is for the treatment of psychogenic and organic amnesia in patients twelve years and over', she added.

'I have to say I've looked at the evidence and it's pretty remarkable. To even be able to run phase III trials and include patients that fall within the psychogenic and organic sides of the condition itself is a major achievement', he gushed. 'And please, call me Nick', he insisted, beaming.

His lilting accent was having a hypnotic effect on her. She imagined herself on a boat in the Caribbean, the gentle breeze swaying. She could almost feel her hands gliding across the water.

'My patients are at the heart of everything I do Midori', he said, his eyes finding hers. OK she was back in the room.

'They are people for whom the world did not exist before amnesia; it's a scary place for them. Amnesia doesn't just affect them, it affects everyone and everything around them. I try to imagine how it must be for the relatives, for the partners of those affected'. He closed his eyes. His voice now low, he continued.

'Imagine, you are married for say twenty years', his eyes opened and stared into hers. Midori sat forward in her chair, she was completely mesmerised. As if mirroring her, Nick too leant forward, his voice soft and honeyed.

'You shared your first kiss, your wedding day, the birth of your children'. He let out a gentle sigh. His voice not much more than a whisper. 'Now imagine staring into those eyes, the same eyes you have stared into for over 20 years, but this time they don't have a clue who you are'. A shudder eased its way along Midori's back. Dr Campbell eased back into his chair and was now looking at her intently. His stare did not make her feel uncomfortable, in fact quite the opposite. She felt safe, secure. God forbid she would ever need a neurologist, but if she did she knew in that moment that Mr Nick Campbell would be the one. He was one of the good guys, who cared. He would fight for his patients no matter what.

'So if all the hype about Centoria is to be believed', he said, a smile forming across his face, 'well then, imagine the transformative effect on all of those lives'. Midori nodded.

His eyes were sparkling, Midori had been given a glimpse into the man that was Mr Nick Campbell and she was not disappointed.

'I understand', she said softly.

'Any side effects of note, any interactions I should be aware of?'

His words managed to snap her out of her dreamlike state, God I hope I didn't look too stupid, she thought. She snuck a sideways glance at Nick; thankfully his eyes were firmly fixed on the clinical paper she had given him. He appeared oblivious to her brief trip to the Caribbean and back.

'Some patients report a change in taste, others a heightened degree of awareness but none of the results are statistically significant. With regards to drug interactions there is some evidence to suggest that tetracyclines should be avoided as patients who have been concomitantly treated with Centoria and tetracyclines have reported cases of blurred vision. However this is thought to be the effect of the tetracycline not Centoria'. Her training had served her well, she thought.

She had put a lot of effort into understanding Centoria and its benefits for patients and now she really got it.

A quick drill on the door made both of them jump. Professor Franklin swept into the room; he had not waited for an invitation. Midori looked up in surprise. It was the man who had been staring at her in the canteen.

'Ah there you are Campbell; Penny said I might find you here'.

His sentence was clipped and direct. Here was a man you really did not want to be on the wrong side of, she thought. Some of her university lecturers had been cast from the same mould. Yep, none of them would suffer fools gladly, that's for sure. He would have intimidated her even if he had not swept into the room so vigorously. There was something Sergeant Major-esque about him. No, definitely want to keep on the right side of him, she figured.

'Ah where are my manners? Professor Franklin, please let me introduce Midori Yates, from KLD. She has been telling me all about Centoria'. Midori stood, or rather jumped to attention, thrusting her hand forward. Thankfully she had managed to digest most of the contents of the coal black liquid, otherwise it would have shot through the air and exploded all over the professor. Professor Franklin stood motionless and stared. He had only just registered that Nick was not alone. She felt on display. She was being inspected. The hairs on her arms and the back of her neck were stick straight and her adrenaline was ramping up. But why?

Not taking his eyes off her, he extended his hand as if in slow motion. His expression was anything but friendly. He had made her feel small and insignificant. He said nothing. His handshake was solid and made her want to run and hide under the desk. Midori felt fear. Maybe it was his eyes that seemed to be burrowing into her or perhaps the gravitas with which he moved. Whatever it was she didn't like it. Nick, however seemed oblivious to the strangeness that had descended on the room. Franklin had not moved from the doorway and was blocking what limited light there was.

'As Centoria is a new drug, is there a chance to try it before I prescribe it?' Nick was continuing as if nothing had changed. He seemed not to have registered the seismic shift in atmosphere or drop in temperature. She however felt positively frostbitten. She mustered all of the strength she could find to continue.

'As Centoria is new to market we can offer samples for named patients but these require a strict protocol to be followed due to its black triangle status', she offered.

Centoria was still black triangle - which meant higher pharmacovigilance and a greater degree of scrutiny from the authorities.

'Well as I said earlier I can immediately think of one young man who would benefit from Centoria. We have tried everything else but nothing seems to be working. I would like to give Centoria a try with the Phillips boy Hugh, what do you think?'

Nick looked towards Professor Franklin. Whilst his expression had softened, there was definitely something not right about him she thought.

'I think that would be a wise move, Dr Campbell, a very wise move'.

Was that glare directed at her? Yes she was sure he was glaring. I need to get out of here as quickly as possible. As if reading her thoughts Professor Franklin turned and opened the door.

'Come and find me when you are finished Campbell, there are a few things I need to discuss'. As quickly as he had entered, he was gone.

Midori breathed a sigh of relief. Why had he made her feel so awkward?

'Don't mind him Midori, he's an acquired taste'.

She looked down towards her feet - was she really that easy to read? Whatever she thought this may have been, it really wasn't, she told herself. 'This' was a professional meeting, nothing more. She bit the inside of her cheek once more.

'I'll send an email back to the office - you should receive the sample pack with a complete summary of product characteristics within a few days. I'll also leave you with all of the trial data I have', she said, pulling out more clinical papers from her bag. 'Thank you so much for your time Dr Campbell... I mean Nick, I really do appreciate it'.

She extended her hand. It was time to leave. For a moment she had thought maybe, just maybe, but no... he was just being friendly.

She left his office with an array of mixed emotions. Not only had she had probably the best conversation about her drug that was possible, she had also developed a crush on the nicest consultant in the entire country. Whilst he had been seducing her with his dulcet tones, she had become aware of two things. He did not appear to be married, well, he was not wearing a ring, and secondly she had seen the way he had looked at her, as if he too had sensed an attraction. But had he or was that just her over-active imagination? He had been attentive, funny, even cracking a few nervous jokes that hadn't been too painful. He had opened doors for her, listened with real intent to what she was saying, and he had held her gaze for perhaps a second too long. She had felt her face flush, as he had caught her off guard staring at him. But, and it was a big but, maybe that was who he was. Maybe Nick Campbell really was that nice to EVERYONE. Then there was the unease she had felt around Professor Franklin. His spikey thorns were filled with venom, of that she had no doubt. But, and again it was another big but, she had no evidence whatsoever - none. Franklin had made her feel scared, but why? Nick had picked up on her unease but didn't seem to mirror it. God, thinking of Nick was making her butterflies do somersaults. How quickly her day had changed! The good news was - it wasn't dull. Maybe she would like this job after all.

Over the coming weeks Midori found a myriad of reasons to go back into the neurology department of QUCH (Queens University College Hospital).She had brought lunch for the junior doctors, spoken with the specialist nurses, and with the help of Dr Nick Campbell she had even managed to attend a meeting with the bristly Prof Franklin, which had been more insightful than she could have imagined. Franklin, it turned out, had been involved in the phase III clinical trials for Centoria. Strangely no one at her office had bothered to mention that fact to her or indeed to Nick Campbell either. Perhaps that's why he had been so stand-offish when she had initially met him?

The neurology department at QUCH were a strange, eclectic bunch. They reminded her of a classic spaghetti western. The good, the bad and the ugly may be a bit harsh, perhaps they were more Blazing Saddles. The department had its own superhero (Nick Campbell), a classic villain (Prof Franklin) and a band of flamboyant outlaws (the other consultants). She herself could play the love interest of Mr Campbell, no trouble. She loved westerns and had watched pretty much all of them at least twice. It had been a passion that her dad had been instrumental in fostering. Having been popular in Japan, Westerns were something of a family tradition, especially at Christmas. Instead of the Christmas day

TV film, they had always watched a spaghetti western. Every year her dad would receive another to add to his collection and every year he would act surprised. She had been the only kid in class 3 to have arrived dressed up as a cowboy for world book day. Everyone thought she was Jess from Toy Story and had been surprised to learn she was in fact Ramon Rojo, the villain from A Fistful of Dollars. Her teachers had been impressed, if a little disturbed, to discover she knew so much about spaghetti westerns at the tender age of eight. It sadly handed her classmates another reason to make fun of her.

The realisation that somehow her family were different had begun to register and her desperate desire to fit in started to take root. Luckily her scrapes and scraps had not ended in a shootout! Yes, the Neurology department at QUCH would make a great cast for a spaghetti western. Henceforth she would secretly call them The Good, The Bad & the Ugly. It would give her something to smile about each time she visited the department. Nick was indisputably the rising star of the department. She also found him the most endearing, but maybe she was biased.

Nick, true to his word, had lined up two patients to try Centoria; a 28 year old female, suffering from amnesia after a road traffic accident and a 44 year old male, whose wife had died suddenly whilst on holiday. Initially he had been in shock, but now two months in he still didn't remember anything. Nick had been fully briefed by Midori and her medical colleagues as to the dose titration and possible side effects to expect.

Three weeks into their treatment Midori received a phone call from Penny asking her to pop in to see Mr Campbell. Her crush on the dishy doctor was most definitely alive and kicking. Her love life was frustratingly non-existent; it had always been Raiden who was good at the romantic stuff, not her. She did not understand the game so how on earth could she play? Her self-doubts and under confidence had shaped her perception of who she was. She hadn't earned the right to sit at the table with the great and the good, how could she, just look at her, she didn't fit in. Her hair was way too straight and her skin was too pale. Her frame had a bit of shape to it, but not enough to make any man turn his head, she reflected. Her eyes, oh god, her eyes were her worst feature. They weren't quite Asian and they weren't western. They were the things she hated most about her appearance. Pits of green pond water, she hated them. No wonder everyone always seemed to stare at her.

Growing up in Langport, Somerset, she had been part of the only 'blended' family in the area. With a Japanese mother and English father she had become accustomed to stares and whispers. Children were good at doing cruel and they had found her weaknesses. She had been called 'ugly bug' and 'alien' on account of her unusual green eyes. As she hit her teenage years her body extended, making her arms and legs gangly. In a desperate attempt to fit in she would bring one leg forward and bend at the knee, trying to appear shorter than she was. She would round her shoulders and look down. Unfortunately it did not have the desired effect and caused more name calling, stripping away her confidence further as with acetone hitting nail polish.

Her brother was her champion. He had always defended her, deflecting the harsh tongues of 7-10 year olds. They made fun of her Bento box lunches that mum insisted she take. They pulled her long black hair so much that after one particularly brutal attack Raiden suggested she get her own back and hide drawing pins within her thick braids. Tracie Evans the gang leader never tried it again, a series of puncture wounds on the palms of her hands made sure of that.

By stark contrast Raiden's experience was altogether different. No one dared to cross Raiden Yates; he was the coolest kid who attended St Joseph's High School. He cut a fine figure even as a teenager. His short, erect raven hair carried natural electricity. No need for the trappings of hair gel or any other type of shizzle for him. His frame was slender but not weedy. He carried enough muscle on his pecs and biceps to make him swoon worthy without being jar-heady. His eyes were, she thought, his best feature – black diamonds against a backdrop of pale white sand. They shone and twinkled as if they too were electrically charged. The affect he had on her friends had now become predictable. She could calculate how long it would take for the first stutter or blush to occur once he had entered a room – usually it was less than sixty seconds. She on the other hand could enter a room and no one would notice, she thought. Any friends she had were as a result of her brother. She was under no illusion - it was not her they were trying to get to know.

Nick Campbell had a similar effect on her, she mused. She totally empathised with her friends Sarah and Holly who found it almost impossible to hold a sensible conversation if Rai were any-where near them. Nick probably has woman fall-ing at his feet, no way would he be interested in plain ol' Langport Dori she thought, as she cir-cled the hospital car park for the third time.

By now she could navigate her way around the crazy corridors of QUCH rather well. As she ap-proached his office she could hear the dulcet tones of his voice. She gently knocked at the open door and slowly peered in. Nick sat dictat-ing letters. He turned and smiled, beckoning her in as he continued with his dictation.

She looked around. Things had improved dramatically since the first time she had been here, although there was still nowhere immedi-ately visible to sit. She hovered awkwardly, des-perate to find things to focus on whilst he fin-ished. The room was still as dark as ever but it appeared fresher, more vibrant: she thought the walls may have had a lick of paint. A very new-looking coffee machine sat pride of place atop the grey filing cabinet, half-filled and smelling inviting. Two posters now adorned the walls. The first poster featured a beautiful tropical beach, white sand and blue sky. She wondered if this was somewhere Nick knew. If she had grown up in the Bahamas she most certainly wouldn't think Somerset would be the go to place. It surely must be a disappointment, she thought. The second was much more telling: it was a bright bold photograph of Andy Warhol, featuring one of his famous quotes - 'the world fascinates me' leaped out in big letters. She understood why he had chosen that print. His whole demeanour sang of learning. He appeared passionate and genuine in everything. A lifelong learner, she thought they were called.

She was anything but. Her school days had left a sour taste in her mouth. University had been different though, that she had enjoyed. Her family had been so proud when she secured her university place and even prouder when she had got her job. She had watched as their faces lit up with delight. Her mum, usually quiet and reserved, had started clapping excitedly, whilst her dad had enveloped her with a big bear hug. Raiden had been equally delighted. She loved her family and had never felt the need to venture too far afield from them. They were her security, the love of her life. She loved making them proud. She knew she was very lucky - not all families were this harmonious.

'I was hoping I'd see you soon', Nick said excitedly as he placed his Dictaphone into his top drawer. He cleared a space on the grey plastic chair beside him and gestured for her to sit down. He seemed genuinely pleased to see her. The room smelt of a mixture of old paper & dark coffee. It was a welcoming smell, if a tad musty. It was the kind of smell you get when you take a very old book off a shelf after many years, flecked with traces of a deep coffee essence. Wafts of fresh Columbian and classic Kenyan occupied the airless room, courtesy of the all singing, all dancing, shiny new coffee machine. She would hazard a guess the coffee machine was on a continuous loop of fill and consume judging by the depth of aroma that had greeted her.

'Would you like a coffee? I've finally found the box my machine was hiding in and can now offer you the real stuff – Jamaican blue mountain no less', he enthused.

Midori wasn't sure if that was good, but seeing his obvious eagerness she would willingly give it a try.

'Yes I'd love some, sorry I don't know anything about coffee, Jamaican Blue...?'

'Oh don't mind me, I am a bit of a coffee snob I'm afraid. I am in fact a qualified coffee taster', he announced proudly.

He poured her a cup of what was obviously the equivalent of liquid gold.

'Crumbs I am in trouble then', she joked. 'How on earth did you become a coffee taster?'

He handed her the steaming cup of precious loveliness. She had to admit it did smell rather good.

'I grew sick of the insipid stuff I drank whilst training, so I made it my mission to try and find somewhere that sold real coffee, the sort I was used to back home. Not a widely known fact, but the Caribbean has some of the finest coffee in the world'.

Taking a sip she was surprised at how good it really was. Bold but smooth with absolutely no taste of bitterness, unlike that first cup he'd served her.

'I found a great place called Douglas on 56th street in Seattle. Not only did they sell great coffee but they also ran fully accredited courses. Everything from a coffee taster pathway, to a coffee buyer pathway. I undertook the taster course. Both were accredited by the SCAA'.

'What's the SCAA?'

'Oh sorry, it's the Speciality Coffee Association of America'. Nick shot her a look and hesitated for a moment.

'What do you think?" he asked cautiously

'I think you're amazing. You must have had to work so hard to fit in all the training to do the coffee thing as well as studying to be a doctor'. She smiled.

'I meant what do you think of the coffee?' He gestured towards her mug which sat firmly clenched between her hands.

'Oh, I... yes the coffee is really good, I mean really really um... bold and well rounded'. She surely knew nothing about coffee but had seen those words used in many a Starbucks to know they may be appropriate in her current situation. She had gone a dark shade of crimson and stared down into her mug with even more intensity. How had she managed to think he wanted her opinion on his coffee diploma or whatever it was? He hardly knew her. Stupid Dori, she scolded herself.

'So how have your patients responded to Centoria?' she asked, raising her gaze. Better stick to safe ground from now on, she told herself. She had caught him off guard; it was as if he were studying her.

'Yes yes the patients', he said absentmindedly. Now it was his turn to blush. 'Well I must say Midori, the results have been incredibly strong and encouraging, that's why I wanted to see you', he said quickly.

She liked the way in which he spoke to her, he always used her name. It made her feel good, confirmation that she had his full attention. Just the way he spoke her name, his voice as smooth as silk, she could listen to it all day long. It was slow and deliberate. A small charge ran through her body.

'I can honestly say I'm impressed, I know it's early days but both patients are responding well and the side effects seem to be minimal'. There was the faintest pause. Nick Campbell looked down at the papers sat in front of him on his desk and continued.

'One thing I did want to check with you and your medical department is the side effects profile. I see from the data you have already sent me that other trials existed and I wondered if you could get them sent through to me as I really would like to see everything?'

'Yes of course, no problem'.

As if by way of explanation he added, 'Centoria works so quickly at restoring the neural pathways and adding to the expanse of the hippocampus that I want to be assured there won't be any rebound at a later date'.

'Rebound?' Midori looked puzzled.

'Yes, it's very common with a lot of drugs, especially neuro ones...and ones that work quickly', he added. 'There is always a chance of rebound after the initial rush of positivity. It's the body's way of trying to rebalance itself. Ever heard the expression it'll get worse before it gets better?'

'Yes, yes I have, OK got it. I'll send an email this afternoon, hopefully medical will be able to get back to you straight away'.

She left Nick just after 12.45pm. She had sat in the canteen and written an email to medical outlining his requests. She hadn't liked to ask why all the neurosurgeons were called Mr instead of Dr - she didn't want to seem more foolish then she already looked. She had a bit of time to play with and Google told her everything she needed to know. Physicians from the Middle Ages had formal university training to practice, thus gaining a degree, hence the title Doctor. Surgeons had usually served as apprentices to a qualified surgeon: if successful they gained a diploma, hence they were unable to call themselves doctor and stayed with the title Mr, Miss or Mrs. Nowadays everyone took a degree. The tradition stuck - in effect surgeons go from Mr, Miss or Mrs to Doctor and back to Mr, Miss or Mrs again. Well who knew? Every day really was a school day and today I didn't look stupid in front of the teacher, she thought.

Grabbing her bag she headed for the car park. She'd better get a wiggle on if she was to meet Raiden for lunch before her meeting at Yeovil hospital; it would take her at least half an hour to get there. She hadn't seen her brother for nearly two weeks, although it felt longer. She had a lot to squeeze into the forty minutes or so they would have together. She'd already told him about her crush on Nick, now she needed his advice. How unprofessional would it be of her to ask him out for a drink, she wondered? Yep Rai would know the best approach.

The traffic leaving the hospital was slow and heavy. It had been raining, always a recipe for disaster. Everything crawled to slow motion. Now however the sun began to once again shine through and as if by magic the traffic started to dissipate. Midori reached for her sunglasses. The trees had formed a union and decided to drop leaves all at the same time, at an alarming rate. The pavements were blanched varying shades of golden brown and rusty orange. Their bronze hue was accentuated by the surreal shine glistening from each leaf as it carried micro-droplets of rainwater atop its surface. Autumn really was the best season, Midori thought. Summer had handed over the baton, its larder full to bursting. The task of storing and making ready; battening down the hatches before the brutal attack of winter appeared was held firmly in the gloved hands of Autumn.

Raiden was sitting at a corner table at the back of the coffee house. She could see he was texting, his manner carefree and unguarded as always. He looked across and waved. He had anticipated her arrival and she was greeted with a latte and ham and cheese panini. He knows me too well she thought.

'It's been too long sis, too long!' He rose to greet her, giving her a heartfelt hug and gentle peck on the cheek.

He was blessed to have Midori for his sister. He had watched her grow from the annoying pre-pubescent who was always trying to get him to play with Barbie and Ken to the thoughtful loving positive person she now was. She had always had such an old soul, even as far as Barbie and Ken were concerned - and that was not easy he reflected. He had never understood her lack of confidence though. It had always been there. She would clam up and he could feel her pain at most social occasions. She did not seem to think she had a choice. She seemed happy letting others take the limelight (including him). The world needed to see who she really was. She wasn't a wallflower with nothing to say. She was bright, funny and certainly cleverer than he was, but she just didn't believe it. When he had struggled with the age old question of 'what do I want to do with my life?' she had given him the most insightful advice – do what you enjoy, what will get you out of bed on the coldest, darkest most hung over mornings ahead. She had of course been right, although this was not something he would open-ly admit; after all she was still his annoying little sister! He could always rely on Dori to give her honest opinion and for that he was grateful. Maybe, just maybe, he could nudge her into turning her crush with this doctor into some-thing more. Perhaps she needed to know she could be accepted by someone other than her family. He would try his best.

Midori had always been spontaneous and quick thinking, even her temper was fast and furious. It grated a bit with him to think his sis-ter was probably a lot braver than he was. He personally preferred a steadier, more laid back approach. He cooked measured, simple meals whilst Midoris were flamboyant and involved every pan in the house. He would shop once a week from a list, sticking to it religiously, whereas she would go armed with a basket and a sense of adventure. Even her flat that he had helped to paint screamed bright and bold. Primary colours screamed out of every corner. Sometimes when she was hung over she really wished she'd taken Rai's advice and not painted her bedroom orange.

Midori understood why her brothers' career choice suited him. An aircraft engineer needed the steady, measured qualities he possessed. Engineering was such a part of who he was. He had always fiddled with odd pieces of dad's old lawnmowers or broken gardening equipment, transforming them into imaginary space craft, completely fitting for an episode in Star Wars. Some of the best even hovered. He came unstuck only once when 'Haifuraiya' - Japanese for 'high flyer' - ended up in the garden pond and electrocuted all the fish. Mum and Dad were not best pleased. However, playing around with heaps of old metal showcased his raw talent. When he was old enough Raiden and Dad entered their creation into the TV show 'Robot Wars' – two kids together. They spent weeks perfecting and preening, oiling and coiling bits of metal. The result was 'Cyclopsinator', a cross between a very small Dalek and a hedge trimmer. It had a long armed probe and a set of razor-sharp edges. They did rather well and were placed overall eighth in the series.

'So, how are things with 'The Doctor'? Tell me everything!'

'There's nothing to tell Rai, sadly. I haven't plucked up the courage to do or say anything', Midori sighed. 'He is so out of my league, I'm not even in the same galaxy never mind on the same planet. I haven't even worked out if he's with anyone yet', she moaned. 'Oh and it's Mr Campbell, not Doctor, for your information'. She was putting her new-found knowledge to good use.

'But you like him, right?'

Midori nodded.

'Oh Dori, you need to just ask him. From what you've told me he sounds like a nice guy'.

'I know, but I just feel so inadequate. He's this big-shot doctor, and me well... well I'm me', she sighed again, this time longer and deeper. Even her sandwich had lost its allure. 'It's as if he's made of stone and I'm made of paper'.

Raiden laughed. 'You do say some very strange things, I don't even know what that means.... and to think we're related', he said, elbowing her in the ribs. 'I hope you pluck up the courage to make your move on him soon sis. You are not *only* Midori, you are bright and funny. Any guy should be honoured to have you as a girlfriend. OK gushing over. I just need to know you're in good hands when I move across the pond'. He shot Midori a look that said: just slipped that in, hope you noticed.

It took a moment before her mouth dropped open and she gawped at him.

'Please Dori, you remind me of those fish I accidently electrocuted, please don't sit there like a dead fish, say something'.

Her silence was making him nervous. He was supposed to be the silent thoughtful type, not Dori. She was the exploding fireball.

When she spoke it was almost a whisper, but he could make out seven softly spoken words. 'Oh my God, tell me everything now'.

'When did you become so Essex?' he questioned, hoping to raise a smile from her now sullen face.

He had worked for 6 years straight at Transcorp Helicopters. Leaving Bristol University with a first class honours degree in Mechanical Engineering he had landed the job straight away.

Due to the nature of the projects he was currently working on, he had been asked to take up a 3-
year research post at the company's facility in
New York, USA. It was the opportunity of a life-
time and he knew it. Telling his sister was scarier
than the thought of living overseas, and that was
scary enough. The words had come surprisingly
easily. Now he held his head low, he couldn't
look up from the table. If he caught her crystal
green eyes he would unravel and start to jibber.
Somehow his sister had always been able to let
him know when she disapproved without ever
uttering a word. She must have inherited that
from mum, he pondered. After what seemed like
a long silence Midori spoke. Her voice was calm
and measured; if there had been any sign of sadness she made sure she'd buried it deep.

'Wow, just wow Rai, bloody hell you know
how to surprise me don't you?' she laughed,
squeezing his hand. Her laugh had been hollow,
although Rai didn't seem to notice. She had tried
so hard to give him the answer she knew he so
desperately wanted to hear. Inside she was burning with grief.

'I know, I keep forgetting that this is really
happening and then when I remember, it's like a

big surprise all over again', he gushed. 'Only thing is...'

He looked up and into her eyes. Raising his eyebrows slightly his expression softened.

'They want me there in two months' time'. He searched her face for a sign of acceptance. He had always been there for her. Now here he was making a decision to move away. He would be too far away to be there quickly if she needed him, and that pricked at his conscience. He had always been there when she had needed him. He was more scared of telling Midori than his parents. That was to be his next challenge.

'Dori?'

'Honestly Rai, I think it's amazing, it's a fantastic opportunity for you. I'm so proud of you. I know how hard you've worked to get where you are. Of course I'll miss you like crazy - but fate has opened the door, you'd be bloody stupid not to jump through it'.

She looked him straight in the eyes. If there had been any element of resentment she had taken an emergency course in 'how to look happy when you're really really sad' and won the Oscar. 'You have to do it, you were born for this Rai, I'm so so proud of you'.

She reached across the table and hugged him. With her head on his shoulder a small tear fell. She realised her brother was forging his own life, and a mixture of great joy and sorrow enveloped her. She was proud of what he had achieved but with his new job came change. She struggled with change, she always had. As much as he needed to go, to carve out his own path, she felt a depth of sadness that she'd only experienced when her grandmother had passed away. Their ties had to be cut one day but she was never ever going to be prepared for it. She felt alone. This was not her moment, she scolded, it was Raiden's. Her melancholy would not spoil it for him. She put on her best smile.

'Well on the plus side I don't suppose you'll be riding around on that death trap of yours in the states', she remarked, trying to break the solemn mood that had overwhelmed her. She was resolute -she would be rooting for him, whatever the cost to her.

'After all these years Dori, you just don't stop nagging do you? It's not a death trap!' he exclaimed 'It's a Motto Guzzi 1981 Les Mans II, a top bike, ridden by a top bloke, yours truly', he said getting a bit artful dodger.

'It's you lot with your company BMWs and Audis that are the real issue Midori Yates, but no I won't be taking it to the States. I've been promised something much more powerful and fast, very fast', by the expression on her face he knew she had nearly believed him.

'Well that's one blessing then. Please tell them you need something with four wheels OK?'

'I'm due to fly out in January; you, mum and dad can come over as soon as I'm settled, you can even bring Dr Thingy if you like. That's if you've plucked up any sort of courage by then.'

Midori looked down at her now empty cup.

'Sorry sis, but you are your own worst enemy when it comes to dating. Far be it from me to give you advice in that department but you were a Kendo champion, where's your backbone hiding?' he jibed. She knew he was right - what was she afraid of?

Outside of her family and Kendo she had never felt truly accepted, and that was the problem. Why would Nick Campbell want her, why would he be different? She wasn't special or interesting or even good looking. He was out of her league despite what Rai thought. Rai was talking so fast she realised she had zoned out and missed a lot of what he was saying.

'They've got an apartment lined up for me and everything. I just can't believe how lucky I am'. He looked so radiant, so happy, she thought. She was happy for him, of course she was. He would always be her big brother and she would always support his decisions. It was the chance of a life-time. He was right about Doctor Thingy too, of course he was, he knew her better than anyone. She was a quick decision maker, a feet first ask questions later type of girl, but as far as love and especially Nick was concerned she couldn't do it. The thought that he may reject her or not find her attractive in any way was too big a risk. That and the fact that she had to work with him: no, she couldn't take the risk. You Midori Yates are very good at giving advice but very bad at taking it, she chided.

4

The end of the week loomed large. She loved her weekends. Not too much planned, just how she liked it. The highlight would be shopping at the mall for some new work shoes and a photo frame for Raiden. She would put a family photo in it to take with him, then a mooch around a few good book stores would be the order of the day. She loved reading. Not many things could compare to that rush you get with a new book you cannot put down. Time took on a whole new dimension. She had sometimes lost days, head buried deep inside a book. She was a lover of all things Somerset Maugham, and The Painted Veil was her favourite novel. She had read and re-read it over and over. If she ever had children, she would make sure that she helped them develop a love of books. Children! Listen to me; I don't even have a boyfriend, she scolded.

Her imagination had been nurtured by her parents' love of storytelling. Their house had been awash with both British and Japanese authors. When she was being bullied at school her mum would sit her down and read her the wonderful tale of Jimusho, the office cat, by the author Miyazawa. It was one of her favourite tales. Her mum would read it in both Japanese and English: she'd put on voices, making the cats sound good and evil - funny, she had always used the English language for the evil cats. Midori loved the tale of an office run by cats and loved the illustrated pictures of the soot cat who was that colour because he slept in the hearth at night. She would snuggle in close, catching her mother's scent of linen and loveliness. Whatever daytime traumas had been inflicted on her paled into insignificance as she sat and listened. Her mother had been as clever as always and chosen stories that could help Midori to understand and cope with life. Jimusho had an underlying story about bullying. Only years later when she refound the book did she realise just how clever her brilliant mother had been.

Maugham had somehow fallen into her lap. She had been trawling the bookshops and they had been doing some kind of special promotion on his works. He had been her first attempt at classics since she had left school. Maugham's style of writing had sung to her: it was crisp, polite and beautiful. She lost days enthralled in his stories, unable to tear herself away to do even the simplest of tasks. Reading was her drug, it helped her to calm down and unwind. She had always been hot-headed, with a short fuse. Less so these days, but the risk of her blowing her top was always lurking, so taking the focus away from herself was a good thing. She seemed to find so much within to disappoint, but she was self-aware enough to know that the less time spent analysing her own perceived shortcomings the better. She had recently finished reading Maugham's biography. Non-fiction wasn't usually her thing but she loved so much of his work she wanted to explore the man. She had been surprised to learn that his initial career had been as a physician. So who knows, she thought, maybe a medical rep can become an author too. Yes, hours lost exploring bookshops was exactly what she needed.

Her small apartment had been doused with its weekly Domestos and she had still managed to get out of the house by 10.30. Smug didn't even come close to how she was feeling; she deserved a bit of retail therapy. Justifying shopping under the guise of a present for Raiden still counted.

Hobson Shoes had done her proud; she had found the perfect pair of patent black leather court shoes within twenty minutes of being in the mall. Even more time to spend in the bookshops now, she thought. A very satisfied smile had taken up residence across her face. She would have a quick latte in the coffee shop and then head to the bookstore.

The coffee shop was not particularly busy. She managed to secure a spot just by the window and sat watching the busy shoppers, another of her favourite pastimes. Her phone pinged. 'Are you free for lunch next week sometime Rx ?' read the text. She reflected on her relationship with her brother. It had gone from strength to strength since they had both left their teenage years behind.Rai had been a precocious horrible little brother and a caring (if annoying) older brother. He was the only person who understood her. Their upbringing, whilst reasonably conventional, had been a little quirky. Their dad Mark and mum Katzuko had met at university in London. Katzuko had returned to Japan to work as a research assistant in one of the leading laboratories near Tokyo. Mum definitely has the brains in our family, Midori thought. It had taken two years of a long distance relationship before she moved back to the UK and she and Mark married. It had been a painful time for both of them. They never really spoke of those years, although Midori knew it had not all been plain sailing and fairy tales. She had seen the way her parents shot each other looks if it were ever brought up.

Katzuko had a love of her home country and would often speak of it fondly. Shimoda, her home town, was a small coastal city in the southern Izu peninsula about 100km outside Tokyo. Midori and Raiden had visited Japan every three years since birth, right up until their teenage years. It was important for her parents to make sure their children were at ease in both cultures. Although nobody else she had known ever had to go to special Kendo lessons at Bristol University, she thought, as she slowly sipped her latte. The memories of her being put on display each time they had visited Shimoda made her cringe. Relatives from across the peninsula had gathered to meet them upon each visit. They had been subjected to her Kendo displays - oh the embarrassment. She got embarrassed even thinking about it. She was grateful her parents had encouraged them to have an interest in both cultures, yet sadly she had never really felt at ease in either of them. How many other kids of mixed heritage feel like this, she wondered? Maybe they don't, maybe it's just me over-thinking things again. Pulling apart that which isn't frayed was her speciality after all. Why was it so important for her to belong, to feel part of something bigger, something outside of her and her family? She and Rai had the same upbringing but when it came to confidence and self-certainty he had got both of their shares.

Kendo had taught her a lot, not about Japanese culture but about herself. At first she had shied away from the lessons, finding every excuse under the sun not to attend. They seemed loud, violent and aggressive, not her bag at all. Yes she was hot-headed and prone to outbursts of anger, but that was her boiling over. It was her reacting to situations. Kendo was altogether on a different level. It was controlled, purposeful. Her mother's subtle, strong approach, coupled with the most amazingly patient coach, paid off. Kendo gave her skills to help her stop and think outside herself. It provided the bedrock of her steps towards self-discipline and depth of character. Her 'Kiai' was a shout as loud as her brothers; it helped her to focus and aided her breathing. She missed practising with her Katana sword; she really did need to get back into it. Sadly her

Sensei had passed away whilst she was at university. He held a special place in her heart. He'd guided and strengthened her belief in herself and had been the only person to believe in her outside her family. Taking up Kendo again without him would be tough. Maybe that's why she had been putting it off for so long.

She stared out towards the shopping mall. Saturday shoppers were now everywhere. She watched as a couple holding hands stopped outside the jewellery shop. My brother will be a good catch one day, she thought, taking a bite out of an extra-large custard cream that had thrown itself onto her tray. How would she feel about that? She doubted any woman would be good enough for him. She answered Rai's text and scrolled through the myriad of emails that had appeared overnight. That custard cream really was rather good. Most of her mail was junk but 'nice' junk, she mused. Maybe she should get another coffee and then she wouldn't feel bad when another custard cream jumped onto her plate? There was a 20% off event for M&S homewares, a Groupon spa day special and a LinkedIn request from a recruitment agent. Since joining KLD she seemed to be inundated with requests from recruiters wanting to 'link up' or whatever it was called. She hit the delete button.

A familiar voice startled her from behind. Immediately identifiable, it sent waves of delight dancing down her spine and made her fingers go into spasms of pins and needles.

'I'll give you a penny for them?' She turned to see Nick Campbell, his smile filling the space.

'I'm so sorry, I didn't mean to scare you!' His expression changed to one of concern.

'No no you didn't.Sorry I was miles away, please please... would you like to join me for a coffee?'

Well that was very bold of me wasn't it, she thought, not sure where this confident version of herself had come from. Maybe it was the shopping, maybe the shopping made her bold! It was a type of therapy after all!

'As long as I'm not intruding?'

'No no, please intrude away, intrude as much as you like... I mean....'

Stuttering and blushing again, the man must think I'm a bloody moron. Thankfully there was no evidence of the oversized biscuit...at least he won't think I'm a glutton as well, that's one blessing.

'What I mean to say is, please sit down and join me'. There, she'd managed to finally spit it out.

She would very much like for Mr Nick Campbell to join her for coffee, sex, a relationship, dinner and whatever else her naughty mind could come up with but right now coffee would suffice. Wicked, that's what I am. Midori was trying hard to sound 'normal' but the giggles on the inside were forming a union and planning their revolt. Nick was still standing, feeling a bit like a patient turning up on the wrong day.

'I'd welcome the company, honestly'. She noticed his hesitation. 'Please sit down'. She pointed to the seat opposite and smiled. Thank goodness reading minds isn't part of being a neurologist. The thought amused her and she smiled again.

Looking back across the table towards her, his nerves were getting the better of him. I really am bloody useless when it comes to small talk, he thought. Why had he thought this would be a good idea? It wasn't as if she had seen him as he'd walked past the coffee shop. He had stood outside and watched her for about ten minutes before plucking up enough courage to propel him through the door.

Nick sprung back up out of his chair.

'I'm going to get an espresso, would you like one or perhaps a custard cream?' I need to stand up I'm shaking like a bloody idiot, I can do this. He clenched his teeth trying to gather some traction over their chattering.

Shit, he had seen her scoff the biscuit!

'No to the biscuit but yes to coffee please, but better make it a decaf, I'll be bouncing off the ceiling if I have any more caffeine'. Why was she behaving like some giggly school girl? God I'm surprised he doesn't just turn and run, she reasoned.

Midori watched as he walked towards the counter. He really was a fine figure of a man. He walked tall, it was a walk that seemed older than his years. Large confident strides carried his well-defined torso. His shoulders were relaxed and sloped downwards, providing the perfect base for his long smooth neck and finely chiselled face. It was a body that exuded confidence. It said: I'm in charge, I can handle it from here. Being around him made her feel safe, and, surprisingly sexy. She wondered what it would feel like to be held by him. To have his beautifully crafted frame surround her. Thoughts of him were becoming her naughty little secret and she was not inclined to push them away. They would catch her unawares, popping into her mind most inappropriately. Last week she had been out on a field visit with Rick and the mere mention of Nick's name had sent her into a hot sweat. She felt the need to cobble together some elaborate reason as to why beads of sweat had formed on her forehead. She was the worst ever liar: thankfully Rick had bought the 'coming down with a cold' routine. Observing him from afar was all well and good, but today fate had given her an opportunity to move things along. Could she?

He ordered the coffees and looked back towards Midori. That was one thing he could do confidently. He had been enchanted with her from the moment they'd met. Good manners and professionalism had served to keep his feelings hidden well enough, but what a stroke of luck seeing her here sitting alone. He had stood across the mall watching her daydream and eating that rather large biscuit, the indecision of what to do pulling him in two different directions. She truly was beautiful. Her long black hair gently stroked the sides of her face, her perfect almond shaped eyes the colour of finest emeralds, shining brightly.

He had been lonely since moving to the UK. His work was all-consuming and he loved it, but he needed to feel alive emotionally and sexually. Midori had appeared on that windy autumn day, a vision of perfection. Had Penny known he would fall for her? Is that why she had been so insistent he talk to her as they;d crossed the car park? Penny had looked out for him over the last six months or so. She could be a bit overbearing but her heart was in the right place, and my goodness she was a good secretary. He had landed on his feet finding her. She had recently returned from working in Europe and was so overqualified it was unreal. If there was such a thing as awards for admin and planning she would have won hands down. She seemed to be happy enough, for how long he wasn't sure, but for every day she kept him organised he was thankful. Penny had made sure he had a list of 'how things worked' in the UK. On her first day she had handed him a book containing every kind of 'what to do ifs...' She made settling into his new life so much easier. Yes, thank goodness for Penny. She had encouraged him with Midori too - he was grateful she had. He had looked forward to the times Midori visited the department. She was a bright intelligent woman who stimulated him both physically and intellectually. He had imagined kissing her many times over the last few months, his large dark lips cupping hers. He'd had to stifle a few awkward moments in the trouser department to avoid embarrassment during a few of their meetings. Now here he was drinking coffee and staring into those enchanting eyes. Could he muster the courage to ask her out? God that would take all of his strength: he'd need a few more espressos and possibly some rum to take that leap.

They sat for hours talking about work and life. She discovered he had a sister who was a dentist and a grandmother Stella who had encouraged him to enter the medical profession. His dad had died when he was only five years old and his mum and Grandma Stella had brought him and his sister up. Grandma Stella had pushed and challenged him when he had wanted to quit.

'A fine lady who I miss so badly', he said. His lilting Caribbean voice was tinged with sadness.

'I only knew my dad's mum Grandma Yates, she was lovely. I didn't know my mum's parents very well. We'd visit them in Japan every few years but we weren't close', said Midori quietly. 'My dad's dad had died by the time I was born. Rai, my brother, met him, but I don't think he would remember. There's only the four of us now, maybe that's why we are such a close family.'

The atmosphere between them had softened and become reflective. Whether it was the discussion of family or the underlying sense of ease that was almost palpable she wasn't sure, but for the first time in a long time Midori felt comfortable and relaxed. The only people that she ever felt this comfortable around were her family, and now, happily, Nick.

'So tell me more about your love of coffee', she quizzed, attempting to change the mood.

His eyes were bright and full of excitement, his passion at the mention of coffee evident.

'It was the visits we made to my grandma Stella in Jamaica that did it', he enthused. 'Every time we went over to visit she always had a pot of coffee on the stove. If I close my eyes and breathe in I can still smell it'. He closed his eyes and breathed deeply. 'It was a rich, almost sweet, smell; it would dance around me. I don't know why but it made me feel excited. It made me feel loved. At grandma Stella's I belonged, I felt I could rule the world if I put my mind to it. It was a depth of feeling that I cannot describe and only ever experienced there...funny how smells and comforts from childhood stay with you'.

She knew this to be true, just the thought of apple crumble and mochi balls and she'd swear she could smell them. They sat in a comfortable silence. Midori had never heard Nick speak so freely and so beautifully. His 'work' persona was logical and measured. Today she was catching a glimpse of the man beneath and it moved her. He was poetical and big hearted. Plans to visit the bookshop evaporated. She could sit here all day.

'As kids, we would stay with her all summer and help out at the plantations. She gave me so many life skills. I learnt a lot about people, but most of all I learnt a lot about myself'.

She imagined what Nick would have looked like as that little boy, and her heart melted further.

'One day, when I can, I will buy a little plot in the Caribbean and start my own small coffee plantation', he added. Midori sipped at her decaf latte. Coffee was not something she had thought too much about. Yes she liked a good cup of coffee, she kind of understood where he was coming from. For him it was coffee, for her it was books.

'So when you were in the states how did you fit it all in, your junior doctor training and your coffee diploma? I thought junior doctors worked ridiculously long hours?'

'I did, but when everyone else headed out drinking and the like I'd give it a miss and work on my coffee diploma. Not really much of a drinker me, well other than coffee of course', he added, seemingly embarrassed. She had not meant to embarrass him, she was genuinely interested. 'Whenever there were days I couldn't miss at college I'd swap shifts with other juniors. Prof. Wallace my senior was very understanding. He said it was good to have an outside interest, it would help keep me grounded – pardon the pun'. Nick smiled bashfully. He really is very attractive, thought Midori, shifting ever so slightly further forward in her chair.

'Well I have to say I'm very impressed. You're the only neurosurgeon I know with a diploma in coffee tasting'.

'Apparently I have great olfactory senses I'll have you know'. He raised his cup towards his nose and started taking in deep breaths. 'Yes, a strong dark blend of Nicaraguan and possibly Columbian', he said confidently. Whether he had done it for effect or in all seriousness she didn't care. Mr Nick Campbell could have told her it was infused with Yak's milk and she would have believed him. An unfamiliar glow had taken up residence in her heart, she could feel its warm embers tenderly caressing her emotions.

Nick surprised her in so many ways. He was only 32 and, in her humble opinion, had the makings of a brilliant neurosurgeon. Unlike a lot of consultants she had met he was humble and funny to boot. His initial awkwardness had given way to a softer somehow strangely familiar Nick Campbell. She was at risk of hanging on his every word. That was not like her at all. It was a risk she had secretly started to embrace. He was a rare beast indeed. His softness coupled with his skill as a surgeon made him a valuable asset to any hospital lucky enough to have him. He cared deeply about his patients too - that was not something that can be taught and rarely came as a natural quality.

'I'd come and work for you'.

God she'd said it out loud. There's comfortable and relaxed, she thought, and then there is downright embarrassing.

'I mean...' Now she was blushing.... Again!

'Would you?' Nick's eyes searched hers. She blushed even more, if that were possible - now what?

'Well, only if the terms and conditions were good. I'm not cheap though', she rubbed her thumb and forefinger together. They both laughed rather loudly, attracting some curious stares from the elderly couple at the next table. Nick looked at his watch.

'Sorry, I'd better get back to Bracken, she'll be missing me'.

What? A big sucker punch hit her square on her abdomen. She had convinced herself he didn't have a girlfriend, how stupid. Why wouldn't he? He's cute, funny and intelligent. Of course he would have a girlfriend.

'Oh of course, of course you don't want to keep your girlfriend waiting, sorry for keeping you so long'.

Letting down her guard had been stupid, she told herself. See what happens? She tried to sound unfazed but inside she felt leaden. Nick was staring; a look of bemusement had begun in his eyes and was now spreading across his face. Starting as a gentle chortle his laughter now filled the cafe. The silver surfers at the next table eyed him with curiosity. Midori frowned: she didn't understand. Why is he laughing, is it because he realises I like him, oh God, no, please don't let it be that... She was now full blush, she could feel the heat emitting from the surface of her cheeks and was in danger of needing someone to spray her with a fire extinguisher.

'Bracken is my dog, although I'm sure that she sometimes thinks she's my girlfriend...'

By way of explanation he continued.

'She belonged to the local farmer, but I kept finding her outside my door. Somehow she just kept attaching herself to me so he said I could keep her. Apparently she obeyed my commands better than she ever did his, although I'm not sure about that'.

Midori was now at maximum redness; her sweat glands were joining the party but she didn't care. It was a mixed bag of emotions, relief coupled with overwhelming excitement. A face which resembled the towering inferno, sweaty arm pits and now relief. This day is getting better and better. A neurosurgeon with a passion for coffee and animals, how much more attractive can he get? She was tempted to bite the inside of her cheek but resisted. She needed to savour this moment, these emotions. Does that mean he is still available, she wondered?

'I love dogs by the way, in case you were wondering.. I mean...'

God I know what I mean, I mean I want you to like me, I want to tick every single one of whatever boxes you have, just for goodness sake please like me ...is what I mean.

'We used to have a lab', she said quickly. 'Her name was Molly. I was about five or six at the time. I always called her Molly Dog. She was very placid. I used to ride around on her back'.

Those were happy days. She and Rai taking Molly Dog out after school. It seemed like they were gone for hours but in reality it was probably twenty minutes, if that. They used to argue fiercely about whose turn it was to take her out, especially if it was raining.

Nick could feel the palms of his hands sweating ever so slightly - nervous was an understatement. It was now or never, he had to be bold.

'You can meet her if you like, she'd really like you...I know she would'.

He hesitated. 'I don't suppose you're free for dinner tonight? I'm a reasonable cook, and to be honest, Bracken could do with someone other than me to entertain. She's good at entertaining; she knows a few tricks and everything. Are you free?'

He searched her face, trying to gauge her reaction. It was impossible. He hadn't been this nervous since when he'd removed his first intracranial tumour as a consultant. His sweaty palms were spreading. He could feel tiny beads of sweat on his upper lip, which he quickly wiped away. It seemed like an eternity before she answered. How odd, he thought – his heartbeat was now pulsating in his ears. He would clearly have to get this looked into if it continued.

'I would love to', she beamed. 'I'll bring dessert'.

As he left he couldn't contain his excitement. Walking back to the car he felt light-headed. Was it really that simple? Had this beautiful girl really just agreed to have dinner with him? Over the last few months he'd found himself thinking of her at the most inappropriate of times. It was as if she had an access all areas pass into his psyche. He'd be sitting dictating outpatient letters and before he knew where he was his mind had wandered and he'd be able to picture her smiling face, those sparkling eyes and full lips. Romance was so not his thing, it unsettled him. He supposed his feelings were what other people felt on a day to day basis, but for him they were strange and uncomfortable. That's not to say he didn't enjoy them, he did. Fact was, he just didn't know how to respond to them. He knew where he was with science, but romance, well romance didn't follow any set formula - and that was bothersome.

As a child he had been slightly disconnected from the day to day, preferring the company of science books to that of people. Most people worked on a different level to him, they wanted to talk about nonsense which did not interest him in the slightest. To outsiders looking in he had been a geeky kid with no social skills. To his family he was just Nick. His mama and sister used to rib him, trying to get a reaction other than silence or agreement. He was the epitome of cool, calm and collected. His mama had remarked that the house could be on fire and he would react as if she'd just told him what was for tea. Ye he felt small talk was wasted energy. Why get so heated up about things that you can't change? He liked to explore the options and find a solution, take the emotion out of it. Maybe that was it. Maybe what he was feeling for Midori, maybe, that was his emotions. Professor Wallace had commented once that love was the only thing in the world that made total sense, yet at the same time it made no sense at all. It was, he'd said, what makes us human. At the time Nick had no idea what he had meant, but now, well maybe now he was starting to understand. He had of course had girlfriends. However, his relationships had been ones of mutual convenience. Nothing had ever broken through like the feelings he had for Midori. He was hard placed to describe what he felt. It was somewhere between the best coffee he had ever tasted mixed with charges of emotional unsteadiness. Now, he mused as he drove towards his home in Chelston, small talk was exactly what had been delighting him for the last two hours, how strange! Today marked a change, he told himself. Maybe this is what Prof. Wallace had been banging on about. Maybe finally he would feel as if he fitted in.

Midori made him feel bold and adventurous. She accepted him for who he was, and that made him feel at ease. He had told her things about his childhood that he hadn't told anyone in a long time, especially about grandma Stella. He had taken a risk and it had paid off. It hadn't felt weird as it usually did. It felt strangely liberating. Midori had said yes to dinner and it had made him the happiest he had been since he had arrived in England.

White noise was all Midori could hear. She was in a daze, a whirling happy daze. He had asked her on a date. A real live, true to the moon and back date – tonight! She had walked around the mall for about an hour without focus – she had been in and out of John Lewis at least 3 times and still came out empty handed! He had found her funny and interesting, he had even laughed at her jokes, God he must like me she thought! Every time he spoke she had been spellbound. She had desperately wanted to reach out and stroke the side of his flawless dark complexion, but no that would have been too weird and very awkward!

Now, here she was dressed up to the nines, chilled bottle of Sauvignon on the passenger seat, slowly driving down Nick's shingle drive.

Drakes View was beautiful, everything she had imagined it would be. Once an old barn, the modernised conversion sat surrounded by a small woodland, out of sight of the road. She had driven up and down the road twice until she realised what she initially mistook for a footpath was in fact the narrow entrance to Drakes View's sprawling drive. Opening the car door, she was immediately struck by the unmistakeable smell of burning wood that hung low in the air. Her four-inch Mui Mui courts were making it a precarious journey as she slowly navigated each step forward. If Nick were looking out of the window now all sense of romance would be lost. She looked like a baby giraffe trying to stand for the first time. Her grip tightened around the bottle of wine – no way was she dropping the wine even at the risk of landing flat on her bum. The wine must survive at all costs!

Bracken had started barking long before she reached the front door. As she drew closer the door flung open wide and a bundle of highly charged liver and white fur bundled towards her. Tail wagging; it reminded her of a helicopter building up speed to levitate. Bracken looked up at Midori and her heart again melted. Who would be able to stay serious and unaffected by this beautiful doe-eyed creature? She bent down and stroked her. Bracken had propelled herself to another planet and somewhere along the way someone had added springs to the bottom of her paws. She bounced gaily in front of Midori, who was just thankful she had crossed the drive in one piece. Her feet were now firmly planted on terra firma. Shingle, a bottle of wine and a crazy Springer just didn't bear thinking about. Bending to stroke the dog had been a mistake, she reflected, as she now had dog slobber all over her face. Not a good look if you are trying to impress, she thought. He'll think - gangly walk, smeared make up and stinks of dog breath – yes very attractive, very attractive indeed.

'Ah I see you've met the crazy dog', Nick said, laughing as Midori tried desperately to stand and walk forward. Bracken had other ideas and was happily trying to pin her down towards the ground.

'Bracken come!' he said sternly. Bracken obeyed and dutifully walked back into the house, head slung low for effect. The farmer was right, she did obey Nick. She really was adorable, if a little smelly.

'You've got her well trained, I'm impressed'.

Midori plucked a tissue from her handbag and lightly wiped her face. She wasn't sure if a peck on the check was appropriate, especially as she had now been embalmed with 'eau de woof'. Thankfully the decision was taken out of her hands. Nick leant forward kissing her lightly on both cheeks. Hopefully that meant she didn't smell 99% canine. Things were looking up.

5

Bright sunlight sliced through the duck egg blue curtains. The realisation of where she was came crashing into sharp focus alongside a thumping big headache. Last night had been everything she had hoped for and more. Nick lay sleeping, the daylight caressing his features. She watched his chest gently rise and fall. She wasn't quite sure how it had happened, but happened it had and she wouldn't change it for the world. Her thoughts were a mesh of spaghetti. All she had to do was find the correct piece to pull. Memories flashed through her mind like streaks of lightning. They were there for a minute, stark and illuminated, in all their saucy splendour, then gone. Her previous perceptions of Nick had been left at the front door. His cool, reserved persona had been wiped away. The reality of Nick Campbell was hot-blooded, passionate and downright dirty. She blushed just thinking about it. They had enjoyed a polite meal, which she had to admit was really rather good. The boy can cook, she reflected. After that the evening took on a rather sultry air. A flashback appeared stage-front in her mind. She had forced him to dance, Oh my goodness how much had I had to drink? Images of Nick's protestations and her insistence filled her. She had deliberately taken a tumble with Nick the fall guy – literally. Her drunken plan had worked. She had landed smack bang on top of him. She could taste his breath as he exhaled, hot and heavy. She had stroked his tight soft curls as he leaned up and kissed her. Gently at first and then as if his life had depended on it. He had reduced her to a quivering wreck. He had been everything she had expected, no everything she had dreamed of - and more. Beneath his outer geeky appearance was a man whose desires and appetite to please her had surpassed her wildest dreams. They had made love four times. His gentle caresses across her body had made her moan with desire. She had lost herself in him, sinking deeper and deeper into a world without time, where only emotions and feelings made each moment. Each time had been satisfyingly different. She wasn't sure that she'd be able to ever sit at his kitchen counter again without a sense of embarrassment and his log store out back had definitely been a first.

Somehow she'd have to check her derriere, she was sure she'd picked up a few splinters. The cold light of day was drilling into the inside of her head. She felt dehydrated and in desperate need of some water but had no idea where the kitchen was. Well you certainly knew where it was last night, you tramp-tastic madam! Oh things were worse than she'd expected, now she was talking to herself. Grabbing her clothes she quietly tiptoed out of the room. She heard soft pads close behind.

'Hey girl, show me where the kitchen is', she whispered.

Bracken eyed her with a look that was as motherly as they come – what time do you call this young lady? it said. Arms encased her from behind making her jump.

'Surely I showed you I ain't no girl'. His voice smooth and playful, Nick gently kissed her left ear.

'I was talking to the ....' But before she could finish her sentence, she let out a gasp of delight. Nick's hands moved slowly across her shoulders angling down her back taking hold of her around the waist. The touch of his lips on her neck and his raspy breath were too much. She turned, her face flushed with desire. She had backed up against the hallway door. Nick gradually worked his way down her aching body, removing the little clothing she'd been wearing. Each tender touch sent her already heightened senses into a further frenzy. As he pushed into her a little further she felt an intensity of heat radiating from him. It was deeply physical and arousing.

'You have no idea what you're doing to me Midori Yates, no idea'. His voice, low and hot, was sending her spiralling out of control once more.

She had no words as wave upon wave of absolute need arose. Hot wet kisses increased with a sense of urgency. This man was making her crazy. Nick leaned against her further and they both tumbled backwards. She had leaned on the door handle. Ah, so this is where the kitchen is. The kitchen was becoming her favourite place in the whole house.

Over the course of the last twelve hours she had become 100% affected by this man in a way she did not understand. Things between them had changed. They had been brave, unmasking their true selves. They had both been bold and it had paid off. Midori knew that Nick Campbell would be the only man she could, and would, ever love. It seemed implausible but true at the same time. Call it love at first sight, call it completeness, call it anything you like, she thought, but I know deep within my soul that without him I will always be missing a part of me.

He was lying next to the most incredible woman he had ever met. That first kiss had somehow unlocked a lifetime of unacknowledged emotion, he reflected. He softly ran his hand along the outline of her beautifully curved body as they lay breathless, side by side on the kitchen floor. The floodgates had opened and he had been liberated from whatever spell he'd been under for the past thirty two years. Work had always claimed him, demanding all of his time and focus. Somewhere along the way his passion and emotions had been hardwired into his career. Last night had changed everything. He had gained glimpses of true emotion the first time he had met her, but as was his way, he had chosen to feed that desire and energy back into his work. Now, though, now was different. That first kiss had released him; it had uncoupled and rewired him. Of course a glass of wine had helped not to send him into his usual state of overthinking and rationalising everything, but that had just been cosmetic. It had been Midori Yates who had managed to cut through all of his barriers. She had opened a window through which a new, raw, emotional wind was now blowing.

The rest of Sunday took on a dreamlike quality. They were together but within themselves, each happily lost in their own thoughts and feelings. They had taken Bracken for a walk in the woods and made love again, out in the open, trees, leaves and everything! Later they had lain by the fire, silently studying each other's features, making love again as day turned to dusk. They were uninhibited and free. She was his and he was hers. Nick's appetite for her grew with each passing hour. She was an addictive drug, from which there was no return. Each moment with this intoxicating woman was more intense and erotic than the last. His desire was insatiable. He had explored every part of her in every way possible. She was sweet and romantic, then he would glance over and she would look sizzling and saucy. She looked at him and winked, removing the only thing she was still wearing - her heels! Moving back towards him it was her turn to call the shots. What she had in mind was hot and dirty, no shoes required, and he loved it!

They lay exhausted as the last hours of the weekend faded. They talked about their hopes and fears, about plans and dreams. Nick had been surprised to learn about Midori's Kendo career, although he could see how her agility would make her a fierce opponent. He himself was a keen cyclist, although since arriving in the UK he had not had time to train. They joked about buying a tandem and getting a dog basket put on the front for Bracken.

'I wonder if this counts?' she jested, kissing his bare torso.

'I doubt it', he laughed.

'Aren't you supposed to abstain from conjugal jiggery-pokery when training?'

'Ah well, my Kendo career was good while it lasted...'

Midori planted a big wet kiss firmly on Nick's soft full lips. Yep, Kendo would be strictly back seat for now.

There was at least one area on which they were poles apart. Midori couldn't cook. Her speciality, she had told him, was cheese on toast, or beans on toast or egg on toast. In fact toast featured heavily in most of her culinary endeavours. Nick however was an accomplished cook. Midori sat and watched in wonder as he filleted and grated various ingredients. The kitchen was definitely her favourite place for so many reasons! Nick served up warm duck and clementine salad followed by steamed salted sea bream with a light ginger and spring onion sauce. Dessert was a sublime Tiramisu, made with his beloved Jamaican blue mountain coffee.

They talked for hours over dinner and into the night. Midori told Nick things she had never shared outside of her family. Her painful experiences, of bullying at school, were still raw around the edges. Even after all these years, if still affected her. She had grown up an outsider looking into her own country. Unhappy school days had a direct line to her lack of confidence. She knew the root of her problem but had no idea how to fix it. Internally she would fly and dream like everyone else, but externally she would clam up, unable to speak. Only Kendo seemed to cut through, well that and her fiery red temper. Thankfully Nick did not need to see or know about that she thought.

'I hate drawing attention to myself, it makes me feel awkward. I'm far happier just being able to blend in. That's why I love science so much. There's no trying to work out what things really mean. I love the black and white of it all. The fact science is so logical and mostly predictable gives me confidence. It's more predictable than people'.

Nick nodded - he understood exactly what she meant, at times he felt the same.

'I've never seen that side of you Midori. You always seemed so confident, so.. well so self-assured'.

'Only around you, oh and my family. The Kendo has helped me a lot. It's given me an inner strength that I can call on when all I want to do is run and hide'.

'I make you want to run and hide do I?' His eyes were wide and clear. They seemed to have a direct line down to her soul. She met his gaze and for the briefest of moments found herself unable to speak.

'Not you, silly. You... you are different.' Her eyes held his in what seemed like some kind of suspended animation. A fit of giggles rose from within her and she began crying with laughter.

'What, what's so funny?'

'Us, we are, we are funny'.

'Why, why has 'us' caused you to go into such a strange crazy fit of hilarity? Come on, share the joke!'

'OK, promise you won't think me crazier than you already do?'

'OK, I promise.' Nick purposefully placed his right hand across his chest.

'Do you remember those Pokemon cartoons?'
Nick nodded. 'I just pictured us as May and
Brock, that's all, it made me a bit hysterical pic-
turing you and me as part of a cartoon...'

'Yep, you have definitely lost it - but if it
makes you feel any better I seem to remember
that Brock was in fact training to be a Pokemon
doctor so maybe you are only a little bit crazy'.
Midori's laughter had become contagious. From
wherever it had been birthed it had taken hold in
the room. Even Bracken, who had been lying
quietly at Nick's feet, decided she wanted in on
the action and began ferociously wagging her
tail.

'You can be Pikachu', Nick whispered loudly
into Bracken's ear. Bracken's tail flew back and
forth as if something amazing had just happened. The day had been perfect in every way.
Midori prayed every day they spent together
would be filled with laughter.

6

Midori moved in with Nick the week before Christmas. A whirlwind romance it most certainly was - but it was the right kind of crazy. Rai had helped move her in. He had immediately liked Nick. He could rest easy in New York knowing his sister had someone she could talk to.

'Don't be afraid to lean in sis, he's got broad shoulders he can take the hit'.

'Am I really such a burden Rai?'

'No, that's not what I meant; just don't go all isolated on him OK?'

'OK'.

'Does he know about your red mist temper yet?'

'No, he doesn't Rai, and it's really not that bad - I have grown up a bit you know'. She was at full pout and inside she had already stamped her feet a dozen times.

Rai acted as navigator, introducing Nick to Mr and Mrs Yates. Inviting them to dinner at Drakes View had been a smart move. They were surprised and intrigued by this man who had managed to sweep their daughter off her feet.

Katzuko Yates was a woman of few words. Gut reactions held more sway for her than any qualifications ever could. She had only once not listened to her inner voice and it had cost her dear. How someone carried themselves and the air with which they moved was as important to her as breathing. Nick's love for her daughter was obvious. She knew he would and could protect her if that time ever came. But it was his culinary expertise that had both surprised and impressed her. Midori had proudly gushed about his ability in the kitchen. She had in fact gushed proudly about Nick full stop! Katzuko and Mark had never seen their daughter so animated. Midori had not exaggerated; his culinary skills were indeed impressive. Katzuko quietly whispered into her husband's ear the Japanese proverb 花より団子 – translated, it means 'dumplings beats flowers' – you can eat a dumpling but a flower will serve no useful purpose. Anyone who could cook this well would make a fine addition to the Yates clan. Mark Yates was completely in tune with his wife; he was pleased to see his daughter so happy. Since leaving school she had started to blossom. Maybe they had smothered her too much when she was younger. It was good that she was spreading her wings.

The new couple now spread their wings further. Nick and Midori drove the eight hours from Calais straight, only stopping for a quick roadside coffee and a rather limp jamon baguette. A week in a pretty medieval town in the South West of France was exactly what they needed. Work had been full on in the lead-up to Christmas. They had jumped at Professor Franklin's offer of a week away at his holiday home. He had said it was payback for Nick being on call for both Christmas and New Year. He had received a last-minute cancellation for the first week of January which they gratefully accepted. It may be sub-arctic but it would be wonderful - just the two of them pottering around little French villages.

Map-reading was not one of Midori's super powers (unlike singing along to Tom Jones and being able to stilt-walk on 5-inch high stilettos). However the N61 towards Bergerac was pretty straightforward, despite the weather. Even her map-reading could cope. She would be hard pressed to get lost. Fields iced with snow littered their route. Hard landscaped industrial zones reminded them they were never too far from a town. Midori found France intriguing. The French were happy celebrating their national identity and diversity, at the heart of everything was their love of the land. Friends, food and love dominated her thoughts. People seem content here, she thought. Life seems simpler...but maybe I have my rose-tinted specs on again...

They reached Monflanquin just before nightfall. Although the journey had not been difficult it had been long. The little medieval town sat proudly on a dome-shaped hill, the lights of the town twinkling. As they approached, the weather had become a cornucopia of vibrant white winteriness. The strong westerly wind had picked up and drifts of snow swirled across the vista. Monflanquin – a snow globe by any other name, she mused. Bracken had slept pretty much the entire journey, only venturing off the back seat when coaxed with pieces of saucisson.

The Gite was everything they had hoped for and more. It sat within the grounds of a large estate - Le Manoir Couder, which, they were surprised to discover, also belonged to Professor Franklin.

'He's a dark horse - he never mentioned this', said Nick as they toured the grounds the next day. Madam Roussel, the French housekeeper, advised them that Franklin visited at least once a month. Her English was faultless. Sadly the same could not be said of their attempts at the French language. A lot of sign language had gone into ordering croissants from the village bakery. Madam Roussel had been most helpful. There were no other guests until Wednesday, when a party of 12 were expected up at the big house. Until then they had full run of the place. That included the 20+ acres of well-maintained gardens, albeit they were currently under a foot of snow, the large heated outdoor pool and Jacuzzi, the tennis courts and the grande bibliotheque which, according to Madam Roussel, was Professor Franklin's passion. He had restored the building four years ago, including state of the art humidification. He had moved the majority of the books in shortly afterwards. The library contained many priceless first editions from across the world. Madam Roussel was insistent that if they were to peruse the library they must wear white gloves and make sure the doors were shut properly behind them. Nick and Midori were in awe at the impressive building. Set on a slope, it had been designed by Charles Holden at the turn of the century. It was similar to his design of Bristol central library. Because of the sharp slope the building had two basement levels at the rear, creating four visible levels there whilst displaying only three at the front. It also appeared there may be further sub-levels. The central light well in the library gave a sense of space.

'You wait until we get back, I'm really gonna ask some serious questions of Hugh Franklin. This place is awesome. I really can't believe he hasn't mentioned his palatial mansion in France before!' said Nick, his voice echoing as they walked through the central body of the library.

'What's down there?' Midori pointed to a staircase which stood at the back of the building. It appeared to lead downwards towards a sub-level with a coded door at the bottom.

'Probably the crown jewels I'd wager', Nick laughed.

They doggedly sat by the pool later that afternoon. The sub-zero temperatures did not deplete their sense of excitement. The sun shone and the blankets and hot chocolate with which they had immersed themselves served them well. It may be cold but it's beautiful, she reflected. Anywhere they were together would sparkle, she told herself. If someone had told her how the last six months would have gone she would never have believed them. Yet here she was throwing snowballs into a heated swimming pool in France with the man she loved. How did she deserve to be so happy? As each day passed she found herself free-falling deeper and deeper. Yes, he could on occasion be annoying, but, she concluded, what man couldn't? Even her brother could infuriate the hell out of her.

They visited the beautiful Bridoire castle in Bergerac where they played a wealth of medieval games. Midori loved watching as Nick behaved like a child in a sweet shop. It was a world away from what he knew - he really is the embarrassing tourist, she thought. The weather was increasingly blustery but it did not detract from their enjoyment.

They had been in Monflanquin three days now and apart from the trip to the castle they had only ventured away from the estate twice, once to buy supplies and once to go out to dinner. Nick turned to look at Midori, his eyes bright and searching.

'I've been meaning to say this for a while', he said, taking her hand. 'Lord knows I am not the best when it comes to this kind of thing'. He squeezed her hand a little. 'Midori, I need you to know how much I love you. These last few months have been the happiest of my life. I'm not even sure I knew what happiness was until I met you'. Nick lifted her hand and gently kissed it. 'You've made my world beautiful Dori, thank you'.

Midori thought her heart would burst. Whatever had prompted him to lay his heart out so openly she was glad. She had needed to hear those words. Maybe he'd realised just how insecure she was. Whatever the reason, it had given her the boost she needed. She needed to believe she was good enough, that he really did love and want her. Why didn't she have more faith in who she was?

'I love you too Nick, I was just a bit scared to say it. I thought you'd think it was too soon'.

He smiled at her fondly.

'Nothing is too soon for us, Midori, it's as if we've waited our whole lives for each other. You know we are a right pair, aren't we Dori?'

'You mean like May and Brock? Yep we certainly are'. A smile etched across her face.

'Do you think by the time you're Prof. Franklins' age we'll be able to afford something like this?' she smiled. 'It could be our Poke gym'.

'I would love to say yes but unless I rob a bank or become some kind of Pokemon ultimate master then it would be a lie. Franklin must have inherited it, either that or he's a European drug lord', he scoffed.

'European drug lord eh? Nah, he's way to clinical for that'.

That night she awoke with a start. A fine layer of sweat had cocooned her. Her feet had somehow become tightly tangled in the myriad blankets that covered them. She struggled to free herself. Was she still asleep? No there it was again, the noise which must have awakened her. It sounded as if a gaggle of jumbo jets were taking off just outside the bedroom window. She listened as the rumbles of thunder seemed to edge their way closer. She loved a good storm, especially whilst lying in bed. It reminded her of snuggling up next to Rai as a child, listening as the storms raged directly overhead then slowly, with a degree of security, ebbing away into the distance. She had always felt safe, despite the noise. Afterwards Raiden would always joke that he had caused the storm - his name did mean God of Thunder after all.

This time, though, she didn't feel quite as safe. She couldn't put her finger on it but something apart from the thunder had made her almost jump out of her skin. She found solace watching Nick's wide frame, his breathing pattern mildly hypnotic. A wide flash of lightning illuminated the room quickly followed by another loud clap of thunder. How Nick didn't wake up she didn't know. It was loud enough and long enough to make her whole body reverberate. These were the times she felt most connected. The charge of electricity from the storm seemed to be coursing through her veins. She felt alive and much loved. She fumbled for her phone on the bedside table. 04:00. She noticed she'd missed a call from her dad at about 11pm. He must have forgotten I'm here. I'll call in the morning. The phone signal was patchy at best but she'd give it a go.

The storm had picked up momentum and with the next peel of thunder the heavens put on a display that would make the world firework championships proud. Even Nick had woken from his slumber. The two of them sat in silence peering out through the window. Nick's arms tenderly held Midori as the show unfolded. The pure white landscape provided a mystical back-drop for the heavenly activity. A chill ran across her exposed feet and sent a cascade of shivers down her spine. They left the curtains open just enough to watch Mother Nature's handiwork. Getting back into bed, the ice blocks hanging off the end of her legs started to defrost.

They had watched the storm for about forty minutes before making love with an unspoken urgency. Holding hands, they lay in silence drinking in the stillness. Now, the only sound was an occasional peal of distant thunder. My feet have warmed up very nicely, surely sex was not the only way to keep them warm, she pondered. A sassy smile spread across her face as the heaviness of her eyelids took control. Sleep beckoned just as the sun began to dance across the sky. Spooning side by side with Nick, Midori fell into a deep contented sleep.

But then once again Midori was woken with a start - what was that noise? Her phone had vibrated its way off the table and onto the floor. She was cursing one of her decisions. Choosing the most annoying of ringtones may have been a bit rash, she thought. The Magnificent Seven theme tune didn't lend itself to French mornings. Although it made her smile, even when it woke her from much needed sleep. Who on earth called this early? It was another missed call from her dad. A hint of worry crept into her psyche. She had missed one call last night and two this morning. She needed to call him, only now she had no signal. Her watch read 11am - surely that can't be right, she thought. She prodded Nick, who stirred briefly before turning his back towards her. She prodded him again.

'Hey you'. Midori bent and kissed him lightly on his shoulder. 'I'm going to head over to the library, I need a phone signal, something's not right at home'.

By chance they'd discovered that the only place with a consistently average phone signal was towards the back of the library - and only if you faced in towards the building.

The storm from last night was well and truly over. Frosty blue sky and bright sunlight greeted her as she opened the door. Bracken came along beside her and tentatively sniffed the ground. She was glad she had packed for comfort. The ice-cold air made her eyes water. Hitting the back of her throat it delivered its sting. Her lungs felt as though they were on fire. She pulled her scarf over her mouth and nose. Picking up the pace she walked briskly towards the back of the library building. At some point fresh snow had fallen, making the landscape once again magical. The pine forest that lay to the west of the property had been lightly dusted and reminded her of the fake trees that had adorned the family Christmas cake. She stopped briefly and took a few photos; her mum would like that. Reaching the back of the building she tucked herself into a stairwell that rose from below ground. Strange, she thought, it doesn't look like it goes anywhere. Maybe a leftover from the renovations. I wonder what secrets lie beneath? She made a mental note to explore the property a bit further when it didn't feel quite as much like Narnia. Her fingers were beginning to stiffen as she dialled her parents' number.

'Hi Dad, sorry I missed you'. She heard her father sigh deeply. 'Dad?'

'Now don't panic Midori - its Raiden', her dad's voice sounded strange, devoid of emotion. It was as if though he was reading from a script. 'He's had an accident... on his bike...he's in hospital. We think you should come home love'.

7

They arrived at the hospital just after 10pm. The journey back to England had been almost unbearable. Nick drove as fast as he safely could. The weather was against them as they made their way steadily through ice covered roads and snow topped villages. Midori had stared out of the window, looking but not seeing. Dad had said very little. Raiden was in intensive care. He had swelling to his brain and they had to operate to relieve some of the pressure. The next few days would be crucial.

Nothing could have prepared her for the small vulnerable scene that lay before her. Six beds made up neuro intensive care, three on each side of the unit. The beds seemed to cling to the sides of the ward as if hanging onto life itself. Each bed had a nurse or in some cases two. It was a ward devoid of vocal tonality, of emotionally charged sounds. White noise echoed out from each bed space. A plethora of wires and machines surrounded each patient. Enclosed by a mechanical circle of prayer, each person quietly fought for their lives. It was easy to forget that real people lay within the mass of technology. Occasionally the dull rhythmic sounds would increase in tone and frequency, calling the nurses to action. But after a brief intervention everything settled back to its steady, almost hypnotic state; a chorus of artificial heartbeats pealing around the room. She struggled to make out which bed held her brother: they were all so still and lifeless. She recognised the large bear on his bedside cabinet before she recognised him. She peered closer - it looked like Raiden, but it wasn't her brother. What struck her most were his eyes, something was different. They were the same colour, same shape, but there was an other-worldliness to them. Tracey the nurse greeted them warmly.

'He's making good progress'. Her face was warm and kind. Nick gently put his arm around Midori's shoulders. He had been quiet. This was his domain, everything breathed familiarity except the reason he was here. Every day he had to deliver information that had the power to cause joy or pain. He never did it lightly. He knew how, within a moment, a life could change. Someone whose prognosis had initially seemed good could suddenly die or someone for whom survival seemed inconceivable lived to make a full recovery. He saw it every day. For him, keeping quiet right now was the best thing he could do. After all what could he say? They didn't even know the facts yet.

'He's sustained a large blow to the head. Thankfully his helmet took a lot of the impact', Tracey said softly.

'Why... why is he not breathing for himself?' Midori could hear herself asking but she felt distant, removed from her own voice. She had hardly been able to look at him. It was his shell, his body, but he wasn't there. The life that was him was missing. The rise and fall of his chest controlled by the ventilator only served to compound her belief further - this was not her brother. It couldn't be. Raiden was fit and strong, not weak and frail. His face looked sallow; any glow of health had been removed on impact. The ventilator's steady sound of compression made the whole scene more surreal than real. Raiden had wires attached to both arms. Some were directed to bags of opaque fluid held high on drip stands, whilst others fed back into an array of monitors. There were charts and graphs on a lectern at the end of his bed. Nick could feel her swaying as he leaned in to support her, guiding her towards a chair at Rai's bedside.

'Do you mind if I take a look?' Nick indicated the notes at the end of the bed. Tracey looked surprised.

'I'm a neurosurgeon at Queens', he added by way of explanation.

'We're not really supposed to, but... I'll go make you both some tea...' Her voice trailed off and she turned away, walking towards the end of the ward. This was all the encouragement Nick needed.

Raiden had been involved in a RTA (road traffic accident). Bike vs car. The driver of the car had suffered an epileptic seizure at the wheel, ploughing across the central reservation and into oncoming traffic. There had been four casualties at the scene and one fatality. Raiden had been lucky. His bike had swerved off the road and he'd hit a tree. His helmet had in part protected him, however he had suffered acute swelling to the brain. Nick skimmed the notes.

'The coma is medically induced Dori', he whispered. 'It's deliberate; it's a way of keeping a close eye on things. He needs the swelling on his brain to go down and this is the best way. They've taken a bone flap out of his skull to give his brain room to swell. All his vital signs look good', he said reassuringly.

Midori stared at her brother. She had never contemplated life without him. Now here he was barely recognisable with tubes and wires all over the place. She did not want to think about a life without him; it was too painful. Twenty four hours ago she had been blissfully unaware, enjoying the storm and reminiscing over childhood memories. Now, raw and numb, she sat and stared at his lifeless body. Closing the door on doubt, she took his clammy unresponsive hand and squeezed gently. Her face carried a tremulous smile. He would recover, he would get better. There was no other option. He had to be OK.

Three weeks had passed since the accident and her brother still didn't know who she was. The accident was taking its toll on her small precious family. Katzuko and Mark Yates visited the hospital each day, their hopes of finding the son they once knew thrown back at them and extinguished afresh each time. Every day was new and every day they had to disguise their disappointment. Raiden lay staring blankly, just as he had since the accident. They were encouraged to bring in photos, music that he had liked. Midori was encouraged to talk to him about things they'd done together, places they'd been. Each conversation was greeted with the same blank expression. There was no sign of remembrance about anything. She could sense his frustration, he wanted to remember.

Why had his doctors not thought to give Centoria a try? She wondered. Everything they had tried so far had not had the slightest impact. Raiden's lack of response to his medication had proved the basis for her first argument with Nick.

'I can't get involved, Dori, he's not my patient', he remonstrated.

'But it's the right thing to do Nick, you know it is. They need to try a different approach, something new. What's their problem?' Midori had seen red. At least this time her anger seemed to her justified.

'Why won't anyone do anything? He's lying there just a shell Nick, he's just a shell. Given everything we know about Centoria he would be an ideal patient to try it on. Why isn't anyone even talking about it?' she shouted. She wanted to scream. Her brother was lying in a hospital bed, there was a drug that had the potential to bring him back to them but no-one had any sense of urgency or it appeared desire to help him. Not even Nick.

'You have to let the doctors do their job, Midori. You have to trust that they will do the right thing for him'.

How many times had he said these words to relatives? He had always thought he'd been reassuring and confident. This time, however, his words sounded hollow and rote-like. Midori was right to question her brother's treatment. If she knew he agreed with her it would likely cause more anxiety. Why weren't they considering Centoria? He didn't want to step on anyone's toes, but if there was no change in Raiden's condition by Monday he would have to intervene. It was the right thing to do. He turned to cradle her as she sobbed.

'He's my brother for god's sake, how bad does he have to be? He doesn't even know who I am. I have to do the right thing Nick, even if it means taking on the whole bloody medical establishment'.

Turning away, her tears continued to fall as she walked from the room. It was probably not the most grown-up thing she'd done but she couldn't handle the rollercoaster anymore. She had to be his advocate; Raiden needed her to help him. Medicine was a world she understood. She would bring down the fires of hell if she had to. She would give Raiden's doctors a few more days to see if any of their treatment regimens were working. If not she would prepare for battle.

Midori had lived a little but had looked and listened a lot. She was as observant as Sherlock. She knew when someone was telling her what she wanted to hear. She smiled back at Mr Davies, Raiden's neuro consultant. She hoped the amount of sugar contained within her smile would be enough to make him hyperglycaemic. One thing her job had taught her was how to be direct and demanding without being rude. It was a skill she had mastered quickly.

'Sorry Mr Davies, please could you explain that to me again, I'm just a little confused?'

Her desire for sarcasm was about to overwhelm her but she managed to keep it in check. She didn't want to come across as bolshie or pushy; she had to bide her time. Mr Davies misinterpreted her need for further explanation; he thought she had not grasped what he'd said the first time.

'I'm afraid I cannot prescribe the drug you mention Ms Yates. It is not a drug we use locally;

it's not available on our hospital formulary, and unfortunately our pharmacy doesn't stock it. The best approach for your brother is, I believe, the approach we are taking. We shall continue to watch and wait. Another few weeks and we can reassess'.

Mr Davies shifted nervously in his seat. This young woman's questions were unnerving him. He was so much happier running sleep clinics and drilling bore-holes into skulls. Dealing with relatives was way too stressful.

Watch and wait? Watch and wait, who the hell does he think he is? I'll give him watch and bloody wait. She could feel her blood pressure rising, any minute now she was about to go nuclear.

Mark Yates gently touched his daughter's shoulder.

'I'm sure Mr Davies is doing everything he can love, we just have to be patient'.

Mr Davies nodded in agreement hoping that the good advice from her father would diffuse the situation. Two more weeks of Rai hooked up to every monitor under the sun, two more weeks looking at his vacant expression. No, he deserved better, she had to make a stand, he needed her to fight for him. Midori turned to her father and spoke softly.

'Dad, I know Mr Davies believes he is doing the right thing for Raiden but I've seen this drug in action. I've seen Centoria transform patients' lives'. She turned to face Mr Davies.

'The neuro team at Queens have been using the drug Centoria. So Mr Davies - I want to ask you a serious question'.

Despite her slender frame and stature Midori's presence had filled the room. She had taken her anger and moulded it just enough for it to become useful. She was calm but her presence was forceful. She felt as if she stood on the shoulders of giants. As she spoke, the room, which had at first felt large and imposing, now became small and intimate. All eyes turned to face her. Her voice was measured and controlled. She was a voice for all of those people whose voices for too long had been stamped on and shut down. She was trying to lift the leaden shutters on a dark lifeless room where protocol and habit had taken up residence. Mr Davies shifted uncomfortably in his seat. He was becoming impatient - relatives of patients always thought they knew best, he told himself. After all what did this mere slip of a girl know?

'The question is a simple one'. She sensed his irritation but she had the floor, she was in control. This was way too important to back down now. Her jade green eyes set Mr Davies firmly within her gaze.

'What price do you place on a life Mr Davies?'

'I'm sorry Ms Yates but I do think you are being a little mel... melodramatic', he stuttered, clearly taken aback by her question. Mr and Mrs Yates looked on agog. They had never seen this side of their daughter. They sat motionless with a sense of pride and amazement, watching the scene play out in front of them. With calmness and confidence Midori continued.

'I ask because I believe Centoria has been approved by the European Medicines Agency has it not?' She was putting her case for the prosecution and although he didn't know it Mr Davies was her star witness.

'It has but...' Beads of sweat formed on Mr Davies brow.

'It is also listed in the British National Formulary, which as I understand it is the book which allows every clinician in the UK to prescribe from, is that not correct?'

'Yes yes but it really isn't that simp....' Mr Davies laughed nervously.

Midori cut in sharper than a fledgling sword on its first adventure.

'So it must come down to cost then. I'll ask again if I may...' she didn't wait for an answer. 'What price have you put on **my brother's life?'** She enunciated the last three words slowly. Everyone was looking at Mr Davies, his face now devoid of colour. When he spoke it was paced and measured.

'The local formulary dictates which drugs we can use locally, I do not have too much influence over that I'm afraid'. He looked down towards the floor.

Midori was not done, without missing a beat she asked, 'When you have a body of experts making clinical judgements, which takes precedence, national or local guidelines?' Midori cocked her head to one side a bit too dramatically to fully convey the depth of her anger.

'Well national of course but I don't...', he realised too late the course Midori had charted.

'So a national formulary with national guidance would therefore top a local formulary with local guidance given your logic Mr Davies wouldn't you agree?' Checkmate Mr Davies, checkmate! Centoria was in the national formulary; it was also included in the latest national guidelines for amnesia. The shutters were not only open but they were just about hanging on by their hinges!

Raiden Yates began his course of Centoria the following day. Within two weeks he had recovered enough to leave hospital. Within three weeks he was back at work. The cost of his treatment with Centoria had been less than the cost of a two-night stay in ITU. Mr Davies had been gracious and fully engaged with Raiden's recovery. He had learned an important lesson. Never again would he allow bureaucrats to have the final say. Clinical decisions had to take precedence. He asked his secretary to start booking pharmaceutical company appointments again.

Raiden's recover was remarkable. So much so that Mr Davies wanted to write up a case study to publish in Neurology Today. Midori looked at her brother across the dining room table. He looked well, if pale. He had been out of hospital a month or so now and was getting ready for his big move to the USA. He had been staying with his parents since his discharge from hospital and was being spoilt rotten.

'OK, what is it Dori, you've been giving me sideways glances all afternoon?'

'I'm just concerned Rai, that's all. It's not that long since you left hospital, are you sure you're up to such a big move right now?'

'I feel better than I've felt for ages Dori, honestly. I get the occasional migraines, which are new, but that's a small price to pay.'

'You're right, I'm just trying to look out for you that's all.'

'Your wonder drug has cured me sis, it really has. I sleep better than ever before, I'm even eating well due to mum's amazing cooking... you should be proud of me sis'

'I am Rai, I really am. Can Nick and I come over for Christmas then?' She looked across towards Nick who had been sitting quietly. He nodded his agreement. He liked Rai, he really did, but he would be happy to have some space between him and Midori. She worshipped him. It was irrational for him to be jealous of her brother but he was. It would be good for her to stand completely on her own two feet. He was her support now.

'We're coming too!' shouted Mark from the kitchen.

'Family Christmas in New York! That's settled then, fantastic'.

8

With Raiden back to full strength and happily living in New York, Midori's life became more leisurely. Its days carried a predictability that she treasured. Her job, whist she enjoyed it, was not her life. No, her life was Nick. Making time to explore life together was her priority. It was where she was at her happiest. They had moved in together so quickly she had not really had any time to think; everything had been here and now. What was it Raiden said? 'You're a long time dead sis, so learn to live'. That was exactly what she planned to do. Thinking of the future made her smile. 'Mrs Midori Campbell' flashed bright and luminescent into her mind's eye. One day, perhaps one day. Nick had been the making of her, she thought as she drove home towards Drakes View. She exuded a new confidence she had never before possessed. Whenever she had felt she couldn't do something, there would be, slowly nudging her. Sitting on her shoulder, whispering in her ear, 'Really? Why not? Why can't you? Who's stopping you? Ah yes that's right, no-one, only yourself'. He had inspired her, giving her the confidence to apply for a more senior position at KLD. Her interview would be in the next few weeks. She'd have to work hard if she was to stand a chance.

She was thankful it was Friday. It had been a long year already and it was only February. The weekend was forecast to be crisp and bright. It was going to be her favourite type of weekend. Long walks with Bracken through the Chew Valley, then maybe a movie on Sunday afternoon or then again maybe nothing but lying around and reading– excellent. Although not as much of a bookworm, Nick enjoyed the occasional read, though his mainly centred around the cultivation of coffee.

Nick's Evoke was parked in the drive. Strangely the house sat in darkness, no lights, no noise. She'd lost count of the amount of times he'd fallen asleep on the couch. The house was deathly silent. Even Bracken hadn't come to greet her. Maybe he's out walking her, maybe that's it, she thought.

'Hi I'm home, where are you?' Her voice echoed in the hallway. She made a mental note to buy a rug for the hall to dampen down the acoustics. Drakes View was a high spec barn conversion. Fine looking Oak beams criss-crossed the high ceilings. A minstrel's gallery stood proud aloft the living room, its two ornate gable ends filled with made-to-measure bookshelves. Nick had rows and rows of medical textbooks interspersed with books on sustainable coffee growing, coffee processing and in fact all things coffee. She had managed to commandeer a section for her not so highbrow romantic fiction. She'd been threatening to buy two rom-coms for every new coffee book that mysteriously appeared. The coffee books 'magically' appeared a bit like her shoes, he'd joked. Walking through the open plan living room that led to the kitchen, the house remained stony silent. She walked through the extension link corridor towards the office. A dim glow peeled out from below the door frame. The extension was as high spec as the rest of the barn. It had been constructed from the original cob of an old derelict barn that had sat within the grounds. The rooms of the extension led directly off a corridor – one room on each side (a bedroom to the right, a bathroom to the left) with the study at the end. As she drew closer she could hear voices. She poked her head slowly around the door. Nick was on a Skype call. She didn't recognise the voice. He waved without turning. His frame slouched towards the computer screen.

'OK see what you can find out Nick, but keep it low key just until we know what's what...I'll do a bit of digging this end, see what I can come up with'.

'Sure Prof and thanks'. Nick's voice sounded fatigued. Bracken padded towards her and was drowsily displaying her tummy wanting a rub. Midori bent down to stroke her belly. She'd fallen in love with this silly old dog as much as with her owner.

'Everything alright?' she asked tentatively. Nick turned to face her, his eyes red and puffy - had he been crying? She had never known him to cry, he was always so in control. He walked towards her, hugging her so hard that for a split second she was caught off guard and slightly winded.

'I'm glad you're home'. His voice sounded different. It was raw and cracked.

'What is it?' She had known as soon as she'd walked through the door that something wasn't right, she'd felt it in her bones.

'I was just speaking to Professor Ellis, head of neuroscience in London; we've been corresponding on our Centoria patients'.

'Centoria?' Midori looked puzzled.

'He's been doing some case studies and I wondered if he would let me see them. He's going to send them through via email this weekend'.

'But why, has something happened?'

He led her to the desk where he proceeded to open a tabular looking document on his lap top. Six tabs each labelled A,B,C,D,E,F.

'I am deeply worried about the clinical repercussions of prescribing Centoria, Midori. In total I've now had six patients on Centoria and all six have made an extraordinary recovery. In fact, too extraordinary. If they weren't my patients I doubt I would believe what I'm about to tell you. I'm not even sure I believe it myself'. His eyes darkened as he hit tab A.

'James Fisher, 44, father of 2, suffered amnesia post his father's death. He managed to run a marathon a few weeks ago – first time ever'.

'Well that is an amazing achievement but I'm sensing there's more to it?'

'It is amazing, for anyone, but even more so for a man who has never taken a day's exercise in his life. His time would even make an elite athlete look slow', he exclaimed.

'You know more than anyone, Nick, people that have undergone life changing events can go on to do astonishing things'.

'Agreed', said Nick nodding. 'I would expect one or possibly two of my patients to behave in unexpected ways, but not all six'. He stood up, agitated, and started pacing the room.

'I have spoken with most of them and each of them in a different way has told me the same thing. These 'gifts' - for want of a better word - were all things they wanted to do before the amnesia, good and bad. Dori - good and bad'.

He was tapping his thumb and forefinger of his left hand together frenetically. Midori had only seen him do this under immense pressure. She gently took hold of both of his hands and he stilled.

'I know, I know', he breathed, deeply trying to gain some composure.

'Not one of them Dori, not one of them has any recollection of how it happened. Take Abby Edwards', he said hitting tab B.

'Abby Edwards, 26 year old teacher. Always wished she could play the piano. Pre accident not a cat's hope in hell, never as much as had a les-

son. But now…now…' His voice was getting louder, gathering speed. 'Now by jingo, now she's
equivalent to grade 8 with absolutely no idea
how'.

'OK, agreed that is definitely weird'.

She needed time to digest the information he
had thrown at her. Surely there was a rational
explanation. He started tapping his fingers together again.

'The police visited me today, about another of
my patients…' He lowered his head.

'A Centoria patient?'

Nick nodded.

'Ed Harris. He had suffered amnesia after a
short brain infection. They have CCTV footage of
him pushing a man from the top of a multi storey
car park. The man died. When they questioned
Ed he had no recollection of it'.

'That's shocking…but I still don't see how or
why you think they're connected?'

'Before the accident Ed and his friends had
been discussing what it might feel like if you
were to push someone from a building, some sort
of conversation about walking close to the edge
of buildings and cliffs. Apparently Ed had started
the conversation'.

'You know - he could just be a psycho, as horrid as it is, he may have done it anyway, amnesia, Centoria or not'. She stared into his eyes trying to offer some reassurance. Nick stared back, his brow heavily creased, his eyes intense. There was something he wasn't telling her.

'Tell me about the other patients', she urged. Nick opened tab D and continued, his voice now devoid of emotion. It was as if he were at a meeting discussing patients.

'Jose Carreras, 17, couldn't even boil an egg. According to his mother he was a very picky eater pre accident. Post-accident and a course of Centoria he's now in the running for MasterChef. Cooks obsessively - everything from classic French cuisine to Mexican. Doesn't even own a cookbook', Nick rubbed his hands through his hair.

'He always wanted to cook though', he added.

'Angela Shaw, 52 year old farmer's wife from Bristol. Sustained a head injury when she came off a quad bike on the farm. Never even been outside of the county, let alone the country. Now fluent in French. Her husband doesn't know what to make of it. Guess which language she always wanted to speak?'

'OK I agree it does all sound a bit, well a bit weird...so what about the sixth patient, what's happened to them?'

Nick looked down towards the floor, the colour draining from his face. Bracken, who had been asleep on the couch, came and laid at his feet. Nick bent down and gently stroked her head.

'Nick?' Midori coaxed.

'The sixth patient was......'

'Was what, Nick?' She whispered, her voice barely audible.

'The sixth patient was my colleague, Dan Hart. He was a consultant Rheumatologist. We were at med school together'. Nick continued small downward strokes over Bracken's back. 'He was an avid cyclist. He sustained a brain injury when he was involved in a road accident on his bike. I tried everything to get his memory back before I started him on Centoria but nothing had worked'. His voice now quivering, he continued. 'Centoria really worked wonders for him, Dori. He'd been on it three weeks and seemed to be back to his old self. He was laughing and joking with everyone, as if nothing had happened'. Nick looked up. 'I went for a drink with him last week Dori. He told me about a charity cycle ride he was set to do in Cuba next month, that's how on top of things he was...'

Nick was now visibly shaking. She pulled her arms around his shoulders, kissing his cheek lightly.

'Go on'

'When I saw him he was Dan, just Dan. He thanked me for giving him his life back'. Nick took a large intake of breath. 'Dan was found dead last night. Apparently he hanged himself. He'd suffered from depression at med school but that was way behind him now...' Small pearl tears started to fall from his cheeks.

'I need to see all the data, Dori, I need to know for sure that this drug had nothing to do with his death or any of the other stuff that's been going on'. His shoulders heaved silently as tears continued to fall. Midori was in shock: how could all of this happen? She admitted it seemed a little too strange for coincidence. She sat on the edge of the desk facing him. She wanted to find the words to comfort him but none came; they were all wedged at the back of her throat unable to find their way out. Tears stained her face before they fell leaden to the floor. They sat in silence, the only interjections small movements from

Bracken as she lay at their feet. The tension in Midori's oesophagus eased.

'I cannot begin to imagine how you feel Nick', her voice whispered. 'We will get to the bottom of this, I swear we will'.

Now was not the time to disclose her thoughts. She didn't know Dan very well, only meeting him on a few occasions. He had seemed stable, for want of a better word, but suicides were more common than people realised.

They worked tirelessly through Friday evening trying to piece together what they knew. They stopped briefly to walk Bracken and grab a take-away. Nick emailed colleagues he knew in other parts of the country to gather case studies from them. He did not disclose his own fears but merely explained he was collecting data for his own research project. It was 3am before they called it a night. Neither of them slept well. The thought that Centoria may be behind the events for those six patients did not sit well with either of them. One way or another they would have to get to the truth.

Midori was amazed at what could be bought at the village post office on Saturday morning. It proved to be stationery heaven – post it notes, pin boards, large sheets of A3 paper. The postmaster was overjoyed; he hadn't had so much business in months. By the time she'd returned home Nick had cleared a large space on the study floor. Skills he used daily as a neurologist came into play. Thankfully he had his patients' notes on a USB. They were to go through each patient's notes systematically - looking for any anomalies. Things of note; family history, medical history, medications and anything that just didn't look right. Under each heading they would drop the name of the patient who fell into that category and go back once completed to re-check the information. So if patient A had a history of epilepsy, for example, they were right to be placed in the medical history category and the medication category (if they were taking meds). Nick was hoping that a trend or pattern would become obvious. His attention to detail was intense. Nothing was to be taken at face value. Time after time he questioned Midori as she trawled the patient notes. 'Go back and check again their family history, check again any side effects from Centoria they reported, check again any other medications'. It was a laborious and slow process. They had sifted through each completed sheet but come up with very few connections.

Midori pushed her chair away from the paper filled floor and groaned. It was now 4pm.

'I feel as if we are looking for a needle in a haystack'.

'I know, but think of it more as a key that unlocks a door, once we have that all this will make sense', said Nick, reaching for his now tepid coffee.

They finally called it a night at 1am having stopped only to walk the dog and grab a sandwich. Nick was asleep as soon as his head hit the pillow. Midori remained restless. Thoughts raced in and out of her mind. As quickly as they appeared they were gone. She looked across towards Nick. His face now relaxed, no more frown lines or pursed lips. He looked serene, peaceful. He must be exhausted. He had been up and out by 5.30am on Friday and not had much sleep or respite since. He'd had a complicated surgical list on Friday morning that had run over by two hours due to an excision of a glioblastoma being much larger than the scans had revealed. He'd just completed his list successfully when he'd got the call about Dan. Midori could not imagine how he must have felt.

Was the weight he was placing on the role of Centoria in all of this his way of dealing with the grief? Did he need somewhere to lay the blame? She studied his features. His dark complexion was flawless, not a blemish or spot to be seen. His finely chiselled cheekbones angled to perfection, impeccably framed his wide enchanting eyes. It was the first time she had really noticed how long his eyelashes were. Jet black elegant rods slightly curled at the ends. No wonder his eyes were so captivating. Then there were his full soft lips: just thinking about his kisses made her want to wake him and experience them afresh. No, he would not have let his emotions send him down a blind alley. She was the emotional one, not Nick.

Nick had perfected the art of maintaining a calm exterior when everything was at sixes and sevens. This had been one of the first things he'd learned as a medical student. He'd had an amazing teacher – Professor Richard Wallace, Head of neuroscience at Washington State Hospital for Neurology. Nick had trained and worked with Professor Wallace before his move to the UK. He had seen Wallace perform some of the trickiest surgery around. During one particularly gruelling, nine-hour operation, Prof Wallace had maintained the same softness of voice and the same steadiness of hand throughout. Nick had observed how he had directed the theatre like a conductor leading an orchestra. He instilled confidence, especially when things hadn't gone as expected. A captain navigating a tricky sea, his eyes set always firmly on the horizon. He had gone on to see the patients' relatives, speaking to them softly, thoughtfully, giving them as much of his time as they needed. He was never rushed and always available. Only when they had both returned to the coffee room did Nick understand the toll the operation had taken on the Professor.

'There were moments in there when I really didn't know if the patient was going to live or die, despite my best efforts', he confided. 'I'd felt scared and out of control, way outside my comfort zone...'

'But you looked so calm and in control', Nick had retorted.

'I had to, it was my operation. People need someone to believe in Nick. If I had openly cracked, do you think the anaesthetist or scrub nurse would have remained as focused or on point as I needed them to be? They would have started doubting their own ability - and that is when you are most likely to make mistakes. If you learn nothing else from me, please remember that people need to believe in you. Even if you are falling apart inside, never let it show. You are the one who is setting the bar high, you need to maintain it. The only caveat is to always and I mean always admit when you are wrong. It takes a bigger man to accept his limitations'.

Nick had carried this conversation with him throughout his career. This is who he aspired to be. He wanted to emulate the Professor. Nick was the next generation of whom great things were expected. He would do all that was in his gift to make the Professor proud. Never had his advice been more poignant than when the news of Dan's death had been delivered.

Over the course of the following week, Nick received sixteen new case reports from colleagues across the UK. The case studies they had sent through were anonymised - all identifies save age and gender removed. The research story he'd concocted had been believed, cases were coming through in a steady stream. He did not confide his true intentions for fear of arousing suspicion or scare-mongering. The data would guide them.

Midori called in sick on Monday morning. She couldn't focus on anything other than getting to the bottom of whatever this was. If Rick had sensed she was lying he didn't say. He wished her a speedy recovery and to keep him posted. She prayed Nick was wrong, that the data they were collected would show no connection, no correlation to Centoria. Deep within her the 'smash glass here' box had been activated and the alarm was starting to sound.

They spent the days that followed refining the system they had used initially. They sub-divided the side effects profiles into KSE= known side effects and NKSE= not known side effects. Nick had set up a spreadsheet on his laptop. He insisted they only review the data once all of the information was inputted. It was a slow, lengthy process. Each consultant had sent the information through in slightly different formats. There was no way she could even contemplate returning to work; she had to find out the truth.

It had been on her insistence that Raiden had been given Centoria - what if she had put him in danger? Every time she thought of it a wave of nausea would hit like a 100 miles per hour train. Diving for the bathroom, she threw up violently, retching until her stomach hurt. She had called Rai on Saturday as soon as she thought he may be in danger. He sounded his usual upbeat self, assuring her he was fine. No, he wasn't working too hard, yes, he was getting enough sleep, who was she - his mother? She hadn't told him about Nick's fears (and now hers) over Centoria. She would wait until they had all of the facts. What if Raiden wasn't fine really? What if their suspicions were right? She ran to the bathroom for the third time in the last hour.

Nick was lucky in that his week mainly consisted of study leave. His only clinic was scheduled for Friday and fortunately he'd got it covered. They would sit down on Friday and review everything. The remainder of the week saw Nick resume his usual stance: he was calm and brimming with confidence, only the occasional look of sadness an indication of his true feelings. Friday appeared quickly.

'Moment of truth Dori'. Nick fired up the computer. Armed with two cups of coffee she followed him into the study. Perching herself beside him, she waited. She felt the suspense may overwhelm her.

It took a split second for Nick to key in the mathematical formula he'd created. His hands worked quickly, inputting the code. He hit enter and they waited. It took just under a second for the truth to reveal itself.

Of the twenty four patients they had knowledge of, all had experienced KSE, mainly headaches and migraines. Sixteen had experienced NKSE, for eight of whom it was a positive experience and eight negative. Astonishingly, two thirds had reported previously unknown side effects. Of the eight negative, three had undertaken criminal activities (GBH, theft and lewd behaviour) - but more shockingly, five had a tag of either accidental death or suicide.

The weight of the silence was heavy. Rain had begun to fall vigorously. A timpani of splashes battled the glass panes. Its clatter was out of place with the burden being felt within the walls of Drakes View. Midori spoke first.

'I have to get to New York, I need to see my brother'.

Her voice was small and trembling. It had taken refuge inside her shattered frame. Nick stared blankly, his shoulders tense and his teeth clenched. His eyes no longer sparkled as they had when the conclusion was still unknown. He had hoped he was wrong. He had learned never to make a judgement until the evidence was clear. His eyes were darker than any rain cloud. He was trying to forge a way through, looking for a measured logical approach. When he spoke, she knew he hadn't found it. The clock in the hall struck 11am. They had sat in silence for the last hour.

'We need to be careful'. Each syllable tension-filled, almost at boiling point.

'Rai could be in serious danger...if I book a flight now I could be there by tomorrow'. The urgency contained within her words flowed forth.

'And do what Midori, do what?' Nick's words had stung her over and over, they were short and spiky. Each one delivered with venom. 'There is no way you should go. We don't know enough yet, we need more data. We need to know if the results we're seeing are statistically important or just... or just anomalies'.

'I don't give a toss if these results are 'statistically important', she scolded. 'People have died, Nick, good people, people with their lives ahead of them. I'm not going to sit here and let my brother become one of your bloody statistics!'

Her face reddened. How dare he talk about statistics. She knew she had upset him by raising her voice, but this was her brother for god's sake. Nick walked towards the window. The rain had not relented; it was winning the battle. Pools of water were collecting across the patio. His voice, no longer measured, became an explosion of urgency.

'So off you go to New York, and what will you do Midori Yates, what exactly will you do??' He turned sharply and caught her eye. She couldn't stand the intensity of his gaze and looked towards the floor. His words had been thrown like daggers. She knew he was right but she felt adrift. She needed to be doing something. Her expression showed how his words had injured her. She felt like a bird unable to fly. Nick's expression softened, arms outstretched he enveloped her. He gently stroked the top of her head as she buried her face into his warm broad chest.

'Dori, you are one person', he said soothingly. 'One person, Dori, against a billion dollar drug company who, knowingly or unknowingly, have commercially released a drug that appears dangerously flawed'.

Midori lightly stepped back and held his gaze. His eyes, bloodshot through lack of sleep, screamed exhaustion. His skin no longer polished chocolate silk, instead lacklustre and muted.

'OK - so what do we do, do we take it to the police?'

'No, not yet. All we have is speculation and I'm sorry to say some anomalies. We need proof. Indisputable evidence that will show one way or another if Centoria really is as flawed as it looks'.

'But don't we have that already, for god's sake - people have died!'

'I know - but as harsh as this is gonna sound, that's not enough. Like you said earlier Dori, who's to say that the people who committed suicide wouldn't have done it anyway, or the patients who broke the law, how do we know they weren't going down that road already? We need to get this right. If these bastards knew and have buried the data, we need to find it and bring them to account'. He paused. Midori could see his mind working. He began pacing slowly, his thumb and forefinger starting to tap tap tap.

'Remember last year when we first met and I asked for all the Centoria data?'

Midori nodded. 'You said you'd got all the data through from the medical department...' she answered.

'I remember at the time thinking it all seemed too good to be true. It didn't sit right. I should have questioned further. Bloody hell, Midori, what if I've put people in danger because I was too fucking busy to do my own research?' Nick's pacing had intensified. She was taken aback by his swearing, that wasn't his style.

'It's not your fault', she protested. 'What about the Federal Drug Agency or the European Medicines Agency, that's their job. They gave Centoria its licence…' she snapped. 'They can ask to see anything they want, they can ask for more trials to be done if they are not satisfied with the data…'

He knew she was right but he couldn't shake the idea that somehow he was responsible. If he had been more questioning, could he have saved Dan?

'You said some of the top neurologists in the country were involved in the phase III trials right?' she questioned. Nick nodded. 'So someone must know something, right?'

'Right, so that leads me to ask why no one has said anything? If you see red flags popping up in the trials, you document it and put it into the data collection - so where is it, where's that information?'

'Professor Franklin was involved in the phase III trials at his last hospital. I'll have a quiet word with him on Monday. If anyone knows anything I'm guessing it'll be him'.

'I think I should look for another job', mused Dori. 'I don't want to be involved at any level with whatever this turns out to be.'

'What? No!' Nick looked confused. 'You need to stay Dori, you need to find out as much as you can from the inside, OK?' He continued, not waiting for an answer. 'You are in a perfect position to ask really searching questions without arousing any suspicion'. Not for the first time today she knew he was right. Staying with KLD did not sit comfortably, but Nick was right. She could ask seemingly innocent questions without too much fuss. She would return to work on Monday with her eyes wide open and start doing some digging. Nick sat at the computer and fired off an email to the consultants who had submitted the case studies. He was hoping they could all make a Skype call for the following weekend, when he expected to have more information. It was his duty to share his theory.

9

Walking down 5ᵗʰ Avenue toward 34ᵗʰ Street made him feel alive. The winter had been heavy on this vibrant city. Four feet of snow and some power outages had tested it to capacity. New York, true to type, had hunkered down and ridden out everything winter had thrown its way. New Yorkers were resilient creatures. They'd bounced back, and now with Spring awakening the city was back to its buzzing self.

Raiden Yates also seemed back on top form. He had arrived just as the last winter snow had melted and with it there had been a change in pace both personally and collectively. Transcorp had secured him an apartment in the East Village, a rent-controlled duplex at an unheard-of reasonable price. Furnished with the basics, he had installed cable and a phone but not had time to really put his imprint on it. Minimalism suited him. As long as there was beer in the refrigerator and a TV he was happy.

New York had come at the right time for him. As much as he enjoyed his job back in the UK, it had started to lose its shine, becoming monotonous. The accident had nearly blown his chances of relocating. And had nearly killed him. He believed now he had finally turned a corner; New York City was most definitely the place he needed to be. It was a city with so much to give, especially if you were ambitious and career hungry. Raiden Yates ticked both of those boxes.

The migraines he suffered were the only after-effect from the accident: an annoyance, but manageable. A small price to pay for being alive, he thought. Returning from his software meeting near Central Park, he was reminded of just how lucky he was. He felt like a goofy tourist each time he walked down 5th Avenue. Everything was 24/7 in the speeding metropolis. He wondered how he had survived living in Hicksville for so long. His co-workers were a friendly lively bunch, mainly guys around his age, with a few senior sages strategically placed to keep the young guns in check. Every Friday after work they would hit the sports bar on 15th Street and watch the baseball or football. The older guys would stay for a quick beer then, citing family commitments and weekends in the Hamptons, they would slowly disperse. Rai and the rest of the singles would stay in the bar for a while before grabbing something to eat at Hunka's Beef Bar. The night always seemed to end in Clubland on 8th Street. Friday nights often got messy. Sometimes Rai fought hard to remember what they'd been doing.

He'd wake up on Saturdays with a banging migraine. The migraines he could handle; it was the not remembering he fought with. He never seemed to remember how the night ended or even how he'd made it home. He'd reek of old smoke and his hair was flecked with ash more often than not. An old grungy BBQ pit somewhere downtown was his guess. None of the other guys seemed to be able to recall too much either. He thought he'd had a good time but couldn't say for certain. He was glad his 'big' nights out were restricted to Friday nights: it took the best part of Saturday for him to feel vaguely human again. I must be getting old. God, old at 25 - what a thought! There was a time not that long ago when he'd been able to exist on a few hours of snatched sleep - not any more. If he didn't set his alarm he could easily sleep until midday. Of late he had felt a bit homesick but a quick trip to Jewel Bako Sushi on 5th street sorted him out. It reminded him of happy childhood memories, of sitting on his mother's knee picking sushi off her plate.

This was the longest he had been apart from his family and it felt strange. The regular Skype calls had helped, although it was not really the same. He hoped everything was going OK with his sister and Nick; she had seemed so loved up when he'd left. She deserved to be happy. They would all be visiting him before too long. He would show them the finest New York had to offer. He would blow their minds with the trips he'd plan. He pictured his mum's face when he brought her to his favourite sushi house, and his dad's expression when they visited the Guggen-heim...yep, he would make it a trip to remember, he thought fondly. A trip to Liberty Island was a dead cert. He would have to build in some time for mum and Dori to shop, otherwise he'd be strung up. Even with his limited understanding of all things fashionista he understood that New York held the high bar. Hopefully he could shake the migraines by then. A pattern seemed to be emerging. Whenever he'd been drinking he would wake up with a head full of cotton wool and a mother of a migraine. It didn't seem to matter if it were two or twenty beers, the effect was the same. He wondered if Centoria didn't mix well with alcohol but the patient information leaflet made no mention of it. He didn't want to visit a physician: sure, he had private health insurance, that was a must. It was more the idea of having to give a detailed history of what had happened. He knew he was fortunate to be alive but everything else he wanted to forget. Doctors and hospitals were not his thing; they made him uneasy. How on earth his sister lived with one he didn't know! He was supposed to have regular check-ups - but hey, who would know! He was thousands of miles away.

He got back to the office with time to spare. Working on the 34th floor of the TransCorp building had its advantages. Easily placed to reach uptown or downtown, TransCorp occupied a large corner plot at the junction of 36th street and Avenue of the Americas. It wasn't the tallest skyscraper in town but it was definitely a skyscraper with 58 full glass floors. TransCorp had the run of floors 34 to 44 whilst a variety of airline manufacturers and software designers filled the remaining 48. The view from the corner office boardroom on the 40th floor was immense and had by far the best view within the organisation. On a clear day you could see right up to Central Park.

Aviation had come a long way over the last twenty years. However, helicopter design and technology really hadn't changed since the first fully operational helicopter the Focke – Wulf FW 61 in 1936. Raiden Yates worked within Transcorp's Project Tachyon - a five year research project designed to look at increasing overall speed of helicopters, thereby making them less vulnerable in combat zones. Working closely with his colleague Brett Allerton, the two of them were asked to design light tactical prototypes based on work already started by the Sikorsky Company back in 2010. One of their largest challenges was how to overcome the copter's low speed at take-off, making it an easy target when evacuating the injured from a battlefield. This has reduced its mission capabilities. Project Tachyon's main objectives involved new and untested hypotheses. They were to design a light tactical helicopter, capable of increased speed with a good overall lift to drag ratio. It needed the capacity to maintain full rotor speed control throughout the flight envelope. Raiden's meeting with Gentry Aerospace had been to explore moving the hypothesis off the table and into a simulated model. A lot was riding on Project Tachyon. If anyone could get it over the line it would be Brett and Raiden. He needed to be fully engaged - if only he could shake these migraines.

10

Monday mornings were always grim but none more so than now, thought Midori as she drove to her first appointment at Queens. Lack of sleep had caught up with her and as much as she tried to disguise it, anyone with half a clue would know there was something amiss. Good job her first appointment was with the hospital pharmacist, a gentle Scottish giant, Angus Finlay. There was absolutely no doubting his clinical knowledge but pure emotional intelligence he lacked. The fact he had to deal with patients was laughable. He should be locked away in a lab somewhere, she thought, he'd be happier there. He was as disconnected as you could get from human existence.

She sat in the pharmacy departments' waiting room and reflected on the weekend. Nick was planning a conference call with all of the consultants who had sent through their data for Saturday. He had included Prof. Wallace in the loop. Wallace had a knack of finding needles in haystacks. After she'd finished with Angus she would go and find Nick, who would be in his office surrounded by a mountain of admin. He hoped to catch Prof. Franklin. He'd managed to speak to him and brought him up to speed just before the weekend. As far as the Professor remembered, nothing of note had come out of the phase III trials, but he'd agreed to revisit his study notes and let Nick know.

She knew the route to Nick's office like the back of her hand now. Her meeting with Angus had been engaging and swift; he too had decamped to deal with a mountain of paperwork. How things had changed since the first time she'd visited. Who knew things would work out the way they did? She had recently made a conscious decision not to visit Nick at work unless absolutely necessary: a degree of separation was good. The line was blurry enough without it becoming invisible. There were plenty of other consultants she could work with. The pharmaceutical industry already had a pretty shoddy reputation. There were plenty of horrid headlines without adding to them. She didn't want her relationship to be one of them. Up until last week they had never talked about work at home. Now things were different.

Midori made her way up the final set of stairs, taking them two at a time. They'd agreed to meet in his office for coffee. Hopefully Nick would have some news from Prof. Franklin to add into the mix. Raiden came to mind again. His being so far away troubled her. What if he needed her, what if something bad happened? She replayed the conversation that was now on a continual loop in her head and tried to reassure herself. Nick was right, so far, all they had was circumstantial at best - it proved nothing.

Nick's office door was locked and there was no sign of him. They'd agreed 11am and it was now ten past. Maybe he'd had to visit the wards. That sometimes happened, especially if they were short-staffed . She checked her phone: no missed calls, no texts, strange. Penny would know where he was. She made her way to the secretaries' offices. There was no sign of Penny but Prof. Franklin's secretary Lucy sat, headphones attached, furiously typing away. Midori tried to catch her eye without being too officious. She knew Lucy had seen her walk in, but as usual had refused to make eye contact. Bloody secretaries, why does she feel the need to go through this stupid act? It's as if I am really inconveniencing her. She knew from experience she just had to wait it out. Eventually Lucy would look up.

'Professor Franklin's not here and won't be back for a while. Please call next time instead of just turning up'. Lucy's tone was curt verging on rude. Only once did she raise her gaze from the screen.

'Oh, I was looking for Penny, Mr Campbell's secretary?' Her voice and tone soft, gentle. She'd played this stupid power game too many times recently to let Lucy know how pissed off she was. For every ounce of venom thrown her way Midori would add a double dose of sickly sweetness to it and throw it quietly back. It disarmed all but the harshest secretarial pitbulls. Lucy was however one of the harshest.

'As I have already stated, it's best to call for whoever it is you want to see - now if you don't mind I have a lot to get on with'. Ouch that was unkind and, Midori thought, you will be paid back tenfold in your next life.

'Thank you for being so helpful'. If there was any tone of sarcasm Midori hid it well. She would check Nick's office again, maybe he had returned.

Still nothing. Nick's office sat in darkness - no signs of life. She rummaged around for the key she knew Nick kept hidden. Strange, it wasn't there. She called Penny, who thankfully picked up: no she didn't know where Nick was, no he wasn't on the wards, yes she could meet her in the hospital restaurant. Maybe Penny could even get the charismatic Lucy to uncoil her defensive posture.

Penny was a great secretary but, Midori concluded, she was not the sharpest tool in the box. She arrived wearing her normal bright smile and her garish dress sense (navy cardigan over rust coloured blouse with green midi skirt and red shoes). The 1970s must have wept with joy at the sight of Penny!

'Why the cloak and the dagger?' asked Penny. Her West Country accent was unmistakeable.

'Well I couldn't handle the death stare from your incredibly friendly colleague. Besides don't you think it odd that Nick hasn't turned up for work?' Midori pushed a latte and iced bun she'd ordered towards Penny.

'Oh he turned up', said Penny taking a mammoth chunk out of the oversized bun.

'But he's not in his office, and he definitely said he had an admin day today?' said Midori looking perplexed.

Midori's patience was wearing thin. It was on-ly mid-day but after the weekend her nerves were shattered. She was worried about Raiden and now Nick was playing hide and seek.

''Appen I saw him on his way in, I'd just ar-rived about 7.30 t'was. I'd know that walk any-where. I saw him crossing the car park. He sent me an email saying I was to cancel his appoint-ments for the next few months as he'd be called away, urgent family business is what it said'. Mouth filled with the remnants of the iced bun, Penny smiled sweetly at Midori. 'Didn't he tell you?'

'No... I er... no he didn't. Has he ever done this before?' Midori's voice kept slow and steady. Af-ter all it wasn't Penny's fault. Nick surely would have called her. What on earth had come up?

''Appen he hasn't, I did think it be a bit unu-sual, but these there consultants they do have some strange ways about them. Poor Lucy she got a call from her Professor Franklin on Friday. He's gone on what thems call a sa-bat-i-cal...' Penny emphasised every syllable, looking to Mi-dori for reassurance. Midori nodded. Her mind was racing. So Franklin's sabbatical had been last minute. Nick had spoken with Franklin on Friday and now Nick had disappeared. She had been trying his phone on and off all morning; it was going straight to voicemail.

'Is everything all right Midori?' Penny's slow and measured voice cut through her thoughts.

'Yes, yes, everything is fine Penny, nothing to worry about. What time was it that you got Nick's email?'

'Oh musta bin 8:15ish I reckon'.

'I'll need to get into his office if that's OK, and I need you to do me the biggest favour too?'

She hoped that Penny was up for what she needed, she didn't really have any other options. Penny was happy to help. Midori wondered if Penny's hapless persona was all a front. To the outside world Penny could sometimes seem a sandwich short of a picnic but Midori had a feeling that underneath maybe, just maybe, she was as sharp as any scalpel.

She had asked Penny to get as much information from Lucy as she could about events leading up to Professor Franklin's rather hasty sabbatical. They would meet back at 2pm in Nick's office. In the meantime Midori would trawl his office for any signs of what may have happened. He'd been gone all morning and she hadn't heard a peep. Now that was definitely out of character...

Penny brought the key and left Midori to it. Strange how it hadn't been taped behind the brass name plaque on the door. The smell of freshly brewed coffee was the first thing she sensed. His all-singing all-dancing coffee maker was full; not even one cup had been drunk and the hotplate was still on. When he'd left that morning he had said he had an admin day. It looked like that's what he had planned, else why make that much coffee? Maybe she was overreacting, maybe there would be a perfectly good explanation for his sudden disappearance. He would not have made a whole pot of very expensive coffee and not touched it, she thought. She couldn't shake the feeling of unease that was crashing into her thoughts in overwhelming waves. She felt nauseous and scared. This was completely out of character for him, this wasn't who he was. He was reliable, open, honest and methodical. If he'd had a family emergency he would have at least phoned, or at least asked Penny to phone. No, something didn't smell right and it wasn't the full pot of Jamaican Blue. She looked around his office; there must be something in here, she thought.

It appeared he had taken her advice. The dishevelled piles of patient notes she had seen previously now appeared to be colour coded and reasonably tidy. There was a red pile, an orange pile and a green pile. Out of the corner of her eye Midori saw another pile, slightly hidden in the foot well of his desk. Not quite as big as the other two piles, it appeared to be tied with gold rope. A bit like the bundle of notes she had seen in a solicitor's office, all bundled together. Why were they separate, she wondered? Anyone slightly suspicious would think they were deliberately hidden. As she reached down to pick them up she saw a flash of orange protruding from underneath the bottom draw. She let out a small whimper. Her heart felt as if it had stopped. Shaking, she reached down and pulled out the iphone hidden amongst the papers. Its neon orange casing screamed at her. It was Nick's, of that there was no mistake. She remembered when he got that ghastly case. She had secretly worried he'd taken a few ill thought out fashion tips from Penny. He had needed something bright, he'd said, for two reasons. Firstly no one in their right mind would be seen with something so ugly, therefore if anyone stole it he could easily spot it. Secondly he could locate it quickly in theatre, a bit like a Belisha beacon, only non-flashing. A conversation had then ensued about his fascination with Belisha beacons. They didn't have 'stripy black poles with orange flashing balls on top' in the Bahamas.

'One of those quirky English things you guys are known for', he'd said.

Now here it was, ironically doing exactly what he'd hoped it would do. He would never have left without his phone. Nick was methodical about everything. If he'd misplaced it at home he would search until he found it, no, he would not have left it. She picked up the phone carefully; it was off. She tried to switch it on, but nothing, no signs of life. What she expected it to tell her she wasn't sure, but at this stage anything would be good. The battery was flat.

She took a pile of notes from the foot well and began flicking through them. They were not Nick's patients but Prof. Franklin's, she noted. Nothing unusual there, consultants often shared notes. They were both working on putting together the Alzheimer's project: after all that's what had persuaded Nick to move from the states. She had no idea what she was looking at. She scanned the pages - blood results, brain scan images. Someone's whole history condensed into no more than a few pages. It made her feel uneasy. She felt voyeuristic. Married with 2 children, worked as a mechanic. Something stopped her in her tracks. She had scanned the last page but something had stopped her. She re read the entry - 'Patient rx Centoria, see additional notes section.' Opening another folder she scanned again, more quickly this time. She found what she was looking for on page 10. 'Patient rx Centoria, see additional notes'. These were not patients with Alzheimer's but patients with Amnesia who had been on Centoria. The additional notes made for chilling reading.

Each one had experienced negative side effects that had resulted in death. They were not names she recognised from the list they'd compiled. These were new cases the Prof. must have given to Nick to add in. She looked at the dates and stopped dead in her tracks. For the second time today she felt light-headed, her heart pounding to the point that she had to place her head in her hands and concentrate on her breathing. The papers fell to the floor. 'Breathe Dori, breathe', she chanted to herself. She sat, head held in her hands and breathed, slowly, rhythmically, in through her nose, and long breaths out through her mouth. She could feel her heart adopting a more normal pattern. She needed to get help, but from who? Nick was in danger, if not worse. Her heart started to speed up again. No, she had to maintain a level head. The dates on the notes had all been the same, 2013 – three years before Centoria was launched. These must have been the patients who had been on the safety trials. She breathed deeply, desperately trying to re-oxygenate her hypoxic body. She needed a clear head. Maybe she wasn't reading this right after all - she wasn't a clinician.

She could hear the voice of her old Kendo teacher echoing in her head. *Trust your instincts Midori.* He had taught and nurtured both Midori and Rai for fifteen years, right up until they had gone to university. Thomas Downes was a master of Kendo – a Sensei whose love of his art was infectious and totally inspiring. Midori had lacked confidence and belief in her own abilities. But by the time she reached eighteen she easily whupped Rai and the other students. She was his 'Chisana hoseki' (小さな宝石) – little gem. Her reactions were sharp and her focus solid and reliable. Thomas had seen her potential and encouraged her to use it. He'd instructed and guided her to use both her physical and mental ability. She had won pretty much every competition she'd entered. Initially Kendo had been a chore, something she had to do to appease her parents, but as the years progressed it had invaded her soul. She had seen how with careful instruction she had been able to control and mould her mind and body. She had been able to harness the power of her anger, directing it through her pursuit of Katana to a purposeful and positive place within the dojo. She had not set foot in a dojo since Thomas had died, but she still practiced her patterns. When stress levels rose, she would shut herself away. Methodically working through her patterns. Concentrating on the art of Kendo brought everything else back into balance.

Her attention turned back to the notes. She needed help, someone who knew Nick but who could also help to figure out what was going on.

Professor Wallace knew Nick better than anyone and he was one of the finest clinicians around. Only trouble was he was in Seattle. It would be the middle of the night now. She would see what she could uncover before calling him. Maybe she'd have to call Nick's family too. Maybe he had had to go back home? A thousand thoughts raced through her mind. She delicately placed the phone in her pocket. It was as if she was handling something fragile and priceless. As an afterthought she found a plastic specimen bag and slid the phone in. Nick's office phone rang, making her jump. Should she answer it? Best not to, it could be anybody. She sat despondent in Nick's chair and stared at the pictures of the Bahamas on the opposite wall. Where was he? She checked her phone for the umpteenth time. There was a gentle knock at the door and Penny poked her head around.

'Tis only me', she said, smiling reassuringly. 'I's knows I said 2-ish, but I figured this couldn't do with waiting'. She paused, waiting for permission to enter. Midori beckoned her in. Funny, she thought, here I am sitting in Nick's chair with Penny sitting opposite me like a patient. Penny looked as if she may burst. Her cheeks were flushed and her bosom seemed even more ample than normal.

'I'ze gotta tell thee now Midori, seeing as I don't wanna forget anything', she said, her breath and voice segued into one. 'Lucy, that be Lucy Edgar, Professor Franklin's secretary, well she be mightily upset with the Professor', she gushed. Midori loved Penny to bits but sometimes, just sometimes she wished she could just get her to talk using ten words or less. Sadly Penny was incapable of brevity. Her wild west country voice could squeeze in at least another hundred words before Midori would be able to guess what she was trying to say.

'Why, why is Lucy upset Penny, tell me?' In five words or under, she wanted to add, but restrained herself. Penny was all about the detail, every last bit of detail would be hung up and admired.

'Well it all started last Thursday you see. Lucy sat down with the Prof as she do most Thursdays, to go through his diary, see?' Midori dutifully nodded. She wasn't convinced Penny had required a response but she needed to convey a sense of urgency: maybe nodding her head vigorously wasn't it though. Penny took a breath so deep she started coughing, her ample bosom now taking off in various uncontrolled directions.

'Here take this', said Midori, pouring out a cup of the brewed coffee. Penny took a gulp and screwed her eyes tight shut.

'Sorry I should have warned you it is probably quite strong. None of this makes sense, Penny.'

'Well let me tell you the rest of the story as I's just heard it from Lucy. Professor Franklin was all ship shape on Thursday when she had her regular meeting with he. She sorted him's diary for the next two months, clinics sorted, surgical lists timetabled, all proper, just as he likes it.

Then lo and behold, Friday she starts getting phone calls from the likes of surgeons in France and Switzerland, see. All saying they needs to speak to the professor as soon as possible. That be Friday morning, by the afternoon the Professor emailed Lucy telling her to cancel all his appointments for the next three months and getting her to sort out cover for his clinics and surgical lists. Said he had some important family issues that needed sorting. He got the hospital trust to sign it off too, so's it must be important'. Penny took a small sip of coffee and tried hard to smile. 'Something ain't smelling right if you's ask me. Tis one thing to says you be needing the time off, tis another to be spotted just this very morning in the hospital when you's not at work...'

'What?' Midori looked astonished 'Are you saying that Professor Franklin was here today?'

'Was as clear as day, I did pass im just after I did seen Mr Campbell this mornin. He did not look good at all, not at all. Now that I is thinking 'bout it tis both of 'em off on urgent family business, what with Professor Franklin and now Mr Campbell. Something don't smell right Midori, not right at all...' Penny's usually happy face looked worried. Tight frown lines had appeared

across her forehead, making her look a little de-
ranged.

'You're right Penny, something is not right...'

How much should she tell Penny? It was a
crazy situation. Was all of this to do with Centoria or just a massive coincidence? Probably best
not to get anyone else involved at this stage, she
thought. Who knows what they had got caught
up in?

'I need to find Mr Campbell, Penny. Do you
think he could have gone off with Prof Franklin?'

'I suppose so'.

'OK so maybe I'll pay a quick visit to the wards
to see if they've gone there. Maybe something
clinical came up that needed both of them there,
if I find him I'll let you know. Then I'm going to
head home to see if he's there. If I have any news
I'll call you, OK?'

'I wouldn't worry Midori', Penny said, 'I reckon tis all simply explained'. She patted Midori's
shoulder gently.

Nick and Franklin were not at the hospital.
She had left Nick's office pretty much as she'd
found it, although she had turned off the coffee
pot. The ward was busier than she expected it to
be, probably due to being two consultants down.
She had managed to find Harry the rather un-

happy looking registrar. Surely consultants carried bleeps - what if it was an emergency, she'd asked ? Harry had looked at her blankly and mumbled something about checking the off duty. A knot of biblical proportions was forming in her stomach. It was now late in the day and she was getting nowhere. She followed gormless Harry to the ward office. Professor Franklin was not on call or even scheduled on the off duty for the next three months. How is that even possible, she thought? Top neuro surgeon takes a sudden sabbatical and no-one thinks there's anything a bit odd about it?

'I know, it's a bit weird isn't it?' said Harry, as if reading her mind.

'Yes, I just wasn't expecting it...'

'That's why we're so busy, two consultants both off for three months. It's really unfortunate both of them having deaths in their families at pretty much the same time. I know the trust have managed to get locums but they don't start for another two weeks...'

Three months! Somehow he had been allowed to leave work, have a major family emergency, but at no time thought to tell her! The knot in the pit of her stomach tightened further, it was threatening to overwhelm her. An impending sense of doom circled. This was not who she knew him to be. Whatever was going on was off-the-scale bad.

Harry looked at her quizzically. Midori and Nick were a couple; even he knew that! He had seen them together a few times at leaving dos and the like. How come she doesn't seem to know what's going on, he wondered?

The colour had all but drained from Midori's face. She grabbed onto the side of the desk. Her heart was pounding in her ears, its pulsating thud drowning out any attempt at clarity of thought. As if to rub salt into a gaping wound Harry turned the page. Nick's off duty stared out at her. Each box where he had been due to work had been changed. A red line had been placed through and A/L had been written on top. She could feel the bile building at the back of her throat. The room started to slowly move out of focus and she felt light headed. Harry took her arm and guided her to a chair.

'I thought you knew, I'm so sorry', said Harry (the gormless registrar now didn't seem quite so gormless).

'Professor Franklin was here first thing, said he'd just seen Nick... I mean Mr Campbell. He'd asked the professor to sort everything out as he had to get the first plane back to the Bahamas. His mum I think...' Harry had crouched down by Midori's side and held her hand. Now she knew something was wrong. If his mum were ill he would have called her, no question. Why was she still hoping this was a big misunderstanding with a reasonable explanation?

Somehow she needed to compose herself. She focused on her breathing. Everything else that was screaming for answers she managed to lock away in a strong box at the back of her mind. What was the first thing she needed to know?

'So Professor Franklin was here, this morning?'

Harry nodded.

'Didn't that seem a bit odd? After all, isn't he supposed to be on a sabbatical?'

'Not really. Consultants are always coming in when they're on leave. There is always so much to do here'

'But three months - that's an awfully long time'.

'They are always going off doing research projects and the like. You'd be surprised how many times it happens', said Harry, trying to be reassuring. He still couldn't work out why Midori didn't know that Nick had left to go back to the

Bahamas...probably best not to pry. He had enough on his plate without having to untangle some lovers' tiff.

'Right, well if you're OK now I'll be getting back to my patients...'

'Yes of course, just one last thing'. Midori had to dig deep, holding onto the fragment of composure that was still remaining.

'I don't suppose Prof Franklin gave any indication as to what he would be doing on his sabbatical?' she asked.

'He mentioned something about a research project he was working on in France, that's once the funeral was out of the way. Plays his cards very close to his chest does Prof. Franklin. Now if you'll excuse me'.

Harry grabbed his stethoscope from the table and before she had a chance to ask any more questions he was gone. Her brain had been on a go-slow ever since Harry mentioned that Nick was apparently on a plane to the Bahamas. It was feasible, she thought, but highly unlikely. He would not even have had his passport, so he must have at some point needed to go back to the house. She would swing by his office and grab those files. They would certainly need further investigation.

She didn't want to think about what any of this said about their relationship, if it were true. Everything she thought she knew about him was under scrutiny. Did she really know him at all? Nick's office door was ajar. She was convinced she had locked it. She still had the key. The papers beneath the foot well were gone, and it looked as though they had never been there. A lump formed in her throat. She felt vulnerable and scared.

Midori called Penny and explained about the missing files. Penny sounded fired up. Which in itself rang alarm bells: after all, West Country accents did not lend themselves to the cut and thrust of intrigue and certainly not anger. Penny's dulcet tones were coming across the hands free loud and clear, the natural ebb and flow of her voice lighting up the Somerset countryside as Midori sped along.

'Towards the end of last week Professor Franklin was getting a lot of calls from a scientist called 'Pieratt'; Lucy said he was quite stroppy when she couldn't find the Professor. He'd insisted he held on whilst she bleeped him. He called at least three times. After the first call the Professor made it clear that Lucy was to find him immediately whenever Pieratt called. It was after that series of phone calls that she booked his ferry crossing to France. I can tell thee she were not happy 'bout it. Taking liberties were her words...'

'So she had never done anything like that before or seen him behave like that?'

'No. Seems Professor Franklin had always done his personal stuff 'imself but last week he be at sixes and sevens. Seems as though this Pieratt fellow had him charging all over the place. T'was one day Lucy swore Professor Franklin had slept in the office, he was wearing the same clothes as the day before and, looked as rough as... excuse me Midori but these is her words... as rough as a badger's arse, honestly I did not know what to say'.

Midori's mind was racing. Pieratt, the name seemed vaguely familiar. Somehow everything must be connected; Franklin's odd behaviour, Nick's disappearance and this Pieratt, there had to be a common thread. The only thing that made sense was Franklin going to France. He had his beautiful home in Monflanquin and it would be reasonable to spend his sabbatical there after all.

'I'm on my way home Penny. I'm going to call Nick's family when I get there and see what I can find out. Thank you so much for your help today. I'll let you know when I know what's happening'.

'Midori, be careful. Who knows what's going on', Penny sounded concerned.

'I will, don't worry...'

The house looked exactly as she had left it that morning. She ran through to the bedroom and flung open the wardrobe doors. She didn't know exactly how many clothes Nick had, but she'd hazard a guess that none of them were missing: the same with the suitcases, of that she was certain. They only had three and they were all present. Should she call his mum or sister? No, she needed to look for his passport first. Bracken sensed something was wrong, her usual wagging tail hung low between her back legs. She followed Midori lethargically, looking as if she had been told off in the sternest of terms. The answer lay in the bureau in the hall. Her hand trembled ever so slightly as she opened the top drawer. Staring up at her was the back of a dark blue passport. Taking it in her hand she turned it over. 'Commonwealth of the Bahamas' shouted out at her in gold lettering.

The light in the house was fading. She did not know how long she had been standing looking down at the passport - the sun had been shining when she had arrived home but now it was gone. She had grown cold, but somehow it didn't matter. Bracken had taken up residency at her feet and was fast asleep. She didn't feel anything. It was as if her mind had overridden her feelings and placed them on lockdown. She could not begin to comprehend what was happening and felt so far out of her depth she was at risk of drowning. She needed to call Professor Wallace or maybe the police or both. Above all, she needed to be coherent and right now that even reality seemed impossible. Her phone vibrated in her pocket. Automatically she answered, her voice somehow managing to disguise the void that had overtaken her.

'Midori, Midori is that you?' Penny's reassuring tones drove deep into her subconscious.

'I've found his passport Penny', Midori said simply

'Stay there I am on my way'.

Penny arrived within thirty minutes, her face flushed and troubled. She had taken charge and they both now sat with a cup of tea. Penny only drank coffee but had felt it inappropriate given Nick's love of the stuff, so a cuppa would have to suffice.

Over the course of the next hour, Midori told Penny all that she knew and all that she feared. She described how they had trawled through data over the weekend, until sheer exhaustion had taken over. How Nick was going to share their findings with Professor Franklin, how she feared for her brother's safety in New York. Penny sat in silence, holding Midori's hand and listening.

'We could go to the police but I'm not as sure what they'll be able to do'. Penny's voice was now soft and controlled. 'I reckon we need to speak with Richard Wallace, Nick's old professor in Seattle. See if he can help'.

Midori nodded and took a sip of the sugary sweet tea. Penny's middle names must be 'crisis management' thought Midori, as her psyche finally started responding to the neurons that had gone unanswered over the last few hours. The tea had helped and brought a degree of sharp focus to the situation. Penny had not seemed surprised when Midori spoke about the unusual amount of suicides they had uncovered. In her line of work the line between life and death was blurred at the best of times and invisible at worst. She had come to expect the unexpected, but even by her standards this situation was unsettling.

Professor Wallace was in surgery. Penny left a message for him to call them back as soon as he was free.

'In the meantime Midori, we shall put together a plan of our own. That way we'll gives ourselves a purpose, not let our minds run away with us', Penny said assertively.

'Do you think it's worth driving over to Professor Franklin's house to see if we can find anything out - maybe he's still there?' asked Midori

'I don't see why not. His ferry was at 3pm today according to Lucy so he shouldn't be there - but it'd be worth checking I suppose...' She shot Midori a crooked smile.

'What?'

'Lucy told me where he keeps his spare key, 'appen I thought something didn't smell right before you told me the whole story so I made Lucy tells me everything she knew about him. Now I thinks the stench is overwhelming'. Penny spread the charts Midori and Nick had compiled out onto the kitchen table. 'There's something more that I didn't say earlier but I been thinking tis all linked together...' Penny shifted uncomfortably in her seat and stared down at the charts.

'What is it Penny? Come on tell me', Midori pleaded.

'It's about you... and your company, Midori, you is not gonna like it...' She met Midori's eyes and held her gaze. She had not wanted to bring more bad news down on Midori but the truth would be the only way they could move forward. It had crossed her mind at the time as being a bit odd, but then, Franklin was a bit odd so that had kind of righted it.

'The first time you came to our offices Midori, we knew who you were'. Penny's voice was small and still. All inflexion had been removed. Penny knew her words would weigh heavy. No embellishment, she told herself, just straight forward, easy to understand words.

'What? What do you mean, that's not possible?'

'I'm sorry Midori but Professor Franklin paid Lucy and I to play good cop, bad cop with you'. Her eyes hovered over the table; she couldn't look up. She felt awful, they had thought they were doing a good thing, helping Mr Campbell and all, but now things had become dark and wretched. Taking a deep breath, she continued.

'He'd come in the week before you had turned up, said that we would be getting a visit from a new KLD rep. Lucy was to give you a hard time but I was to be nice and helpful. He said there was a new drug that he was fully aware of but that Mr Campbell would need to be brought up to speed with, and we could help him by making sure it was Mr Campbell that the new rep got to book an appointment with. Two weeks later he presented us with M&S vouchers. Said we had worked so hard, that we were never rewarded and because of all the nice things we did this was his way of saying thank you. He'd never done anything like that before. Now I thinks about it, makes me sick to my stomach. I thought he was trying to help Mr Campbell but now I thinks he was paying us to set you up with Nick...I mean Mr Campbell...' Penny's face was redder than ever. 'I'm so sorry Midori, If I'd of known then what I's knows now.....'

'Did he mention me by name?'

'No, appen he did not, I'm so sorry Midori I really am'.

Penny had slumped forward, holding her head in her hands. Midori wrapped her arms around Penny's shoulders.

'It's not your fault Penny, you or Lucy'.

Her thoughts now crowded in. She thought through every blank canvas that presented itself.

What did it mean? How had Franklin known who she was and why had it been important that Nick knew about Centoria?

Midori started pacing the room, a habit she had picked up from Nick.

'Did anyone from KDL come to see you before me Penny? Was there anyone else the consultants used to see?'

'Yes there was', she said brightly. 'A nice chap, always smiling. He got on really well with Prof Franklin, they were always going off to lunch. Lucy was always taking calls from him, even last week I took a call from him while she was at lunch. I think his name was Rick, yes that's right Rick Clunie ..like George', she added.

Midori's head began to spin. Why was her boss such good friends with Prof. Franklin and why had he not once ever mentioned it? He knew she'd had a hard time in the beginning to get in and see people, why had he not disclosed his relationship with the Prof? And why for fuck's sake had she been set up to meet Nick? Things were starting to unravel: she felt like a spectator in her own life. It made her feel uncomfortable and slightly scared.

'OK I think I do need to pay a visit to the Professors house, see if there is anything going on there. Penny can you stay here and wait for Richard to call?'

'Sure, don't worry Midori, I'm sure there is a reasonable explanation for all of this...' Even as she spoke the words out loud she didn't believe them in the slightest. Not one for emotion, Penny was churning up inside. Why? That was the question she kept coming back to. She had started to formulate her own opinion but prayed she was wrong. Sooner or later she would have to reveal what her real role in all of this was. Medical secretary she may appear to be but Midori deserved to know the truth now. Well, at least her real role in whatever the truth was. She was certain they had only just scratched the surface. They'd found the one bad apple but somewhere there was a whole barrel full. She had been in the business long enough to know when something was rotten to the core. Could Midori handle the truth, the real truth? She'd have to gamble that she could. Things were moving faster than she'd anticipated. She waited for Midori to leave and then picked up the phone. They would need more help: it was time to call in the big guns.

11

She had taken Bracken along with her. Although she was a big softy at heart, Bracken could growl with the best of them. She would drop her off at mum and dad's on the way back. She had been a bit vague when they asked if she and Nick were doing anything nice. She couldn't tell them Nick was missing; they had been through enough with Raiden. No, she would wait until she at least had something other than speculation to offer. She couldn't even call his family - what the hell would she say? And why had Penny been so sure the police couldn't help?

Quite what she had expected to find at Franklin's house she wasn't sure, but she had to do something. All roads pointed to him. She would have a snoop around, even if it only gave her an insight into the man - that would be better than nothing.

The wind had started to kick up, branches of trees were strewn across the roads as she drove towards the professor's house. Midori had been to Professor Franklin's house once for dinner with Nick. It had been a pleasant enough evening, although on reflection even then something had seemed not quite right. At the time she'd put it down to the streak of arrogance that seemed to run through him like words through a stick of rock. Now though, she wasn't sure. She had not mentioned anything to Nick, after all what could she say? Prof. Franklin is rather arrogant? Him and 80% of the other consultants, he would have replied! Hopefully he would be at home and she at the very least could find out what was going on.

Compared to his house in France, The Cedars was an exercise in all things modest. It didn't really fit with his other life. A reasonable sized three bedroom detached modern house set in two acres in Wellington, Somerset vs a twenty-acre-plus large country estate, complete with pool, library and housekeeper in Monflanquin? She knew which got her vote. It was hard for her to marry the two with Hugh Franklin. He had lived at The Cedars for the past eight years since the sad death of his wife Anne. It appeared to Midori, or anyone bothering to look, that cash was not an issue for Franklin. Maybe Anne had some sort of hefty death insurance, who knows?

He had evaded a discussion about finances over dinner, but she had thought at the time there was more to it.

Dusk turned to night as she headed towards Wellington. She killed the lights of the car as she turned into the drive. She'd seen it often in movies - somehow it had seemed the right thing to do. The house sat in darkness. If he was here he was doing a pretty good job of looking like he wasn't. She parked away from the house, put Bracken on her leash, and headed towards the front door. A detective she was not. At the first sign of trouble she hoped she would not buckle. She found the key under the large wisteria to the left of the door, just where Penny had said it would be. There was no sign of an alarm, which was good. She felt on edge as soon as she walked through the door. She dared not turn on a light and the torch she'd brought was only a cheap old thing, more of an afterthought really. Its weak soft focus beam didn't illuminate much. Carefully unlocking the door, she listened. The house sat in silence. What the hell was she doing? This was insane! She stepped into the hallway. A large circular hallway with a central staircase stood before her. Its memory brought her back to the front of her mind. Yep she was insane. How the hell could she even explain what on earth she was doing here? She was breaking the law, acting very suspiciously, and did not even understand what she was looking for. I have really lost it now, she thought as she shimmied forward in the semi-darkness.

All downstairs rooms branched from the hallway. The kitchen towards the back, dining room to the left, living room to the right. There was a downstairs cloakroom just by the entrance. The only door she didn't remember was the one just next to the cloakroom. She assumed it was Franklin's office. As good a place as any to start, she thought. The smell of ageing paper hit her as she entered the room. The room appeared darker than the rest of the house and her eyes took time to adjust. The curtains were drawn, their density all-consuming. You would have no idea about the world outside in this room. She wondered if the curtains were drawn to stop people outside looking in or to block whoever had been on the inside looking out? The temptation to turn and run overwhelmed her, and, for a moment, she paused. What was she thinking? If Franklin was as rotten as she was starting to think, would he really leave stuff lying around? What if she'd got it all wrong? What if...?

Her thoughts were interrupted by the ringing of a phone that sat somewhere towards the back of the room. There was not much for it she would have to turn on the light, she couldn't see a bloody thing. The phone sat on top of a bookcase, one of three that filled the room. There was a desk with a computer, the usual kiddie type holiday photos and a desk lamp. A 'normal' type of office, if ever there was such a thing. The desk had a series of three drawers on each side, all were locked. The answerphone clicked in and she heard Franklin delivering the standard 'leave a message after the tone' script. She could hear someone breathing at the end of the line, but no message, just breathing. As if things weren't creeping her out enough, she stood and listened. How stupid, why am I holding my breath? There is no way whoever is at the end of the line knows I'm here, she reasoned. Still, she could not escape the feeling that whoever had been at the end of the phone indeed knew she was there. *Clarity of thought Midori, clarity of thought*, Sensei's words echoed through her mind. He was right, she needed to find some clarity. She could rattle around here for days and not find a thing.

So if I were a crazy Professor, where would I think of hiding secrets? She surveyed the room.

Everything looked normal, which was infuriating. The only things she found a little left of centre were the inordinate amount of books, they were everywhere. She knew from the time they had spent in Monflanquin that this was Franklin's passion, so nothing bizarre about that. Without warning Bracken leaped to her feet and started barking furiously towards the window. Midori peered from behind the curtain: a car had pulled into the driveway.

Oh shit, this hadn't been in her plan. She grabbed hold of Bracken by the collar and gently placed one hand around her muzzle. 'Sshhh, good girl, quiet now, sshhhh quiet now...' she whispered. What on earth should she do. *Focus Midori, focus* - Thomas' voice calmly insisted.

Great, my defence me lud is that on the said night in question I had clearly lost my marbles as I was forever taking direction from a voice in my head.

There was only one thing for it. As stupid as she knew it was, she would have to hide behind the curtain. She could hear the slamming of car doors and feet meeting shingle. Oh God there's more than one of them. The curtain now seemed like less of a good option. Grabbing tightly onto Bracken she darted back across the room, out into the hall and into the downstairs cloakroom. She had just managed to close the cloakroom door behind her when she heard footsteps entering the hallway. At first there was silence, then to her relief she heard Penny's unmistakable voice.

'Midori, where you be?' Penny's accent softly chimed out. Midori's sense of relief was palpable.

Opening the cloakroom door she was faced with Penny and Gormless, aka 'Harry'. Bracken rushed past her, furiously wagging her tail.

'What's he doing here?' The surprise in her voice blatant.

'Penny called me to see if I could help'. Harry caught Midori's eye

'I've been on Franklin's team for just over a year now', he said by way of explanation.

'Penny?' Midori cocked her head to one side.

Penny caught her gaze and held it.

'We needed help Midori, Harry knows Franklin as best as anyone...he wants to help us', she added.

'OK fine'. She wasn't happy about bringing more people on board. She didn't even know what this was but it felt pretty bad.

An awkward silence was quickly broken as Bracken took the opportunity to break wind.

'That dog can certainly handle herself', laughed Harry.

''Appens she can, but you Midori - you'd make a lousy spy', chipped in Penny.

'Why?'

'You's gone left the bloody light on', Penny pointed towards the office. 'And the front door was wide open'. Penny rolled her eyes

'Sorry, this is not normally what I find myself doing on a Monday evening', Midori jibbed. 'I'm glad you're both here, honestly I am', she sighed. She walked towards the office. 'I'm at a loss, I have no idea what I'm looking for...'

'Do you mind if I take a look?' Harry asked.

'Be my guest, in fact be Franklin's guest'. Harry was grating on her. Why did she find it so hard to ask for help? Everything was just a bit too surreal. It felt as if the fabric of her life had been woven with cheap thread and was now starting to come apart at the seams. Two weeks ago she had been blissfully happy. Now? God, now everything was a mess. Centoria, Nick's disappearance, her paranoia, everything!

As if seeing the cracks Penny drew alongside her. 'Stop beating yourself up girl. There's nothing you could have done to change any of this'.

She placed her arm gently around Midori's shoulders.

'I just feel so helpless, we don't even know if we're on the right track'.

'Oh we are', said Harry from the other side of the room. He was examining one of the book cases.

'I brought him up to speed in the car', said Penny hastily.

'Come and look at this'. Harry was holding a copy of Professor Franklin's first published book 'Neural pathway redevelopment in immunocompetent patients'. A gold thread similar to those that had been tied to the patient notes in Nick's office dangled along its spine. Harry opened the book to where the thread bookmarked the page.

'Got ya', he said proudly. Dangling from the end of the thread was a key, which at a guess would open at least one of the desk drawers.

'See Harry, your army training is standing you in good stead', said Penny proudly.

Midori looked at him curiously.

'Long story, medical corp', he replied.

The top drawer had the usual bits and pieces you would expect to find lurking: business cards, photo I.D. for the hospital, a few pens and pencils. The second drawer however was a lot more giving of its secrets: receipts for an android phone, a high spec set of walkie-talkies, binoculars. The receipts were all dated within the last week.

'Maybe he enjoys rambling, this could all still be quite innocent', offered Midori. Penny and Harry shot her a look that said – WTF?

Bracken had started to make small whining sounds; she was moving only her back legs from side to side. 'We're both starting to get a bit creeped out being here'. Midori bent towards the dog, gently running her hand across its back and patting it softly.

'Just another minute, I think I've found something'. Harry had been exploring the remaining drawer. In his left hand he held a USB. 'OK, let's go...'

'Can we really just take it? Isn't that technically stealing?'

'Well if we're getting 'technical', isn't entering someone's house without permission technically breaking in? Honestly Midori, come on, let's just go. You can get all righteous on me once we know what's on it'.

From nowhere Harry had taken command. She didn't have the will or inclination to fight about it. Maybe he could be helpful. He seemed at ease with the situation, must be that army training or whatever it was, she thought. Sitting in the car she realised just how bone-tired she was. It was her tenacity that had got her to this point. She wasn't sure what came next but was thankful for Penny and now Harry's involvement.

The memory stick was exactly what they'd hoped it would be. It contained files and files of data. The trial patient data it contained proved beyond a reasonable doubt that Centoria was flawed from the outset.

'The amount of similar side effects to the ones you told me about are immense. I can't believe they knew all of this and blatantly hid it. People's lives have been at stake for fuck's sake!' The anger in Harry's voice was unmistakeable. He had been scanning the data for the last two hours. They all now sat in the study at Drakes View. With Bracken safely dispatched to her parents, the house felt very lonely. Midori rustled up some pasta, although no one had an appetite.

'This is big, too big for Franklin to have been working solo', said Midori. Penny and Harry shot each other a look. 'Sorry - did I miss something?'

'I suppose now is as good a time as any...you'd better sit down'. Penny motioned for Midori to join her on the sofa.

'Harry and me haven't exactly been 100% forthcoming .Truth is we both, well, we both work for a special unit within the European Medicines Agency – EM3'.

Midori's eyes widened.

'European Medicines 3, not very original I know but that's what it is'.

Penny shifted uncomfortably.

'About two years ago a scientist working on Centoria came to us with concerns about the drug's safety profile. Naturally we have to take all reports seriously, especially when they are from such an eminent source. A full investigation was launched, as you know for yourself the overall trial data seemed spotless so...' Her voice trailed off.

'So the investigation closed – no case to answer', continued Harry. 'Then about a year ago the original whistle blower, scientist Dr Gunther, committed suicide. His family insisted there was no way he would ever commit suicide, so the case was discreetly passed to EM3. We deal with, let's say, the seedier side of the pharmaceuticals industry...whilst the police go ahead and conduct their investigations we go ahead with our own. Our investigations always centre on drug safety...'

Midori's mouth was on the ground.

'You mean, you mean you are like drugs spies?'

No way was this for real, how the bloody hell could buxom Penny Longstocking and Gormless Mcfucking Gormless ever EVER be proper bone fide spies? You couldn't make this shit up, she thought. Just when she thought things could not get any weirder!

'We do work mainly undercover and our work is quite secretive so I suppose at a push you could call us spies - but I prefer to call us drug safety investigators', Harry said proudly.

D.S.I no way, no frigging way!

'But...but... you are so normal...' The disbelief in her voice was possibly a tad too much. Both Penny and Harry gave her a death stare. 'Sorry, I mean, you are obviously good at your job... I didn't mean....' That's right, keep on digging... 'I just meant I didn't see that coming. It's taken me by surprise really...'

'The unit investigates drugs companies independently. If there are concerns about new drug safety we get brought in. Technically we don't exist. Everything we do is so commercially sensitive that we really do have to tread carefully. We must be 100% sure of our facts. If there is doubt around original data used to get a marketing authorisation then we step in and take a look, but we do it covertly so as not to draw any unwanted attention to ourselves. No one in the hospital knows our true identity; we work hidden in plain sight. Most of what we do results in no need for concern, which is reassuring. But every now and again you get one that smells rotten to the core. Up until now with Centoria we didn't really have much to go on. We were due to close the case next month but now, well now...' Harry turned back to the screen. The display showed graphs and pie charts and lots and lots of numbers.

'But you are from the West Country Penny, you're just a regular person?' Midori's look said - reassure me, tell me I've got this wrong. OK I know I'm starting to sound a bit hysterical now, but really Penny of all people, a spy? Thankfully she hadn't said any of this out loud.

The first time Midori had met Penny was in the neuro secretary's office. She looked just like a secretary: ordinary, anonymous. If she hadn't have had to visit the department often she would have been easily forgettable, well her name anyway she reasoned, not her dress sense. That was most definitely memorable!

'Just the ways it worked out, Midori. I broadened my accent for this investigation, but it's always been identifiable, I really am from around here. It's nice to be home for a while to tell you the truth'.

Stop staring at them, she told herself. They are still the same people. Or are they? She didn't know what to believe anymore. Nothing had changed but somehow in an indescribable way everything had. Events had moved from surreal to frighteningly real. This was big boy stuff. Stuff she didn't have a road map for.

'So what happens now, do the Police take over?'

'No, no Police, not at this stage anyway, not until we know the extent of the damage', Penny said quickly.

'Damage? This is not damage. This amounts to murder from where I'm standing. Plus possible kidnapping, God only knows where Nick is now...' She started pacing, she needed to be active. Sitting around thinking gave her too much time to imagine all sorts of nasty possibilities.

'Please Midori, sit down, I need to concentrate'. Harry's voice was firm and controlled. A few small things now started to make sense. She could see how his act of being gormless would gain him insight into the Professor. She slumped down into the armchair opposite the computer. It was the same chair she had sat in the night they had figured out there was a problem with Centoria. The night she and Nick had argued about her running off to New York to make sure Rai was OK.

'Oh my God, my brother Raiden, I have to make sure he's OK, he's been taking Centoria, he's on his own in New York!'

Penny looked at her, concern etched across her brow. 'We know, we have a list of every patient currently taking Centoria. Has he been acting strangely?'

'Not that I'm aware of, but how would I know, being so far away?'

'Don't worry about your brother. You concentrate on helping us figure out where Nick might be. I'll make a few phone calls and see if we can put a tail on Raiden for a few days just to make sure he's OK'. Her smile was weak, but it was a smile.

Despite recent revelations Midori trusted Penny. She was honest and believable and that comforted her. It was 2am. Harry had spent most of the evening breaking into the encrypted files on Franklin's email account. Midori was convinced Franklin would take Nick to Monflanquin.

Nick's phone beeped a fully charged signal. Taking it from the charging deck Midori switched it on. Maybe there was something here that could help them. Nick had been clever and set the voice memo on his phone. The time read 8:04am. It had recorded what must have been his last known conversation.

'You won't get away with this Franklin, I just can't believe it took me so long to see you for who you really are'. She recognised Nick's voice immediately, he sounded confident and strong. There was no hint of fear in his voice.

'For someone seemingly as smart as you, I'm surprised you haven't figured everything out...' Franklin's voice, unmistakably smooth and measured.

'You know Nick, this game started way before either of us were born. I'll let you into a little secret - what's happening with Centoria is nothing new. Have a think, cast your mind back – where do you think the Nazis got their drugs? Eh? Or the US military? Eh? They got them from reputable pharmaceuticals companies, that's where.

Then there's thalidomide? Any pennies starting to drop yet Nick? These are not isolated incidents Nick; these are only the ones you get to hear about. Centoria sits somewhere on that spectrum. What is it they say eh? You have to crack a few eggs to make an omelette'. Franklin's voice had become distant, as if he was moving away.

'You can't be serious - people are dying, Hugh. Good people are dying. This isn't war or some kind of bad clinical trial. There is no mistake here - this is deliberate'. She could hear the anger building in Nick's voice. 'Why would you be involved with something like this Hugh? We try to save lives, not destroy them...'

'I was like you once, Nick. I wanted to make the world a better place, to do good. That's why I'm involved with Centoria. We are so close Nick, so close to finding the right formulation for Centoria, for Alzheimer's. Think of the lives that we could save. If my wife was still around, imagine the difference this drug could make to her and thousands of others? She could get her life back, the life she deserved to have. Not the life she got'.

'So you've done this for her, for Anne?' Nick's voice had taken on an edge of aggression, of incredulity.

'Not just for Anne, for everyone. You know Alzheimer's is the largest threat to mankind there is right now. Imagine, Nick, imagine where we could go with this?'

'But we haven't started the trials yet for Alzheimer's, we've only just got ethics approval. Based on what I'm finding out about Centoria there is no way it's going to be approved even for a safety trial'.

'Step back Nick, look clearly. The trials have been on-going for years; the first step was to get Centoria to market. To open up the prescribing to a wider cohort of patients to really see the drug in action'.

'But...but... so you're saying this whole thing is a... is a stepping stone... an experiment...... on people. Sick, vulnerable people? You are willing to try out a drug which may not, no, has not, proved safe - for your own warped sense of purpose?'

'Why do you think I wanted you on my team Nick? I saw your work with Prof. Wallace, I saw your passion, your commitment, how you wanted to move neuroscience on to the next level. You can still be a part of the future. Work with me on this. Together we can make it work, I know we can!'

'I can't believe how far you have gone Hugh. I really looked up to you. But now I'm seeing who you really are. A sad delusional mad man. I want no part of your sickening plans. The sooner the authorities find out about this the sooner it will come to a stop'.

Midori could hear the sadness in Nick's voice. Everything he believed in was crashing around him.

'I'm sorry Nick, I really am. You will come to see the power that Centoria has, you will. You'll see, Nick, you'll see. We're playing with the big boys now and they don't like losing. Right now though, I need you to do something for me'. Franklin's voice had grown clearer, closer.

'Hugh, what are you doing?' The sounds became muffled - perhaps a struggle? Then a thud - the phone must have been on Nick's lap and fallen to the floor. The three listened intently, trying to make out any sounds. More muffled noises, then silence. What had happened, had Franklin drugged him or injured him, or both?

Franklin's voice now distant but audible. 'It's Franklin, I need you in Campbell's office. Bring a trolley and some scrubs. He'll be coming with us. Get another space booked and make sure the paperwork's watertight. We can't afford for any slip-ups. The sooner we're in France the better'.

For the next few minutes there was silence, then unknown voices. 'We brought the wheelchair, thought it may work better than the gurney. We'll get him loaded up. We're booked to sail this afternoon'.

Although she didn't recognise the voice she knew the accent, it was broad and Scottish.

'Good, you go ahead with him. I have to tie up some loose ends here just to avoid any suspicion. I'll need to do a bit of tap dancing with management but I'll make sure it's sorted. Get him settled at the facility and I'll be over tomorrow. He should be out for at least ten hours, I've given him a rather large bolus - that should keep him under control. Just keep an eye on his vitals'.

Midori looked at Harry and Penny. Any doubt in their minds had just been completely washed away.

'We need to find that bastard'.

Midori had never heard Penny swear; it seemed somehow out of place.

'I think he's taken him to Monflanquin. Nick and I were there earlier this year. I think he's got some kind of facility beneath his bloody library'.

It was decided that Midori and Harry would go as quickly as possible to France whilst Penny would await news about Raiden and also bring Professor Wallace up to speed. If need be she could jump on a plane to New York. She hoped that would not be necessary, she had not seen Professor Wallace since she ended their relationship two years earlier, but she had thought about him every day since.

12

He'd awoken from a dreamless sleep. His head felt heavy. How had he missed it? It must have been staring him in the face for months. These were the questions imprinted on the inside of his skull, but he had no idea why. Missed what? What had he missed? His memories were not forthcoming. His mind felt foggy and full of cotton wool - had he been drugged? The room was dark and felt gloomy. A few chinks of light displayed eerie patterns on the wall. He was lying down on what he presumed was a bed. He shifted the pillow beneath his head, it felt starched and cold. He felt different, somehow disconnected. Bloody head, he couldn't even think clearly about trying to think clearly! He ran his hands along the sides of his body. His clothes felt odd. They too felt starched, cold and most definitely unfamiliar. How was he so sure? Anaesthetic, only anaesthetic would give him the kind of mother of all headaches he was experiencing. He was struggling to make out pretty much anything in the near blackness of it all. He needed to fix on something that may help to explain what was happening. He felt his arms for a watch - nothing. Scrubs, he was wearing scrubs, he was certain of it. He sat up slowly. He didn't feel right, waves of nausea flooded over him as the room started to spin. Laying back down, the nausea subsided. OK, think man, think. Nick lay still and closed his eyes. What could he remember, oh God, what could he remember? Panic gripped him and squeezed tight. His memory was as dark as the room: he remembered nothing.

He'd been there two days, possibly it was longer. He had been marking the iron bed frame with the plastic cutlery they gave him. He knew how to count so at least that was something. In fact that was pretty much everything. Why did he think it necessary to make a note of the days and hide it? His struggle was with what he was being told. Both mornings a medic had appeared with a hand full of pick and mix drugs, two red and two yellow. On the first day he had refused. He remembered the needle being driven into the back of his neck, then nothing. He had woken disorientated, cold and shivering. Each time he refused to take his meds it would be done the hard way, the medic explained. The hard way appeared to be a needle in the back of the neck and further memory loss. He felt drained and hungry in equal measures. The men in white said he was a volunteer for a drug trial, didn't he remember? He had been included because of his bad memory, did he not remember? Each afternoon he had left the room and was taken to a scanning room. He was put into an MRI (how he knew its name he had no idea). The facility was clinical and glaringly bright compared to his dark room. Why was his room always so dark? He felt like a veal calf awaiting its fate. At night he'd heard voices. They chanted a multitude of miseries that had invaded his soul. They were not the voices of hope. They were the sounds of despair, of utter wretchedness. Were they real? He hoped not. He slept little, preferring instead to maintain his hyper-vigilant state. He felt like an imposter in his own body. Nick's sense of entrapment at times overpowered him and he slumped to the floor unable to comprehend how or why he was here. He may have forgotten much but somewhere in the back of his inadequately functioning mind he knew this was not good. He was in the eye of a storm without a compass to navigate his way out.

Had he really volunteered for some kind of trial? Why? Who was he? Why would he do that? He had nothing by which to flesh out his thoughts or feelings. Each time he tried to remember he hit a brick wall. What if he did volunteer for the trials? Had his mind been in any fit state to realise what was involved? Questions plagued him. They raced through him at lightning speed, depositing their uncertainties. He was left feeling haunted and preoccupied. Whatever was happening here was not good, he didn't need a memory to tell him that. Carving a hole into the underside of the cylindrical bed leg he stored the remnants of today's pills. Thankfully no one had noticed. He had behaved in a subservient and compliant manor during the morning's drug round. He had put all of the pills into his mouth under the watchful eye of Medic number 1. A loud bang from within the facility had proved timely, distracting both medics and giving him enough time to pop the pills into his scrubs pocket. They had turned back just in time to see Nick downing a cup of water. He knew he could not have faked swallowing the pills. The large and more obtuse of the two had his finger in Nick's mouth giving it the once over before Nick had a chance to blink.

His clarity of thought seemed to improve throughout the day although sadly his sense of self was no clearer. Maybe he was in the medical profession or worked in a hospital? He seemed to know a lot of the clinical terminology they used around him. Only when they had to perform tasks such as the drug round or cleaning did the lights in his room go on. That afternoon his lights went on and a familiar looking man appeared flanked by the two medics. Nick seemed vaguely to recognise him but could not place from where.

'So Mr Campbell, I hear you are having trouble remembering things, would that be fair to say?'

Ah so my name is Mr Campbell, good, at least that's a start. The man's voice had thrown a chill over his body - this man unsettled him. His voice was familiar in a foreboding way. Alarm bells began to ring. His subconscious was hammering on the door with an important message. Each time he tried to open it the door jammed. He caught a glimpse of the message. It read 'do not trust him' in large neon letters.

'I think so', was all he could manage.

'Good, well let's see what we can do about that then'. The alarm bells had been replaced. Air raid sirens now sang from every fibre. Any minute now this experience was going to get worse.

'We need to prep you for theatre tomorrow Mr Campbell. We're going to have a good look around and see if we can see where the problem is'.

'I, I don't think I understand...' Nick's voice was no more than a whisper.

'We need to identify the area of your brain that isn't working properly and kick start it'. The man's voice had become snappy and impatient. 'Prep him for theatre tomorrow. Make sure he's good to go first thing'.

Nick felt sick. Two thick-set men stared at him, their faces blank, expressionless. Directed to change into another set of scrubs he sat upright on the trolley, visibly shaking. The panic that had gripped him subsided. Panic had left the room kicking and screaming, what now sat on his shoulder was far darker – terror.

13

The unlikely pair of Midori and Harry set off just before dawn. Neither had slept particularly well. They agreed to hire a motorhome in Kent on their way down to the Ferry terminal to France. The motorhome would provide a good cover story, useful if they needed to 'blend in' whilst travelling through France. No one would suspect a young couple on a camp site, even if it was late winter. The last time she had been in France had been so different. They had been happy days. Monflanquin had been the place Nick told her he loved her. She had been so exuberantly joyful she had wanted to burst. It had also been an anxious time: it was where she had first learnt of Raiden's accident. Maybe that's why she had not at first glance taken on board the suspicions that lay within Le Manoir Couder - now they seemed blindingly obvious. Are there certain places on earth that draw you to them, she wondered? Places where for whatever reason you have a connection, some unknown ethereal tie? Maybe it was the place where it had begun or ended for them, in some previous existence. Had they once been citizens of Aquitaine? She stared out of the window. Once she had sat in awe of the passing landscape, now numbness, anxiety and fear were her companions. Why had they been fated to travel to Monflanquin in the first place? It had seemed like a random act of kindness on Professor Franklin's part. A chill ran down her spine - random? No - kindness? She doubted it. Monflanquin certainly seemed to have a hold over them.

The motorhome was making good progress. They would be in Monflanquin by nightfall. They approached the city from the North. Midori directed Harry to the small campsite she remembered from her last visit. The night was casting its shades of velvet across the landscape by the time they arrived. She had thought the campsite would make a great spot for future holidays. Now, her heart hung heavy. She prayed Nick was here, there were no guarantees. She still wanted to hope beyond hope that there had been some dreadful mistake and there was a perfectly reasonable explanation for recent events. She knew she was on her own with that theory.

The owner of the campsite was delighted to see them. Business had been slow on account of the bad weather, only a few motorhomes and a couple of tents were pitched. Tents, in this weather! Maybe the owner had put them there for effect, to make the place not look quite so bleak. She couldn't imagine anyone bedding down in a tent! To the outside world Midori and Harry looked like everyday holiday makers, a young couple exploring France. The campsite backed onto woodland that bordered the estate of Le Manoir Courder. They picked a pitch parallel to the edge of the woods. It would allow them to come and go without attracting too much attention. They had picked up some supplies at the Carre Four in town. Thankfully Harry had been thinking straight. Alongside the pate and olives that found their way into the shopping cart, Harry had picked up a torch, some rope, two small cans of hairspray, a TV remote and a first aid kit. The hairspray, he explained to Midori's amusement, was to spray into the eyes of any hostiles they encountered. The TV remote could help to signal their whereabouts should they be captured.

'Are you serious, a TV remote, what's it gonna do? Switch the nearest TV Channel to 'Help I'm an unlawful investigator get me out of here?' Midori's voice reached fever pitch: it had been a long confusing day. Ignoring her sarcasm, Harry stuffed the items into her rucksack.

'If pressed and held skywards a drone or radar station can pick up our whereabouts. It emits an infrared signal. We have to report in every three hours via phone. If we don't they will start to monitor our last known location. It can act like a beacon'.

'They' must be EM3, she concluded. This shit was real and serious. She needed to stop thinking it was a mistake or a deluded dream and accept the reality of it all. It would be a long night. Waiting for the fullness of night to form they settled down to a dinner of pate, bread and olives which they ate silently.

At 2am Midori and Harry walked through the woodland. It brought them out towards the rear of the tennis courts on the estate. They had a good view of the library from here. Anger rose from the pit of her stomach; the bile hitting the back of her throat made her gasp. She was struggling to believe what she was seeing.

Concealed beneath a calm French country estate lay what appeared to be a state of the art, highly functioning research facility. A facility hidden in plain sight below an authentic library. She had not clocked any of this the last time she was here. I had only seen what I wanted to see, she thought sadly. This does not bode well, this does not bode well at all. They still had a few hours before the dawn chorus. The fencing surrounding the tennis courts had provided good cover.

'There are cameras everywhere', whispered Midori pointing to the CCTV cameras at the side of the bibliotheque. She had not noticed these either on her last trip. The only way she could think to get into the facility was via the library entrance. She prayed the door was unlocked. Having approached from the rear of the building she now saw for the first time what had been there all along. The building had been cleverly designed to display less at the front than at the back. Two further lower ground floor levels sat steeped in amber lighting. She guessed there were even more sub-levels. Her eyes caught air vent shafts littered around the patio. She must have been so head-in-the-clouds last time she was here that she had not noticed any of it. OK so it had been snowing, but really? She had even stood in the stoop of the lower ground floor to get a phone signal and still not seen anything.

Such a beautiful place holding back so many secrets, she thought. A rash of goose bumps danced up and down her spine. She shuddered, who knew what they would find?

Thankfully the main door to the library was unlocked. Harry and Midori clung to the shadows as they navigated their way through the main atrium. The same musty old paper smell hit her senses. Everywhere was in darkness and apart from the hum of a distant generator silence reigned supreme. They found the stairwell with ease: she hoped it was what she believed it to be.

'Bugger'.

'What?' whispered Harry, who was now so close behind her she could feel his words breathing onto the back of her neck.

'The code to the door, I forgot there was a bloody code'.

'Let me have a look'. He shone his Maglite down the stairwell and onto the keypad.

'Do you think we can do it, can we get in?' Midori's face looked anxious.

'I bloody hope so, it's been a while since I had to unscramble one of these but I'll give it my best shot. Let's hope that Franklin wasn't too much of a nerd when it comes to security eh?'

From somewhere Harry produced a small roll of miniature instruments. Was there was no end to this man's talents? After all, a neuroscience SPR who also doubles as a spy come European Drug agency law enforcer – what else didn't she know about Harry Jay?

Her thoughts drifted to Nick. She had managed to stay so 'task' orientated that now, standing waiting for Harry to weave his magic, she had time to think. What if he wasn't OK? What if he wasn't even here? Harry shot her a look. She signalled she was OK and he continued. Why did she believe Franklin had kidnapped Nick: what did he have to do with anything? Her brain hurt too much to think clearly. Harry's voice cut into her thoughts.

'We're in, no alarm bells going off either which is good. You ready? We'll meet back at the wagon at 5am regardless OK? If either of us are not back by then we go straight to the gendarmerie OK? I'm going to find the control room and disable the CCTV, it'll probably kill the lights as well. You got a torch?'

Harry studied her face. It was a big ask to expect a civvie to undertake such an operation, but from what he knew of Midori she was tougher than she looked. Midori nodded and held up her phone. It was now or never, she would have to deal with whatever flew out of this, whatever the fuck this was.

The overhead lighting was the first thing that struck her. Its hue and glow not more than an ember escaping from a fire someone had forgotten to stoke. It made everything seem 'soft focus', with burnt amber undertones. Despite the darkness of the library Midori's eyes still had to adjust. What presented itself was not the bright white clinical scene she'd been expecting. The corridor was low ceilinged and narrow, only just wide enough to stand side by side. At the end was a T junction, the lighting here was somewhat brighter, more in keeping with a clinical unit. Although she had never been down a mine Midori imagined that the claustrophobia she now felt would not be dissimilar in one. Harry tapped her shoulder. From his gestures she read that she would take the left side and he would take the right. She pulled up her hood and dragged her scarf up and over her nose and mouth. If she did get caught on camera there was no way they'd know it was her. Midori paused at the T junction and watched as Harry slipped off silently down the right hand side of the corridor. He quickly looked back towards her and signalled the all clear before slipping into a side room. It was now or never. She had to believe that every step she took would be bringing her a step closer to Nick. It was her turn to be brave.

On either side of the corridor lay a series of rooms and directly ahead was what looked like a staircase. She moved slowly, clinging to the cold smooth wall. A smell she could only describe as medical invaded her nostrils. Bar the regulated sound of a distant monitor the corridor was silent. Sweat was building beneath her scarf. She hoped Harry was OK and had managed to find the control room. She peered through the window of the first room. It sat in darkness, save for a spotlight hanging low over a white desk. At the back of the room sat a tall bank of computers, their tiny lights randomly low-glow flashing. They reminded her of Christmas lights set on intermittent. Why the hell was she thinking of Christmas lights? She crossed the corridor and peered through the window. This room was more in keeping with what she had been expecting. A tall white man lay deathly still on a hospital bed. A variety of machines seemed to be carving out some sort of medically induced tune. He was alive, of that she was certain: she could make out the rise and fall of his chest beneath the crisp white starched sheet. She was relieved it wasn't Nick. The door opened with ease and she silently slipped inside.

The room looked much the same as any hospital room. It reminded her of the private hospital in Bath she had visited when her mum had been a patient. The monitor emitted a slow rhythmic chime – a lullaby for those in a drug-induced haze. 'This is not a hospital, this is not a hospital', she chanted quietly. But what the hell was it? No way could Franklin have done this by himself. She had not really taken in what Penny had told her. But here, now, standing in the silence with only the sound of a ventilator keeping time, did she start to theorise. What did Franklin have to do with her getting the job? Why had he insisted she hook up with Nick, to what end? Where the hell did Rick and KLD fit into it all? This level of funding needed serious cash. The sooner she could find Nick and get out of here the better. If all of the patients were like the man on the bed it would explain why no staff were needed. Maybe patients in induced states could be monitored centrally somewhere; maybe Harry would figure it out.

Why is he keeping patients here, hidden? He certainly never mentioned this to us when he offered for us to stay. Surely if you had some kind of facility on your estate you would think to mention it – wouldn't you? Patients, I can't believe I'm calling them patients. But if they're not patients what the fuck are they? As warped as Franklin was, there must be some sort of reason, she thought. He's a bloody neuroscientist! Her racing thoughts stopped for a split second. She listened to the mechanical throng. The effort of breathing now controlled by an electrically supplied surrogate. She shifted awkwardly. She was an intruder, whatever her intentions, the fact remained she was most definitely an intruder. She had barged her way into a life she neither knew nor understood. She had no emotional connection to the man lying in the bed so why did she feel so rotten? Any minute now she would wake up, any minute now Nick would tell her to get up from the sofa. That bloody sofa had a lot to answer for!

Still more questions haunted her: what is this man's story? How did he get here? The whole place gave her the creeps. Girding her courage she edged closer. A large white bandage encompassed the top of his skull. Two IV lines flowed through one cannula, their drip rates slow and steady. There must be something here that may help? Inching closer towards the bed she could feel eyes on her. Was she being watched?

She is freaking herself out. It is all she can do to maintain her balance. It is the man's eyes, they are watching her. They are haunting and vacant. His eyes are open, wide open. Sunken, soulless caverns staring upwards towards a magnolia expanse. He lies motionless, no hint of movement from any extremity. But it is his eyes that are disturbing. They stare out, empty and expressionless. She had never seen a dead body before but she is convinced this is what it would look like. This man however is clearly alive. Slowly and carefully she touches the back of his hand. It feels warm and soft. A sigh of relief escapes from within her, yes he is definitely alive.

Her attention is drawn to a low rumble of voices that seem to be drawing closer. Scrambling into the en-suite she pulls the door ajar behind her. She dare not look. Two possibly three people have entered the room. One of them is definitely a smoker. The stale nicotine cloud hits her at the back of the throat. She cannot make a sound, she must not make a sound.

'No change, he's stable but remains unresponsive'. The voice is male, the accent thick and broad. Scottish for sure, maybe Aberdeen at a guess. Is it the same voice she heard on the recording? She can't be sure.

'He's ten days post temporal lobe resection with no change, prognosis poor...'

'OK initiate protocol N34, go get the Professor, we're gonna need his sign off'. This time a new voice, light and French.

One of the men has paused at the door. Did he sense she was there, hiding for her life in the shadows? Midori closes her eyes; it was something she would do as a child. If she closed her eyes no one could see her, she was safe. As crazy as she knew it to be, she closed her eyes tight and prayed.

'That doctor guy downstairs will need to be fast tracked. I'll make everyone aware that we'll move him into room 3 later. He's still playing nice so things should run smoothly for tomorrow. You OK with that?'

'Sure just make sure you run it by Franklin first, he has a soft spot for that one. Make sure you treat him right OK? I've had enough of clearing up your fucking mess'.

OMG that has to be Nick - it must be Nick they're talking about. Midori could feel her heart thumping out of her chest, beads of sweat started to slide down her forehead and into her eyes making them sting and weep. She tries to focus on what she has just heard, not on the pain that is searing into both eyes. Closing her eyes tight shut for the second time she tries to put the pieces together. Deconstructed bursts of information fire around her brain – Nick – where – how – why him? – Harry – find him – game plan? – keep calm – think.

The sound of scraping furniture grabs her attention. Voices, low and whispered dance on the stale air. Why were they being so quiet, surely it was not out of some misguided respect for their patient? It's not as though there was anyone around to overhear. Not unless they had sussed she was there? Oh god, no. No they would have done something by now. Get a grip Dori, you're getting para.

Peering through the crack between the door and its surround she can make out Franklin's frame. He has entered the room as if swept in with the tide. Sweat is coming thick and fast across her brow. She wants to freeze and run at the same time. She can feel the bile once again hit the back of her throat. Not now Dori, not now. Keep it under control, deep silent breaths. She wants to sigh a big heartfelt sigh as the nausea subsides but she dare not. Her sense of terror has receded just enough for it to become manageable. The French man begins to speak.

'We'll make the necessary arrangements Prof, we'll make him disappear. A fishing trip I think'.

'Do what's necessary, but no loose ends OK?' Franklin's unmistakeable voice, hushed and measured.

'No loose ends Professor, no loose ends'.

'Make sure patient 7 is stepped up'.

His voice is ordinary, as if this was just another regular ward round. Patients to see, notes to write, all very every day and yet completely out of place. All part of that excellent service from your everyday, run of the mill, we've got your back psychopathic neurologist!

'We'll make sure he is first on your list tomorrow Professor'.

'Good, good. I think we are almost there, gentlemen. We are so close. I think patient 7 may be able to help close this circle. I have a good feeling about him. We just need to make sure he doesn't cone. Right better get on with this then, do you have the propofol?'

'Right here Professor'.

The sound of equipment being moved and metal on metal invaded her ears. The monitors that had been so rhythmic and steady start to ring out with pace and vigour.

'Turn those bloody machines off Ted will you?' Silence.

Franklin's voice hard and cold. 'Time of death 02.46pm. Do what you must gentleman, do what you must'.

Midori hears the door open, the lights are cut. She can hear the trail of voices growing muffled and further away, then silence. She can't leave. She has rooted herself so firmly to the spot that she cannot move. She doesn't want to move. She knows what the world outside the bathroom holds. The smell of death is gradually making its way towards her.

Steeling herself, Midori pushes open the door. The room is in darkness except for the frosted light casting a shadow from the hallway. The machines have been pushed to one side in a neat row and sit silently. Shuffling closer to the bed, she can see a sheet has been placed over the man's face. She feels horrible. She stood by, she let it happen. She was not who she thought she was. She had thought she was brave. She was not, she was a coward. A coward who stood by and let a man die because she was too scared and too selfish. She could argue with herself until the cows came home about how she was outnumbered or how she didn't have any weapons but that wouldn't make her feel any better. Human experiments, that's what this was about. Life here carries no value. Here lies a man with a story, with history. This would not happen again, this could not happen again. She finally had the measure of who she was dealing with. Now she would be prepared. No more life would be lost here if she could help it.

The stairs at the end of the corridor offer only one direction of travel – down. She descends quickly and quietly. In front of her is a corridor not dissimilar to the one above, except this one has only doors, no windows. The air is stale and decaying. Its' aroma familiar. It's the same as in the room above but stronger. It's the smell of death.

Her legs feel as if they have been fused with lead, every step derived from forceful, focused effort. Light-headedness grips her. It reminds her of the time she tried to climb Mount Fuji. The air had been so thin that she had struggled to breathe. Thankfully she had not suffered altitude sickness, but it had been a close call. She had turned back at about the halfway point. Maybe they deliberately kept the air thin here, she thought, pushing forward slowly. She wanted to leave this place - it had an undercurrent that was messing with her psyche. It said: everything here is bad, nothing good exists, only misery and pain. Nick was her priority: she needed to hold onto every last piece of courage she had and drive herself forward. She moved sluggishly, gulping in vast quantities of stale air. It was a pace which allowed her to breathe without too much effort. A sound not like any she had heard before made her stop. It was a deathly sound that made the hairs on the back of her neck stand to attention. It was not a particularly loud sound, more a low guttural cry. It was hard to work out if the cry came from a man or woman, or even if it was human. Midori once again found herself glued to the spot, her breathing now shallow and rapid. The hallway took on an ethereal quality; the walls began to blend into soft focus. This was no time to have a panic attack; she had to stay in control, stay alert. Every sinew screamed for her to hold on and not go under. She leaned against the wall and untied her scarf. She breathed slow and steady into the scarf counting in 2,3,4, out 2,3,4, just as she had been taught. A finger of clarity returned. The animalistic sound had dulled to a whimper, a low level, pulsing whimper. It was the sound she imagined a slightly injured dog would make and it appeared to be coming from the room at the far end of the corridor. Bracing herself, she stood tall and walked slowly forward. The end of the hallway would have to wait. She approached the first door and her heart almost skipped a beat: 'Patient 7'. She inhaled deeply and without hesitation entered the room.

The woman who had entered his room seemed vaguely familiar. Did he know her? Her large green oval eyes were troubled but displayed kindness. He stared hoping for a light bulb moment. Neither spoke. Each second of silence became cavernous. He wished he could remember her, he really did. This woman did not look like the others. Her presence was somewhat out of place. Why couldn't he remember?

'Nick, it's me – Midori', her voice said, soft and tender. She longed to wrap him in her arms and never let him go. His appearance shocked her. She tried hard not to display the turbulence of emotions that had hit her upon seeing his face. Within the space of a few days he seemed so different. He was definitely Nick, but without his presence.

He sensed she was nervous, her voice, although calm, gave a hint of distress. He stared at her, why couldn't he remember? She moved towards him and took hold of his hand. She felt warm and soft, but not familiar.

'I've come to get you out Nick. We have to go quickly before they know I'm here'. The pace and tone of her voice quickened. Should he trust her? Nothing made any sense.

'Why are you here?'

'I've just said, to get you out of here, we have to go'.

'I'm so sorry but I have no idea who you are'. He withdrew his hand from hers and took a step back. He was perplexed. 'I need to stay here so that I can get better... I need to finish my treatment'.

Midori felt the life drain from her. Reality started to stab at her. Of all the things she had envisaged and been fearful of, this was not a scenario she had played out. Somehow over the last few days the Nick she knew was gone. What now stood in his place was his shell. What had they done to him? She needed to be stronger now than at any moment in her life so far. Every word she uttered needed to count. Her words needed to convince him that going with her was better than the alternative.

'OK, I know none of this must be making any sense to you, but you need to trust me OK?'

He studied her face. Unlike the clinicians who'd been looking after him he wanted to trust her. Something about her gave him confidence. But who was she and why did he need to go?

'We don't have long Nick, if they find me or Harry here who knows what they'll do. I need to get you out of here as soon as possible. Please, please try to trust me'.

'Who's Harry?'

'You worked with Harry at the hospital, he was your senior registrar. He worked for you and Franklin. Don't you remember?'

She needed to keep it simple, there was no point in going into the details of how he came to be here. Nick shook his head. His brow had furrowed and he seemed completely lost. She wanted to wrap him in her arms to tell him everything would be OK.

Midori sat on the edge of the bed, indicating for him to join her. She turned to face him. She needed to be calm. Inside a seething mass of molten lava was about to erupt. Thank god for Kendo, without it she would just be a very angry woman right now. Think before you speak Midori, she told herself.

'OK, so this must seem very strange to you but you need to believe what I'm about to say...' If he didn't believe her she was out of options.

'I'm Midori, I'm your girlfriend. We live together in Somerset in England...'

'England?' Blimey, how could I not know that?

'Yes, you moved there at the beginning of the year. You're a consultant neurologist. You work with Professor Franklin, who for whatever reason has gone rogue and is now conducting unregulated experiments on people. I believe he is using you as one of his guinea pigs. You did not come here of your own free will. Harry and I managed to find out where you were being held and we really, really need to get you out of here'. Midori took hold of Nick's hand again.

'Nick - you have to believe me. Bad things are happening here, really bad things. I want you to be safe. I want to help you get your memory back'. Midori held his hand up to her face.

'I'm your Midori, Nick...' She could feel her eyes starting to prick, no, no, she had to keep it together.

He believed her, he didn't know why but he did. She was right, something here was bad. He had felt it too.

'OK, what do we do?' he asked.

Nick quickly changed out of the gown he was wearing. Feeling slightly self-conscious - it was as though he were undressing in front of a stranger. There were only a set of clean scrubs at the back of the cupboard and no shoes anywhere. Why had he not twigged before, surely if he were here of his own free will he would at least have some clothes and shoes. Whatever the drugs were they'd been giving him had dulled his mind as well as his memory. He had felt he had not really been thinking at all and now this confirmed it. He was glad Midori had shown up. Who knows what would have happened?

He could understand why he had been attracted to her, he thought, as he watched her curvy frame. She turned to beckon him over towards the door and he blushed.

They were to make their way back up the stairs, retracing the way Midori had come. As they reached the stairwell they were plunged into darkness. Sirens emitting a high shrill began to sound. It would seem Harry had found the control room. Taking the stairs two at a time they entered the upper corridor that led to the library. The light from her phone guided their path. She could make out the T junction just up ahead. As they turned the corner the emergency generator kicked in and they were bathed in a sea of white light. She was standing face to face with one of the goons she recognised as being in the room of the now very dead man.

'Run Nick, run!' she screamed, turning and fleeing as fast as she could back the way they had just come.

A combination of surprise and shock had disorientated the man just long enough for Midori and Nick to get a head start. She did not turn but knew he was gaining on them fast.

'In here, quick', she said, pulling Nick into the room containing the banks of computers. She knew there was no way out of the lab but she felt calm. If it was her destiny to die here, then it was to be the way of her line, but she didn't feel ready. She would front it out and remain calm, she told herself.

'OK Nick you need to really listen to me. I want you to go and hide underneath one of the tables. Do not come out until you hear me give you the all clear. Got it?'

'But I can help you, I can fight besides you', he argued

Her tone was sharper than she had intended.

'No, absolutely not, you are not strong enough. Do as I've asked, quick, we don't have much time. I can handle this'. She was right, climbing the stairs had all but knocked him out: his mind was willing but his body was listless, probably the cocktail of drugs, he thought. Finding a spot just under one of the tables he pulled the chair in behind him. From here he had a direct view of the door.

All she needed now was a Shinni or anything that vaguely resembled a Kendo sword. A quick scan of the room revealed a pole standing in the corner that was used to open skylights. It will have to do, she thought as she pulled it away from its coupling.

Within a heartbeat the thick-set man was in the room; within two strides he stood opposite her. A sly grin widened across his face.

'That is not going to help ye lassie', he said, taking another step closer to her.

Your spirit must be quiet Midori, make yourself as a mirror, reflect your opponent's anger, have courage and you will be victorious. Thomas Sensei invaded her thoughts.

With one almighty scream she launched, her Shinni raised above her head ready to strike. She had the advantage of surprise, her first strike cracked the top of his head, her second, a vigorous blow to the throat, had sealed his fate. She had struck harder than she had ever done before. With the force of ten thousand Samurai within her she had broken his windpipe and he had crumpled to the floor unable to breathe. Her journey of a thousand miles had begun with that first single step. She had been at one with her sword, her training had just saved both their lives.

Nick sat captivated. He marvelled that out of such a petite graceful woman had come such aggression and anger.

'We need to go now Nick, quick!' she shouted. She grabbed his hand and ran back out towards the exit. Turning the corner for the second time she could make out Harry up ahead. He was carrying something, no, he was carrying someone. The body appeared limp and lifeless. He was struggling to decode the door back through to the library. Midori ran past him and took charge of the frail woman he had been holding. Her complexion was insipid and her skin was chilly.

'The codes must have reset due to the power outage, bugger. This is gonna take a bit of time....' Harry sounded anxious.

'She is dreadfully dehydrated, she needs some fluids as soon as possible'. Nick had come alongside Midori and was now studying the woman. How he knew what to do he didn't know, he just did. Midori placed her rolled-up coat under the woman's head.

'We're sitting ducks here, Harry, we need to have a plan B...we can't stay here'. Her voice sounding fractured and high-pitched.

'It's OK I'm done'. And with that the door unlocked.

They stuck to the edge of the tree line where possible, stopping every now and then, Harry carrying the girl who was still unconscious.

'What happened Harry, where did you find her?' Midori asked, trying to keep pace with him.

'She was down in the sub-basement. I thought the sound was coming from an injured animal but it turns out it was Laura'. He nodded down towards the girl.

'You know her name?'

'Yeah, it was on the notes at the end of her bed. When I arrived she was conscious. She just looked at me and begged me to help her. It chilled me to the bone, Midori. It was just after I'd promised to help her that she became unconscious. I checked her vitals and she seemed OK. I couldn't leave her there'.

'I wonder if there are any more people being held there?'

'We'll report it as soon as we can, look we're almost here...'

They crossed the small clearing making their way towards the dimly lit motorhome. The lamp they had left on was shining out like a welcoming beacon of hope. Thankfully the handful of other campers at the site all appeared to be sleeping. Nick had held up well. The frequent stops had helped him to acclimatise to his surroundings. He had no recollection of how he came to be at the facility. A chill ran down his spine as he looked towards the crumpled shape of the girl, enveloped in Harry's arms. He knew he had been lucky to get out alive.

'She needs a doctor, she really does'.

They laid Laura across the pull-out bed. Nick had given her as full a neurological assessment as he could. Everything came to him as if it were second nature. He used the phone torch to see if her pupils dilated and a prickly hairbrush to test the soles of her feet for a reaction. When he had finished he let out a big sigh. 'Her biggest problem right now is hydration. Obviously I can't do any blood tests or the like to see if there is anything else amiss but if we can't push fluids into her she will deteriorate further. At least if she were awake we could get her to drink something...'

His voice was calm and steady, with a touch of his old bedside manner creeping in. Midori smiled, it was good to have a part of the Nick she knew back. At least now she could hope.

'OK, OK we'll have to move. Not ideal, but necessary. The idea was to stay here in the camper van until morning, not attracting too much attention. Fly under their radar, but driving around now at 4.00am... well...' Harry looked at Midori, then at Nick and finally at Laura who looked dreadful.

'OK, we'll just have to pray that once they twig Nick and Laura are gone they start looking towards Bergerac and not Agen, which is where I propose we head for'.

'But they'll know we are going to need a doctor', pitched in Midori.

'Agreed, they will, but there are so many directions we could take they will have no way of knowing which hospital we will plump for. They won't be able to cover all of them - and by the time they've figured it out hopefully the authorities will be onto them, we will be the least of their worries'.

'OK, Agen it is then. Do you know if they have a neuro unit?'

'Yes they do. All the hospitals around here have good facilities and a good reputation. They will have a hard time trying to guess which one we've opted for.'

They left the campsite as quietly as they could. Harry drove without the assistance of lights for the first couple of miles. He wanted to put some distance between Monflanquin and their small vulnerable party of four. The night was still and silent. They passed no one. It was as if the little motorhome with its precious cargo was the only vehicle in the region of Lot-et-Garonne.

Midori had fallen asleep on Nick's shoulder. This petite beautiful girl had saved his life. He had been amazed at how she had delivered the throat punch to their adversary. His head thumped as he desperately tried to pull back some semblance of who he was. Was it true what Harry and Midori had told him? Had he been drugged? Had they somehow erased his memories? There were some they hadn't managed to get rid of. He was thankful that somehow his subconscious had stored some of his medical training. What about the rest of his life? What about Midori? Why couldn't he remember her or their relationship? His head continued to pound. A wave of nausea rose over him. He couldn't remember the last time he'd eaten.

They were a good forty minutes into their journey. Harry started to relax his shoulders and his breath became a little more natural. He was confident they hadn't been followed. The only traffic they had seen had been going in the opposite direction. He had made it to the N21 with no trouble; they should be in Agen in no time. They had stopped for a breath of fresh air and he'd made the call to the local police nationale. His superb French meant they were able to fully comprehend the urgency of the situation and in turn had enlisted the support of the gendarmerie nationale. He also placed a call to his boss at EM3 who would set the wheels in motion at his end: no doubt it would involve Interpol. Harry was under no illusion: Professor Franklin would be a slippery fish to pin down. They needed to cut off his escape routes ASAP. As they inched towards Agen, he was confident they would get Franklin and the other guttersnipes who were further up the food chain. Glancing into his rear view mirror his heart melted. Midori and Nick were both fast asleep. He would call Penny once they were settled at the hospital. It was the first time he'd thought about Penny all day. He wondered if she had any news on Raiden. They had been on some strange cases together, but this one was definitely the most traumatic and brutal. Usually they were looking at fraud but this was on another level. Harry had worked under Franklin all year and had to admit he was a dazzlingly brilliant neurologist. What on earth could have driven him to this? Greed? Surely not, no, there had to be more to this picture than what they were currently seeing.

The hospital was easy enough to find and the car park was pretty much empty. It had just turned 5am and Harry could hear the first flutterings of the dawn chorus.

'OK we're here'. Harry spoke softly into Midori's ear. She immediately bounced up to attention, still asleep but aware she needed to be awake.

She gently shook Nick's shoulder. 'Come on sleepy head, time to wake up', she whispered.

Something was wrong. Nick did not respond. His head lulled over to one side and his eyes remained closed. He was cold and clammy to touch. It was as if he were in a deep, deep sleep. She raised her voice and shook him with a little more aggression this time.

'Nick, Nick, wake up we're here at the hospital'.

Nothing. Knots formed in her stomach again. She felt his wrist for a pulse. Relieved she found one. It was shallow but regular. But he was still not responding.

'Nick I really need you to wake up now – Harry's gone to get the doctors and they'll be back soon. Please open your eyes' - nothing. 'Please Nick, please, you're scaring me now, please wake up...'

The passenger door opened and two medics stood alongside Harry.

'He's not waking up, he's not responding...' She knew she had spoken the words but somehow they weren't hers. She could hear the words being spoken, she could feel her mouth speaking them, but they were not hers. A slow steady trembling took hold and her body started to shake violently. Get a grip girl, get a grip, she told herself, but it was too late. A low sound seemed to be being beamed out of her and then she blacked out.

The room seemed harmonious and peaceful. Soft low chimes rang out from the monitors. A nurse stood with a clip-board at the end of the bed, her smile soft and warm. Midori thought she might cry at any moment. The weight of events had begun to pull her down. Her body burned, it felt battered and bruised. The last time she had felt like this had been after a gruelling Kendo championship. She had lost so badly that she had gone immediately back to the dojo in Bristol and practiced against Thomas Sensei until she could no longer stand. Never again would she let anyone win because of her lack of commitment. This was different, she had fully committed but it had been her emotions that had let her down: she was weaker than she had believed. She loved Nick; he had broken through her barricades quite by accident and now she was disarmed. She didn't know how much more she could take. She prayed he would be OK. She dared not think of the alternative.

'It's OK, everything is OK', said the nurse tenderly. 'The doctors say you have exhaustion, you need to rest'.

Midori eyed her cautiously, dare she ask?

'Nick, where is Nick, is he OK?' Midori's throat was as dry as sandpaper and just as brittle.

'Don't worry, he is being well looked after. The doctor you sent over from England is with him now. I'm sure they will do everything they can, he's getting the best care possible'.

She had a lilting raspy French accent that soothed away Midori's concerns. She laid back onto her pillow. Finally this whole sorry affair would soon be over. She smiled towards the nurse.

'Thank you, yes, Harry is a good doctor isn't he? If it wasn't for him none of us would be here...'

The nurse looked at her quizzically, as if she hadn't quite understood. She continued placing dots on the observations graph she had in front of her.

'I'd like to see him if possible, oh and the girl Laura, how's she doing?'

Despite the metres of cabling that she was now connected to Midori wriggled to the side of the bed. For a moment the room didn't move, her brain, slow, started to re-engage. She wasn't sure how long she'd been out for but it could not have been too long. The sun was starting its approach. The darkness of the night had started to move aside. She could hear a wealth of birdsong above the gentle chimes of the machines. She looked down. She was wearing a standard issue green hospital gown, not the most attractive look she'd ever cultivated.

'They are fine Ms Yates, but you are my patient and you need to rest, you may still be a bit unsteady on your feet, please do not try to get up just yet...'

The nurse's badge read: Natalie Huval. Yes she looked like a Natalie, thought Midori.

'I only want to see him - I know Harry will be doing a good job but he is only an SPR after all, a junior really, what about your.....'

'I think you misunderstand me Ms Yates, Harry is not in charge of their care, the Professor is'.

'Professor? What professor?' She could feel the adrenaline of the last few hours starting to surge back to life. Surely not, surely not that professor, she thought.

'The one from England, the one you telephoned. It was lucky he was already in France, what a kind helpful man. So very polite and so how do you say... so English', Natalie giggled. 'Is something wrong Ms Yates?'

Midori griped onto the side of the bed. God no, he couldn't have found them. He wouldn't be so brazen as to..... She felt the colour drain from her face.

'Please Natalie, describe him to me?' Her voice sounded harsher than she had intended.

'Well he is tall, an older gentleman let's say, silver hair, very pleasant gentleman, very English...'

'Where are they, where is Nick?' Alarms started to ring out as she frantically pulled at the wires. She had to be sure, she had to help Nick, no way could this be Franklin, no way, but she had to be sure.

'Please Ms Yates, I do not think you should be doing this, I... I think maybe you misunderstand me, please get back into bed, you are not very well, you need to rest...'

'You have no idea what this man is capable of, I didn't call anyone'.

Her feet almost buckled as she made contact with the floor, no way was he going to harm the man she loved any more, no fucking way. It must all be a misunderstanding, Franklin wouldn't dare – would he? Where was Harry for God's sake?

'Please Natalie, you need to tell me right now where Mr Campbell is, do you understand? He could be in a lot of danger'.

The tone of her voice had inferred there was more to this than Natalie understood. Midori held her gaze. The depth of her jade green eyes desperately tried to convey the seriousness of the situation.

'Right now Natalie, you must tell me right now! If this is **the** professor both of them are in serious danger - they might die. We didn't call anyone...I think this professor may be the one who is trying to harm us. He may be the man we were running from', she pleaded.

Whether it was the look of sheer panic in Midori's eyes or a gut feeling Midori wasn't sure, but she was grateful that Natalie was disconnecting the last intravenous line from her arm.

'Mr Campbell is on the fourth floor in the neuro unit. Here, you will need this', she handed Midori a lanyard with a bar-coded pass attached.

'Thank you, thank you, now go and call security and get them to meet me there, then call the police - tell them that Franklin is here and he is dangerous!' She had slipped back into her clothes that had been folded besides the bed. She didn't have time to figure out where her shoes were, damn it she would have to go barefoot.

Fuck, fuck and fuck, she climbed the stairs two at a time, her body screaming in agony. She was slightly breathless with sharp shooting pains running up her left arm. This is not the time for a frigging heart attack she cussed. Level 4 shone out ahead of her. She would die defending Nick if that's what it took - where on earth was Harry? She prayed nothing awful had happened to him.

A wisp of sunlight bounced off of the motorhome. Harry lowered the visa. He had just finished talking with Penny. He took a deep breath in. If he had not have given up smoking last summer, now would be a good time for a smoke. He remembered how he used to feel as the nicotine took hold, invading his blood stream. God it had felt good. The last 24 hours had been crazy, but finally everything seemed to be drawing to a close. This case was bigger than anything he and Penny had ever handled. It may well prove to be the biggest case of his career. Franklin was just the tip of the iceberg, he was relatively small fry. This unhinged human trial was global. Who knew how many people in how many countries were affected? This level of planning and organisation was way beyond anything Franklin could be capable of. The sign-off for something like this came from someone far higher up the food chain than Franklin. Was it really all about money, he wondered? Franklin was an excellent neurologist - why destroy that? Why become a murderer?

Penny had informed him that the EMA had acted immediately and issued a class 1 rapid alert to all countries. The MHRA in the UK had done likewise, issuing a class 1 urgent withdrawal and recall of all Centoria products. This was on a scale and at a speed that neither of them had seen before. Penny was now in New York where she had met up with Prof. Wallace, who had flown down to meet her from Seattle.

Midori had been right to be concerned about Raiden. He had met with Penny earlier that day and had agreed to be admitted to the Langport neurology centre in Chatham New Jersey. His blood work had come back that evening and revealed some rather startling results. His white cell count was up, as were all of his inflammatory markers, yet he showed no sign of illness or infection. His MRI scan was even more alarming. His frontal lobe had taken on an unusual shape and was a very odd colour. The brain's cortex, usually a pale pinkish colour, had turned a dark shade of mustard yellow: this was not a shade usually seen on a scan. The radiographer had adjusted the contrast of the screen but no matter how many adjustments she made, the dense mustard yellow remained. What this meant no one could tell for sure. Professor Wallace drew up what he considered to be his 'best guess' at an optimal care plan and set about contacting the best scientific minds he knew. They would begin by slowly lowering Raiden's doses of Centoria. He would have regular cognitive tests and a series of scans to compare results. Rai's original medical records were still in the UK and Wallace needed to cross check them, just to be sure he wasn't missing anything. If Rai started to deteriorate he could prescribe further medication, although without his records he would be flying blind.

Rai trusted his sister implicitly. She had sent Penny; now he had to trust her and Professor Wallace. He knew he had to talk openly about the nights of no memories. It was difficult for him; he was always the strong one, the one in control. Midori had always relied on him, the big brother, problem-solver extraordinaire. Now he felt weak and vulnerable, on edge as each night approached. Unsure if it would be a 'normal' night or not. No, he had to tell them everything, maybe they could help him.

Penny and Professor Wallace listened as he described waking up clothed in sweat, his hands blackened, the smell of smoke cocooning him. He had wondered why when he closed his eyes and tried to remember all he could see was a wall of mustard yellow. Penny shot the Professor a sideways look but said nothing. Raiden described how he would close his eyes and systematically retrace his memories of the night before. All would be clear up to a point. It seemed to follow the same pattern each time. He was always alone, never when any of his friends were around, well he didn't think they were. He would always wake up at home with no recollection of how he got there. His head would be banging beyond belief, more than just a normal hangover, and he was scared. What followed in his words were his 'darkest times'. He felt a despair that ran through him so deeply he wasn't even sure he would make it through the day. He was petrified he was losing his mind, that somehow his accident was to blame. He would spend hours in the shower scrubbing at his hands, trying to wash away the burnt scent that had overnight invaded him. It was on those mornings, the mornings of no memories, that he was at his lowest ebb. He had struggled to regain control of his thoughts. It was as if he was on a predetermined path of destruction which he couldn't do anything about.

Penny placed her hand gently on his. Had there been a time at any stage where he had wanted to end it all? Rai nodded, tears in his eyes. Yes, yes he had. Each of those mornings he'd had to fight with his sanity. He had used every ounce of strength he had to battle and keep from walking across that line. He didn't know if anything he said made sense but he needed to speak it out, he wanted help. He had been guarded about seeking any help for fear of losing his job. At the first sign of anything other than full health his company would pull him off the project. Transcorp were a good company who treated their employees fairly. However, right now they needed everyone to be at the top of their game. There was no room for a weak link. They had placed so much trust in him, he didn't want anything to get in the way of doing the best job possible. Penny had assured him of absolute discretion. He had holiday owing so could easily take a few days without raising suspicion. They sat with him throughout the afternoon. Reassuring him, helping Rai to see that his thoughts and feelings were not isolated. Without giving him any details that may push him over the edge, Professor Wallace explained they now believed Centoria may be behind his experiences. Recent cases indicated that Centoria had an added side effect profile that had only recently come to light. Wallace was at pains to stress that it was not unknown for this to happen with new drugs. Now they needed to work on finding a solution.

Piecing together his movements, Penny had drawn up a list of dates and times Rai had given her when he felt he'd 'lost time'. It had perfectly matched the dates on which serious arson attacks had taken place across town. Thankfully no one had been hurt. The damage to property however had been significant. There was a total of five incidents, with two of the buildings having to be demolished. She didn't share this information with Rai, only with the Professor and now Harry. It was his call if he wanted to share it with Midori, she'd said. Harry hung up and reflected on their conversation.

Poor Midori, he thought, her boyfriend lay in who knows what kind of state with who knows what chance of recovery, her brother thankfully not so critical but still affected - and she works for the company who manufacture the drug, what a mess. Some people get all the shit, he thought. There was nothing to be gained by telling her just yet about Raiden, he concluded. He needed her to stay focused here. He wound down the window. The sun was starting to rise. A light dew reflected across the grass. A carpet of jewels laid out for the morn. He watched as steam started to evaporate from the bonnets of the parked cars. God he really could do with a cigarette. His attention was grabbed by raised voices somewhere near the hospital entrance. He checked his watch – 6.30am. What now?

Midori flew into the room with no regard or forethought of what lay inside. All she knew was that right now Nick was in danger. Her eyes darted from left to right trying to pick up any sign of Franklin or his goons. Nick lay peacefully on the bed, undisturbed by her sudden entrance. His machines hummed softly, making the whole scene appear almost dreamlike. She felt a slight sway of air behind her and without a second thought she turned. Her journey of a thousand miles was about to take another step forward.

Franklin had been behind the door. He had heard the commotion in the corridor as nurses tried to grab Midori's attention. That bloody girl, he would deal with her the same way he had the others.

Midori entered the room at speed. She had spun around so fast she was unsure of which direction she was now facing. Franklin felt the cold slap across his face as her foot made contact. This was immediately followed by a series of short sharp deep punches to his chest and torso. Bloody girl was stronger and a lot tougher than he'd given her credit for, but she was on uncharted ground. He, however, had been down this road before.

She caught sight of the hypodermic too late as Franklin drove its bevel towards her. Then darkness.

She was a tough cookie but her frame was light. He hauled her up from her slumped position and over his right shoulder. He knew this hospital like the back of his hand. This is where some of his finest participants had been found. He was jeopardising everything by staying here even if he still needed Nick Campbell. He would have to wait. The night nurses had followed Midori and were now just outside the door. If he had to he would kill them both.

'Get out of my way!' he screamed.

From his left trouser pocket he draw a Glock 9mm. The nurses backed away silently. Franklin edged slowly towards the fire exit leading to the stairwell, his eyes firmly focused on the two women. Once through the door he took the steps two at a time and headed up to level 6. Level 6 was empty - under refurbishment. No-one would be around this time of the morning. Oh the joys of knowing the hospital so well, he thought. He'd had enough drama to last him a lifetime. This was not supposed to turn out this way. Damn girl, turning Nick's head like that. She was supposed to be on his side, for God's sake. Did she not know who he was? He'd been on the verge of trusting Nick with the truth. He'd shown him glimpses of what he'd been working on, even let him stay at the facility in Monflanquin. But then he started asking questions, the wrong kind of questions - bloody idiot. He was one of the brightest neurologists around - did he not realise what was at stake? Some things were bigger than individual lives! He propped Midori up against the bottom step and went in search of a gurney. The department's equipment lay under dust sheets. It didn't take him long. Dragging Midori's small limp body through the corridor, he carefully lifted her onto the gurney. He was a shadow, darting through the half-light towards the new extension block. He scurried into a staff changing room on route, grabbing some scrubs. Quickly and deftly he changed. He could hear Midori's slow dull groans. He would have to hurry. He headed towards the service lift. He could escape undetected through the basement exit. Franklin drew up another dose of Lorazepam, pulled out Midori's right arm and stabbed her hard. He covered her face with a thin white sheet: that should keep her quiet for a while. This was not what he had signed up for. His face was flushed and a two-day stubble was playing across his jaw line. When had he gone from caring to cut-throat? Yes he would have killed those nurses if he had to, he reasoned. They were collateral damage. He had done worse, much worse. He pushed the gurney out and through the small fire door at the back of the hospital. Thankfully, this was regional France, there were no CCTV cameras here. He'd taken Madam Roussel's car. By the time she realised it was missing he would be safely out of France.

Triggering the alarms had made him think on his feet. Thankfully he had planned for every eventuality. A small part of him had anticipated this day. Now that it was here, he felt alive, he could focus better under pressure. Something about the risk he was now taking made him as horny as hell. He thought about Midori now slumped across the back seat. He remembered the hard-on he'd got the first time he'd seen her. She reminded him so much of her mother. He'd had to leave the hospital that day because his desire for her was out of control; he was out of control and he loved it. He'd given his mistress a real pounding that day. Of course the cocaine had helped but my god - this girl turned him on. A bit too much of a pounding as it had happened, he'd ended up dumping her body in the estuary. Midori had been the itch he couldn't scratch. The lengths to which he'd gone to make sure KLD had hired her. He knew exactly how he would take her and where. She would not survive the night but he'd have some fun with her first, oh yes, he would definitely have some fun with her. She wouldn't get away from him as her mother had.

Harry stopped abruptly as he reached the door to Nick's room. His heart had been racing ever since he heard security shouting something about intruders in ITU. Two nurses stood behind the nurses' station, ashen and shaking. They were being comforted by the ward cleaners who had recently started their shifts.

'What's going on?'

'The Professor, he... he pulled a gun. I think he drugged a girl who was in the room...' He pointed to Nick's room. Hatred rose in Harry. He could feel his jaw clenching as the security guard continued.

'The nurses say he took her with him, she was unconscious. We have sealed off all the main entrances and are waiting for the police...'

The guard looked uneasy: the most he'd ever had to deal with was a patient with dementia going walkabout. The ward sister appeared at the door to Nick's room.

'He's stable - there doesn't seem to have been any change. I don't think he's been given anything but I've taken some bloods just to be sure. We'll know the results in about an hour...'

14

The effort she needed to lift her head made her groan. Her head pounded and her ribs felt bruised. She sensed someone else was in the room, watching her.

'Are you comfortable Midori?' It was a familiar voice which she recognised instantly.

'Why are you doing this Professor?' Her mouth felt as dry as the Sahara and just as gritty.

'Please call me Hugh, no formalities here Midori, please...'

He drew up a chair alongside her; a faint trace of body odour disguised with sandalwood accompanied him. Her hands were bound tightly with tape behind her back. Sitting up straight relieved some of the pain. Her feet had been bound and taped securely to the chair legs. Her clothes had been removed. She sat feeling exposed in her underwear. She noticed a white sheet overlain with a sheet of plastic beneath the chair. There was no doubt in Midori's mind: whatever he had planned was not going to be pleasant. Small electrodes had been placed either side of her breastbone. Her ample breasts were covered in a pale glutinous liquid. Oh my God, he had... had he...? She gagged at the thought of Hugh Franklin abusing her in such a way. A perverse smile spread across his face.

'I'm glad you're awake Midori Yates, it's time to play a few games...'

She tried to remain calm as his hand made its way towards the top of her thigh. She could feel his stale breath on the right side of her neck.

'Don't forget Midori, I have access to all sorts of naughties here you know', he whispered.

'You have caused me no end of problems Little Miss, now it's payback time. There's no point in thinking of escape or screaming, no-one will hear you. We are very much alone'.

She had to think fast; she needed to kick-start her cloggy, drug-filled mind.

'Do what you want with me, it doesn't matter. If it ends for me today all well and good - but please, please just answer me one question?'

He removed his hand and sat back to face her. For a man of his age Hugh Franklin was in good shape. His tanned firm body showed only small signs of aging, a wisp of grey hair here, a small wrinkle there. Good on the outside but rotten and twisted on the inside, she thought.

'One question you say, then I get to do what I want?' He stared directly at her breasts.

Midori lowered her gaze; she felt queasy and bare. She nodded slightly. She prayed that whatever he had planned he would have to untie her first. At least then she might stand a chance. It was at that moment she knew what she had to do.

A halo of light emanated from behind her and lit the room dimly. It cast an arc of light about four feet in front of her. The floor was wooden, a dark mahogany, covered with rugs of varying shapes and sizes. The room felt old and stately. With much effort she lifted her head again. The walls were panelled, probably oak, and a high ceiling held some sort of intricate wooden chandelier in which only three of the eight bulbs seemed to be working. A variety of stuffed heads, boars and stags hung regally on the walls to the left and right of her. A pair of fine crossed swords held pride of place above the large stone fireplace directly in front of her. She could not discern any windows but had a sense that they may too be subject to panelling, possibly of the shutter variety.

'Do you know what Alzheimer's is, Midori?' His voice, clear, directed. As if he were asking a student a question.

'Yes of course I do'.

'No'. His voice now stern and booming. 'No, I don't think you do. I don't think you understand the full complexity. It turns people into sponges, vacant sponges. It robs them of their souls and tears and shreds any sense of self they once possessed into.... into mush...' He began to pace back and forth. His arms extended, animated as he spoke. 'Ten years ago I came home to find my first wife Anne not quite herself. To begin with it was small things, forgetting where she had put something, we all do that, right? But towards the end she didn't even exist. Any semblance of who she was, who we were, had been washed away. It was a death sentence I could do nothing about'. His tone had changed: he was staring at her, through her, he looked tormented and in pain.

His eyes flickered and the glint of steel was back. 'You say you understand but you know nothing!' He lunged towards her and grabbed at her left breast, twisting it so hard that she let out a cry. With his other hand he slapped her across the right side of her face. Pulling her hair sharply he yanked her head back and she stared up at him. His expression was one of bemusement and he began to laugh. 'You really don't have a fucking clue, do you?' He shoved her head forwards, making her chair wobble.

'On the day Anne died, I vowed to do everything I could to stop this disease. A few months later I was approached by a scientist working for KLD. He asked if I wanted to get involved in some clinical trial work for a new drug that may have an impact on Alzheimer's. I jumped at the chance. It was a molecule I had worked on during my time in Japan'.

'Japan?'

'You don't know do you? You don't fucking know...'

He was jumping around all over the room. One minute she caught sight of him to her left, the next to her right. Now he was behind her, mumbling to himself. The sound of glass against metal made the hairs on the back of her neck spring to attention. She needed to keep him talking.

'So how did you get from clinical trials to here?'

The movement behind her stopped. The silence was deafening. She couldn't even be sure he was still in the room. She knew better than to try to turn around. She could hear chopping noises, sharp at times, with the occasional scraping, akin to the noise fingernails made when they were pulled down a blackboard. She shuddered. Whatever he was doing was not good.

'Is that your one question?' His voice putrid and hollow. 'I tell you I worked in Japan and that's the best you can come up with? You ask too many questions...'

A strong smell of antiseptic was slowly creeping towards her; an invisible tide was rising that she needed to turn. Midori tried to tune out whatever was going on behind her. She needed to focus on somehow getting out. There was very little in the way of clues. The house must be old. It was a grand house, judging by the height of the ceilings and the wood panelling. The air was stale and static, no through flow from an open window or door. OK so what could she hear? There was a faint sound of running water, no voices and absolutely nothing else. Fuck.

She needs to takes a deep breath in; it needs to be the deepest breath yet, it needs to overwhelm and bury her desire to scream. No-one is listening, of that she is sure, so why not just scream? No, it may just tip this psychotic animal over the edge, no, for now she will just listen.

Most of the clinicians she'd met had always been driven by a desire to do good. She could handle the larger than life egos which were paraded like a badge of honour. As misguided as Franklin was, maybe, just maybe, deep down he still cared. It was worth a shot. She had started to feel dizzy. Even if she managed to break free, how far would she get before collapsing? A sharp pain seared through her chest. Had she broken a rib? She was uncomfortable but resisted the temptation to move, she didn't want to draw his attention back to her. From her position she was not able to see a door. She needed him to trust her, just enough.

'It must have been very satisfying working on something you knew would make such a difference...' Midori injected a tone of optimism into her voice, it sounded light and airy...a normal conversation in a far from normal setting.

Franklin stopped what he was doing. He stood to her left. Her heart sank. He was wearing a surgeon's gown and scrub hat. In his hand he held what looked like a cross between a pair of scissors and a drill.

'It's an endoscope; good for not leaving scars', he said matter-of-factly.

'In answer to your question, yes it was very satisfying. We were making real progress. Each test we performed, each piece of data we collected provided us with more insight into how Centoria worked. The phase III trials had given us great hope that we were on the right track. We were really getting somewhere'. His voice now animated, he began pacing. 'Yes of course there were a few glitches. I wanted to iron them out but KLD needed to start seeing a return. They wanted their pound of flesh, I couldn't really blame them'.

'So you agreed to suppress some of the data... in order to get the regulatory approval?' She needed to tread carefully. She had altered the tone of her voice in an attempt to sound less confrontational.

'You make it sound straightforward: it wasn't. We needed a bigger pool of patients, to really know if what we were seeing was real. We needed to know if its effects could be replicated in the population as a whole.'

'So what happened?'

'We started to see some anomalies. Centoria had a few issues with 'Forbidden Colour' syndrome."

What the hell was 'Forbidden Colour' syndrome? As if reading her mind he continued.

'It's where light interacts with the central nervous system at a physiological level. Centoria somehow seems to unlock the limitation of the filters we hold on seeing colours. So for instance we can't see ultraviolet or infrared light, agreed?' She nodded. 'But there are so many other 'forbidden colours' we aren't even aware of everyday. But trust me they are there. The limitations within our vision are there for a reason. By unblocking our ability to see these colours, our brain gets sent into stimulatory overload. This threw up a few challenges, I can tell you, but it was exciting and we were on uncharted ground. We found that Centoria worked on many levels. It removed the block, our filter. Patients would not be aware of it, the changes to the spectrum of colours were subtle, almost subconscious, but they were there. By being able to see the forbidden colours it proved to have a positive effect on the temporal lobe. It not only restored our ability to remember; it improved our memories. We found that areas of the hippocampus actually increased in size. Can you imagine?' The passion is his voice was clear. His sentences were gathering pace and his gesticulations were escalating.

'Damaged areas within the brain were being restored and replenished because of the over-stimulatory effects of being able to see these forbidden colours. It had an amazing cascade effect...'

'You said there were some anomalies?' she pushed.

'Yes, we found there was a direct correlation between the size of the hippocampus and emotional response. The hippocampus is anatomically connected to parts of the brain involved in emotion. Therefore if the size and structure of the hippocampus start to change there will be a change in emotional responses – i.e. depression or elation. It's a part of the brain that also receives modulatory input from the serotonin, norepinephrine and dopamine systems. We know that due to its chemical make-up Centoria depletes tryptophan, an amino acid that converts to serotonin which would explain why some people feel depressed and suicidal. So it's a double whammy, anatomically and chemically'.

'By taking Centoria not only do patients get back their old memories but they regain memories and skills which are new - playing the piano, speaking another language, that type of thing. Acoustic nanoparticles fire off within hours of taking the tablets, quicker if given intravenously. On first pass Centoria coats the inside of the targeted nerve cells. The proteins embed themselves within the dendrites of each nerve. They then feed back to the brain a variety of messages. The RBap48 nanoparticle is encased in gold and carries the protein to its target within the hippocampus, where it starts to repair and rebuild those cells which have been damaged or lost'.

'Could you not modulate the uptake of Centoria at the receptor site, reduce its ability to bind?'

'You see, I knew you were as passionate about this as me, I knew it!' he said excitedly. She could see Franklin frantically trying to pull off his gown. He pulled up a chair opposite her, his face alive and animated. 'That was exactly my thought initially. We could play around with the levels of chemical uptake, trying different formulations until we got a good range. However this was complicated by the need to control the amount of stimulation provided to the temporal lobe by the forbidden colours. How much was too much, we just didn't know...'

'Would it be possible to have some sort of clothing, Hugh? I feel... I feel a bit, well a bit...'

'Yes, yes of course, here...' He covered her with the surgical gown. Not quite what she wanted but it would do. He hadn't taken off her hand ties but at least this was progress. Bloody hell, he is a real life Jekyll and Hyde - but maybe a little more unstable - she thought. In the space of a few minutes he had gone from captor to carer. Whatever she was doing she needed to continue: it was obviously working. Betting on his passion for science was paying off. She just needed to make sure she maintained it. The last thing she needed was to tip him back over into super fucking crazy Franklin.

'We needed to stabilise the side effects profile before we went live but KLD were having none of it. The best way to collect data was to look at the surveillance data once the drug was on the market, they said. KLD sampled Centoria to key centres with amazing results, and from my patients not so amazing side effects, which for the greater good I... well, let's just say I held back. A decision was made to suppress the papers with the unfavourable data and go with the positive trials'.

'I still don't get how you got from there to here though Hugh?'

'I was asked to continue with my trial work even with the drug on the market, that's why we had such a big uptake of Centoria in my department'.

'But people have been dying, doesn't that bother you?' Shit she shouldn't have said that. Franklin's face darkened. His voice was low and measured.

'People die all the time Midori, it's just that no-one is interfering in the way you and Nick have been. We have been quietly working behind the scenes, trying to come up with a solution. I just needed a bit more time...'

He looked beaten and dejected. As unhappy as he looked there was no way she could ever feel sorry for him. No, that was never going to happen. He stood before her a broken man. He had become so caught up in the ideal of Centoria that he had deliberately excused or ignored the warning signs that had rung out from the phase 1 trials. If the writing had been on the wall any larger it would have been visible from space. No, like a parent refusing to accept that their perfect child was not going to be the next president or the next top athlete, so it was with Franklin. He had deliberately blinded himself from the truth. She thought long and hard before she spoke.

'The only crime of the people you murdered was to have forgotten their memories. They were good people, Hugh. People whose families have now been changed irreparably because of your ideal, can you not see that?'

Silence followed. It was a space in which she allowed herself to become optimistic. Whatever delusional cloud he was under, there was a slim chance that reason and acceptance of reality may lift it. She hoped the radiance of the truth would cut through and free him. Even if she died right here, right now, she would be able to die knowing she had at least accomplished that.

In those few moments she reflected on the life she had lived so far. Her life had been exceptional. Not in any kind of Hollywood way, but in small seemingly insignificant ways. She had spent her childhood feeling like an outsider looking in, an invisible wall erected by her mixed heritage. She had a foot in two camps but a sense of belonging in neither. Her parents had surrounded both of their children with love. Their unlimited, selfless commitment to each other and to her and Raiden had been immense: only now did she understand the depth of love her parents had for them. She thought about Nick lying in that hospital bed in Agen. Midori inhaled sharply, fighting back the waves of sadness that crashed upon her spirit. Their life together over before it had really begun. No, this would not be their story. She had accepted she may die but she would now put all her energy into finding a way to live. She glanced at Franklin. He seemed almost lost, transfixed inside his own mind. His version of reality seemed to be on continual replay inside his head. His responses had thus far not thrown out any leads on which to build. She would have to cast her net wider.

'Of course I see it Midori'. His voice matched hers in softness of tone. Was he being sarcastic? She wasn't sure.

'Good people die every day Midori: cancer, car accidents, every day. My wife died because no-one was brave enough to do what needs to be done. You sit there in your ivory tower and have no idea of the living hell people have to go through'. His voice was now flecked with sharpness and disdain. 'No fucking idea.' He turned and walked out of view.

'Your one question is well and truly over.'

Shit, she was about to lose him: no, she had to think quick.

'So how can we solve this Hugh, how can we really solve this?'

If he was not capable of engaging empathetically, she would try to work with his sense of logic. If she could persuade him to hand over all of his data and come clean about the suppressed data...no, now she was too far ahead of herself. First she had to get him to believe she was on his side. Appearing beside her he looked at her quizzically.

'I understand Hugh, I do. I really get what you are trying to achieve. I may not agree with how you've gone about things but I do get it. You have to defy convention when you are trying to answer one of the 21st century's biggest challenges. What was it Da Vinci said? Knowing is not enough, we must apply. Being willing is not enough, we must do'.

Christ, she had pulled that out from some old science lesson somewhere, thank god for good teachers. Now all she could do was pray. Franklin paced slowly back and forth.

'I'm not sure if I could help, but I would like to... I mean if you want me too?' she continued. 'I could help to bring Nick back to you - he's obviously important to your investigations'.

She stopped, holding her breath, waited. There was now quietness about the place. She imagined the expression on Franklin's face: thankfully he hadn't seen hers otherwise she would have been undone, she was a lousy liar.

'You would do that?'

'Yes I would, I've realised how important your work is. I hadn't really thought about the implications of how many lives a treatment for Alzheimer's could save. Now I understand...'

Her eyes were lowered towards the ground but she sensed Franklin had moved from the back of the room and now stood once again in front of her.

'You have no idea what hearing you say that means to me'.

He had crouched down on one knee and gently lifted her chin. She was staring eyeball to eyeball into the face of a psychopath. She could feel the nerve endings at the side of her mouth start to tremble. Taking a deep breath in she slowly moved her head to the right, Franklin lowered his hand but his gaze remained. The glint of a scalpel he held in his right hand caught Midori's eye. This was not how she had imagined dying, this was not her time. With every part of her soul she cried, silently. Franklin was smiling. It was a smile that signalled a change, his face lightened. He raised his hand and she flinched. He cut through the thick tape that had bound her hands and then did the same for her feet. Midori dared not move. She didn't know this game or its rules. If she moved would he revert to the cracked, demented man she believed him to be or would he continue to be the man she thought he once may have been: calm, logical and reasoned? She did not want to take the risk. She remained statuesque.

'I knew it, from the moment I chose you and told Rick to hire you, I knew you...'

'You... you did what? How... how is that even...'

Her voice trailed off. Now she moved, sitting forward on the chair, the surgical gown struggling to maintain her modesty. Had she heard him correctly? God, she may have been drugged but there was nothing wrong with her hearing. His words sank like a stone into a pond, cutting through the warmer waters on the surface and penetrating to the cold depths below. The weight of his words began to disperse through her thoughts as she tried to make a connection. He had struck a blow she did not see coming, hitting her where she had not even thought to be guarded. Somehow Franklin had got inside her head, his poison sending its talons into her heart. He knew her, how? Everything was out of control. She'd never met Franklin before working at KLD... whoa, he'd planned, he'd.... She could feel her breathing becoming shallow. Nothing made sense...he had some connection to her, but what? Everything was now in slow motion.

'I'm going to find you some clothes and then we'll talk', he said matter-of- factly. 'I know now that my feelings about you were right, I know I can trust you', he said, placing his hand gently on her shoulder. She wanted to be sick, she felt defiled. She imagined this must be what a patient who'd been examined inappropriately feels like. It took her a moment or two to release herself from her own inability to move. She seemed unable to get her body into motion. She heard a door close behind her. Midori turned sharply - her theory had been correct, the door was directly behind her. She needed to kick herself into some sort of order, she wasn't thinking clearly anymore. Time was precious, Franklin would not be gone more than a few minutes. She had to make those minutes count. An inner struggle now raged and threatened to overwhelm her. She wanted to sit tight, to hear what he had to say, to try to make sense of it all. How did he know her, why had he chosen her, what was their connection? But this was not a game; it was her chance to survive. She had come this far without knowing, she reasoned. Her efforts had to focus on staying alive and getting as far away from this psychopath as possible. Her original plan would still work she just needed to put a few things into position before he returned and then she'd be set.

Franklin re-entered the room carrying two bags and her rucksack.

'Here', he said, handing them to her. She had sat back in the chair but had turned it to face the door.

'I took your phone, you won't be needing it, but I left your make-up bag and toiletries', he said. The other bags contained new clothes by Armani and shoes, beautiful shoes by Manolo Blanik. She looked up puzzled. Franklin smiled. 'I bought them for you a while ago - I held onto them in the hope that one day things may work out between you and me...'

'Work out?'

Whatever he had injected her with must still be playing with her head because there is no way this is reality, she thought.

'Please get dressed Midori and tidy yourself up, we have much to do'. He saw the uncertainty in her eyes and laughed. 'I really don't think now is a time for modesty, do you? I own you right now, just remember that...' Midori turned her back towards him, trying to maintain the only strand of dignity that remained hers. She dressed quickly. Pulling the brush from her rucksack she unknotted the strands of hair that had matted together and tied her hair back into a ponytail. If he had chosen the clothes himself she was both disgusted and impressed. A black long sleeved cotton shirt dress with delicate sliver breast pockets reached to her mid-thigh, while the Armani jeans she wore beneath the dress hugged her slight frame. Along with the whole craziness of her situation, two things about the clothes disturbed her. The new underwear was from Agent Provocateur, not your everyday undies store. She could feel his eyes on her as she tried to navigate the mesh bra. It seemed to have a series of straps that needed a degree in engineering to figure out. Midori wasn't sure if this had been Franklin's plan all along. She was starting to suspect that maybe it wasn't Nick he'd wanted after all. She reached back into the bag. As she pulled out the shoes her eyes widened. She hoped she had not displayed any emotion but feared she had. The shoes were troubling. Not only were they a perfect fit but they were similar to a pair she had been eyeing up the last time she and Nick had been in London. That was at least three months ago.

'Please can you explain to me what is going on?' She turned to face Franklin, whose smile widened.

'I take it you like the clothes then?'

Midori nodded uncomfortably. She didn't want to upset him but she certainly didn't want him to think she was enjoying this. He was erratic and most definitely unstable. She slowly and purposefully walked towards him. Not taking her gaze away from his she stopped just beyond touching distance. Her moves deliberate and calculated. She held his gaze. Taking a deep breath she summoned all of her strength. She did not want to come across as scared, though the truth was she was petrified.

'Hugh, I just need to know what's going on, you can understand that can't you?' She felt sick but needed to carry on.

'Come, let's sit', he indicated the leather chesterfield towards the back wall, as far away from the door as you could get. Midori joined him on the sofa, keeping as much distance between them as she dared. 'You look so like your mother, Midori, it really is quite extraordinary'. Franklin moved towards her, leaning forward he gently brushed a wisp of her hair from her face.

'How do you know my mother?'

'Your mother and I go back a long way, Midori, back to a time before you and your brother. Back to a world where life seemed simpler. Maybe that's how it is when you are young. The world is full of hope and promise. Problems, well, problems don't seem that way. Everything is possible, right?'

Midori nodded because that's what he wanted her to do. Right now, nothing seemed simple or possible. Franklin however had gone back in time, his face more relaxed than before. His eyes appeared burdened with sadness.

'I first met Katzuko in Japan. She was vibrant, full of laughter and clever, so, so, clever. I was there undertaking some clinical research. She was on my team. We spent the best part of a year working together. We became good friends. Anne became my wife, but your mother, ah well - your mother was my passion'.

Her mother had never mentioned Franklin. Even when she had got the job at KLD her mother had not mentioned she'd known anyone in neurology. Strange. Now that she thought about it, her mother did not really talk much about her time before marrying Midori's father. She was aware she had worked in the scientific field but she'd given that up when she'd had children. She was the best mother, attentive and loving. She had a steely determination to do things the right way plus the ability to debate for days. Her mother was a thinker, capable of deep levels of thought that were at times beyond her children. Midori had inherited her mother's passion for debate. No matter how hard she tried she was, however, unable to master her mother's patience. Katzuko jested that her fiery qualities stemmed from her father's side of the family. She felt sick hearing Franklin call her mother his passion - how fucking dare he! She was nothing to him, nothing.

'I'm still not clear though how you...how you got me the job at KLD and why?'

So what, he knew her mother, that didn't really explain anything...why had her mother or father never mentioned him – ever?

'We stayed in touch over the years, Katzuko and I - the odd email, Christmas cards, you know the sort of thing. She and your father came to Anne's funeral; that meant a lot to me. They didn't need to come but they did. She was so proud of you and your brother, of what you have both achieved'. He said was...did he mean to say was? 'She was right to be proud, I saw you debating once, at Kings'...'

Midori looked at him quizzically. Oh I didn't know you'd be there, but I knew you were her daughter the moment I saw you. I'd gone up to do a talk on what the future holds for neurology. I was asked to build on the back of the TED talk done by biochemist Gregory Petsko. I got in early and saw your debate – right to choose? Why we treat our pets better than we treat each other or something like that...'

'Yes, it was called 'the right to choose, the way ahead'...'

'You were very good Midori, you displayed eloquence with passion, not easy to do. You reminded me so much of those happy days I'd spent in Japan with your mother. I just knew you were her daughter, you are the spitting image of her. Your mother had mentioned you were finding it hard to get a job, so I helped out, that's what friends do...'

Midori sprung up, taking a few steps away from the sofa.

'Stop it, stop it - you have no right talking about my family like that. My mother is not your friend; she has never even mentioned you, ever. If you were such good friends why has she never mentioned you?'

Her voice raised and angry she wanted her words to sting, to hurt. She needed him to know he was not part of them, he had no hold over them; they owed him nothing. He couldn't be telling the truth, could he? Her mother had never mentioned him as far as she could recall. Franklin sat silently. 'Did she know, did my mother know you got me the job?'

'No, I never told her. Midori you need to calm down', he chided. 'You got the job for two reasons: because you were good and because I insisted. KLD owed me and ... they owed your mother...' He paused and stared at her; his eyes had once again begun to darken. 'Now... you owe me. Funny how things work out. Three degrees of separation I think they call it'.

'Six, it's called six degrees of separation'.

Why did KLD owe her mother? Hugh Franklin was talking rubbish. My mum never worked for KLD. The question which had been formulating in her mind had made its way to the tip of her tongue and before she could rethink whether or not she wanted to know the answer it was out.

'Did Nick know... is that why he?' Her voice trailed off. Too many thoughts rushed in and out of her head. He had come to find her on the day they had met; he had gone out of his way to find her in the car park. No-one does that do they? Why only now did that strike her as odd?

'No, Midori, as much as I wish I could take credit for that, no he didn't know. You and him, well, it's complicated things. I admit I should have seen that coming. If only you two had left things alone, it could have been so perfect. I was planning on bringing Nick in on this trial as soon as he'd settled in. With him by my side and you at KLD we would have made an amazing team'.

Franklin rose from the sofa. His facial expressions began to change again. Midori was coming to realise that his moods could be predicted by his visual expressions. He was once again beginning to look tortured. His eyes beamed wildly, his pupils dilating by the second. His frame took on the appearance of increased size and his bodily movements became frenetic and jerky. He turned sharply.

'They were watching you both, you know? Almost from the moment you began working at KLD'. Franklin cocked his head to one side, his sinister expression reminded Midori of a Velociraptor.

'Who... who was watching us?'

Even his movements were becoming raptor-like as he quickly paced up and down. His neck seemed to have become hyperextended from his body, his arms were pinned tight into his sides, his fists clenched. He began to laugh in a way which suggested that somewhere deep within him lay a molten pit of hell. The hairs on the back of her neck stood tall, goose bumps erupted across her body. It was at this instant Midori had no doubt that Franklin was capable of anything. She felt vulnerable. The sun was setting on Franklin's rational thoughts, the darkness of his psychosis was about to overwhelm him. It crossed her mind to run, but even without the stupid heels her positioning was wrong. She needed him behind her or at the very least to her side, not directly in front of her. She was being stalked: as an animal shadows its prey so Franklin was with her.

'You seriously think it was me that put all of this together?' he shouted, his arms gesticulating wildly. 'Me? A humble consultant? No, no, no. All I had were the brains and the passion, no, this is bigger Midori - so much bigger!' He was approaching her fast and she had nowhere to go but back towards the wall.

'Who then, who?' she screamed.

'I should have stuck to the plan see? They will not appreciate my deviation, they won't understand our connection. It won't be pleasant but it will be quick, I owe it to your mother...' The sound that followed echoed throughout the room. It was the scream of a banshee signalling death. It was a cry that said run, the alarm is raised and Armageddon is coming. There was no doubt in her mind, he was going to kill her.

Midori darted for the door but Franklin had anticipated her move and was quicker. He lunged and caught hold of her hair wrenching her backwards. Her whole body whiplashed. Sharp, painful movements exploded as she fell towards the floor. She heard something crack as she fell. Her face was ground downwards. A mixture of fresh blood and beeswax filled her mouth and she started to choke. She thought of Nick, of the one person who completely understood her, who made her feel like she belonged. She was not ready to give that up, her journey was not yet over. Taking as deep a breath as she could she started to build her Kiai. Her Dantian emitted a guttural slow moan emanating from deep within. Each syllable more powerful than the last. For anyone with ears to hear her sound became the voice of many. It said 'beware my sword is now my mind'. Quickly and powerfully Midori brought her elbow up and back: she'd managed to hit Franklin into the side of his ribs, unseating him enough to gain some traction and flip over. Bringing both feet up and bending her knees as much as she could she aimed for his head and with as much power as she could muster kicked him square on with both feet. Her blows were powerful enough to launch Franklin back by at least a metre. Shaken and now gushing blood, Franklin was disorientated.

'It doesn't have to be this way Hugh, surely we can work this out?' she cried as she ran towards the fireplace. She turned to face him: this would be his last chance. She didn't want violence but if there was no other way then so be it.

The look on his face told her everything she needed to know. There was no way back. She pulled the sword off the display. It was heavier than she had expected. Making some quick adjustments to her stance, she stood side on facing Franklin. Holding the sword's hilt with both hands at shoulder height, she pointed the blade downwards.

'It really doesn't need to be this way', she whispered.

'Ah but that's where you are wrong Midori, that's where your mother was wrong too. We are but pawns in a game of chess, things will never change, people will always die and today it will be either you or I'.

Getting to his feet, his eyes shot to the left. Hers followed in quick succession. Laying on the steel instrument table was the Glock 9mm. Now everything depended on focus and speed. *Remember Midori nothing is impossible, get beyond your thoughts rise above them, now you shall do what is right,* Sensei's voice encased her. Whether she was successful or not did not matter, doing nothing was not an option. With her sword now raised she knew she would only have a split second to disarm him. Neither of them moved. She had only ever competed with a bamboo sword. This would be her most difficult battle yet, losing would mean the end. The distance between her and Franklin was about ten feet. It was about the same distance from Franklin to the gun. She closed her eyes and in that ever so brief moment everything became clear. Her Kiai emitted power and strength but above all it sounded a cry for hope. Running as fast as she could, she mounted the chair on which she had been tied. Spring-boarding from here she now stood directly between the gun and Franklin. Franklin had not anticipated her guile. He had seen her sprint and assumed she was heading for him. It was a split-second decision that was to cost him dear. He ran with as much force as he could muster towards the gun. It was a moment too late that he realised Midori's end game - by which point he had impaled himself onto her blade. Midori dropped the sword and stepped back. Coolly and calmly, she took charge of the gun. Falling to his knees, Franklin tried in vain to stand. A shrill cry echoed through the room as he removed the blade in one powerful move. He edged towards her, his face an eerie shade of grey. Blood now sang out both front and back, creating a death march of woe. A malevolent smile spread across his face.

'Bravo Midori, bravo', he slurred. Falling to the ground, Franklin breathed his last breath.

She stood for a while, not comprehending. Seeing but not understanding, she felt nothing. No anger, no guilt. She did not trust what her eyes told her. Any minute now Franklin would rise like a phoenix from the ashes and all would be lost. She dared not believe it was over. To get to the door she needed to step over him: she was not ready for that - after all he may just be pretending. No, she would wait a while. She righted the chair and sat, her vision fixed on the corpse laid out in front of her. Her senses still on high alert, all sounds were quickly assessed and categorised. She pulled the surgical table towards her, keeping her eyes firmly on Franklin's still frame. She could see the table in her near vision and still have a clear view of Franklin's bloodied form beyond. The table was a cornucopia of pills and potions. Several straight lines of white powder had been laid out on the stainless steel worktop, and alongside them sat a small drinking straw. Her best guess was cocaine, but what did she know? It would certainly explain Franklin's erratic behaviour. A smaller silver tray the size of a small platter sat to the left of the lines of white powder. It contained three small vials with hypodermic needles attached. She could make out the label on one of the bottles – diamorphine.

She didn't know how much time had passed. Her mind had been blank, only watching for the smallest sign of life. None came. She walked towards Franklin, her legs like wobbling jelly. Keeping the gun by her side she approached his body. His face was now devoid of colour and looked even more punishing. Blank lifeless eyes stared back at her. She gently kicked the back of his leg. It was solid, unyielding. Rigor mortis had begun its cascade. Midori walked towards the door.

What greeted her was a surprise. She was in the hallway of a large sprawling house, not dissimilar to Le Manoir de Couder. She took off the crippling shoes. Running fast had to be an option. The house appeared empty. Dust sheets covered most of the furniture. All of the windows were shuttered; chinks of light had found their way through the cracks casting bright linear beams. Where was the phone, was there a phone? She stopped and listened. Nothing except the sound of her light breathing filled the space. No traffic noise, nothing. She made her way hesitantly towards the windows and peered through a crack in the wooden shutters. Swathes of patchwork fields filled her vision. There was nothing for her to get a handle on. Surely someone was looking for her now? A dull muffled hum caught her attention. It was coming from behind one of the doors in the hallway. Maybe a generator, maybe she could find a phone. She could always go back to Franklin and search him, she knew he had her phone somewhere. Yet the thought of having to go anywhere near him made her shudder. No, she would explore the house, there must be something. Opening another door, her heart sank and fear once again injected itself into her blood stream. In front of her were a series of steps, at the bottom of which sat a coded door – identical to the one in the bibliotheque at Manoir de Courder. She stumbled backwards. She needed to get out of here. She had no choice, she would have to go back to Franklin.

A sense of foreboding hit her senses as she navigated her way back to the lounge. Franklin was gone. The instrument trolley was gone. Everything that had spelled death had gone. Only a small patch of dried blood remained on the mahogany floor. Run Midori, run, don't stop just run. She turned, grabbed her rucksack from the corner and ran.

She felt the cold wet long grass on her legs. She had no idea in which direction she had taken off. The front door had not been locked and she had run. Her heart was pounding and her breath was coming in raw bursts. She had to get as far away as she could. She knew not why but she darted in varying directions. A deer being stalked would probably stand more chance than her. She was sure her feet were cut but she couldn't feel them: they, like the rest of her body, had gone into adrenaline overdrive. She headed towards a clump of trees on her left. She needed cover.

Only when she had reached the trees did she dare to look back. Nothing! No-one following her, nothing out of the ordinary. Was she going mad? No, she had killed Franklin, she had sat there watching him turn to stone! He was dead. So who else was there? She had heard nothing, not even the smallest of sounds until the generator had kicked in. She needed to get her breath back and think. She had no phone: what did she have? She emptied out her rucksack onto the floor. Make-up, hairbrush, hairspray, TV remote. TV remote! That's it. Now what had Harry said? Find the highest point and keep the buttons held down. Which buttons? She had no idea, she would have to try them all. Ahead lay an area of open coppice. She could try from here. She prayed they were looking for her.

Harry paced up and down. She had to be somewhere, she could not disappear. He hoped they would find her in time. How could Professor Franklin have walked into the hospital so freely? Support had arrived from EM3 in the form of his two colleagues from Belgium, Inge Maes and Lucas De Vos.

They set up an incident room within the hospital. The local police had been most accommodating but Harry knew it was a big ask for them to understand the subtleties of a case like this.

They were focusing all of their efforts on locking down the facility. More bodies had been discovered and they had at least four people in custody. Until Harry had the proper clearance he could not interview them. Bloody protocols and paperwork. It was an essential evil of the job but it made everything move so slowly.

'Boss, look'. Inge pointed to the radar screen. A hazy signal was pinging intermittently about fifty miles to the west.

'Can we get a drone over that area?'

'On it'. Lucas had already picked up the phone and was talking rapidly in Flemish.

They had very little to go on: CCTV was sparse and no-one was quite sure how Franklin had left the hospital.

'We may have a lead, the housekeeper has reported her car missing', said Inge, replacing the handset.

'Cross check it through all of the intersections where there are cameras; check all the gas stations too, maybe we'll get lucky. Any news on that drone?'

'On its way'.

Maybe they hadn't seen her. She had stood for two hours she guessed, randomly waving the remote in the air. Holding down different buttons; swirling it up and down, round and round. Nothing, no-one was coming. Her arms ached. She had no idea of the time but at some point it would get dark. A rather dishevelled pack of Skittles found at the bottom of her rucksack had been a welcome sight and she devoured them slowly. She needed a plan. Civilisation could not be far away. A farmhouse, a petrol station, anything. Picking up her belongings she decided to keep walking as far away from the house as possible. No-one had come looking for her, not friend nor foe. A multitude of questions crowded her thoughts. Why had no-one come for her? Someone knew she had killed Franklin. Why did they leave her? Why weren't they after her? Who are they? She stopped and listened. She had never known the sound of a car could make her feel so good. There must be a road nearby. Relief flooded in. A little longer, just a little longer and she would be safe.

As she stood on the side of the road a van appeared on the horizon. Gratitude was swelling inside of her. As it approached she froze. Rick, it was Rick Clunie! In a split-second the van would be alongside her. She had run out of options. She could run back into the woods, but then what? If Rick was here that meant he was a part of it. Franklin had indicated as much.

The screeching of tyres came loud and sharp. Another car appeared. A black Mercedes had approached from behind the van and rear ended it at speed. Gunshots rang in her ears. Everything went black.

15

The 747 rose above the fluffy white clouds as the sun slowly allowed the day to be drawn into focus. A beautiful Autumn morning lit the horizon. Hues of soft pink cut across the now clear azure sky. As the plane turned, Midori felt the solar rays warming her face.

'Sunshine', she said out loud.

The man next to her looked as if she'd just told him she was carrying a bomb. One day she would escape the tedium of cattle class. One day she would be able to say 'sunshine' and there wouldn't be anyone close enough to care.

Her shoulder, though uncomfortable, was healing well. The shot had gone clean through. She had been saved by the TV remote she'd stowed in her breast pocket! Harry told her that one day she would look back on all of this and see the humour in it. She doubted it. Her love for Spaghetti Westerns had waned as a result of being shot by a real life bullet. Harry and his colleagues had found her in the nick of time. They had tracked her via her remote signalling and cross referenced it with CCTV of Madame Roussel's car. Franklin had jumped a light on the D122 which confirmed her location. Le Manoir Coulder had not been the only facility. Midori had been taken to a chateau in St Emilion. It transpired that the chateaux held secrets of its own.

Owned by Rick Clunie, the chateau had been used for clinical purposes two years prior. A team had discovered a series of shallow graves towards the back of the property. Tracing the money trail was ongoing and there was now a dedicated team of six trying to unravel the complex off shore accounts that had so far drawn a blank. Rick Clunie had said very little. KLD had distanced themselves from him. The fact that he was carrying a gun and a variety of controlled drugs would help to secure his conviction. He had pleaded ignorance about the clinical activity at the chateau, claiming it was a holiday let that he sublet to Franklin.

From above the clouds everything looked peaceful. She was detached, aloof. The world was a better place from up here, she concluded. No-one was trying to cause her harm, no one looking out for their own self-interests, causing endless chaos. Just clouds and the gentle hum of the Rolls Royce engines. Finally she was starting to feel a sense of peace. Small as it was it was there, growing between the cracks of the last few tumultuous months. Leaving Nick in hospital had been difficult but she was buoyed by the fact that he would be transferred to the care of Professor Wallace in Seattle as soon as he was fit enough to be airlifted across the Atlantic.

He recognised her now. It was a small step but he was heading in the right direction. He had just been woken from his medically induced coma. The doctors believed he had PTA – post traumatic amnesia. How much he would remember no-one could say. Franklin had given him a cocktail of drugs, some of which they had difficulty identifying. They believed he'd been fed a combination of experimental drugs, the long term effects of which were not clear. The drugs appeared to have reduced the size of his hippocampus. From the papers they'd found they believed Franklin had been trying to induce Alzheimer's in his victims. The notes indicated that Nick's genetic coding was slightly different from that of most people. He had a greater sensitivity to picking up the spectrum of forbidden colours. Franklin had wanted to induce dementia and then use varying doses of Centoria to reverse it. He had been targeting patients with known amnesia and known dementia, although dementia patients were more difficult to access without questions being asked.

Unbeknownst to Nick, he had been the potential key to years of illegal research. Franklin had targeted Nick four years previously when Nick had sat a light test at one of the Professor's seminars. It had flagged his affinity to being receptive to the forbidden colours spectrum. He had hypothesised that if he could find the direct level of light penetration and the right dose titration for Centoria then it could become as simple as wearing coloured glasses and popping a pill. None of what had happened was by chance. Franklin and his cronies had planned this for years. What they had not foreseen, however, was the relationship between Midori and Nick. Thank God they were now safe, that was all that mattered. She could leave the authorities to take it from here on.

She had sat by Nick's hospital bed each day, filled with a new degree of hope. It really was one day at a time. She had been advised that he may never fully recover. No one knew for sure what the prognosis was, they were on uncharted ground. He may have fits of agitation, aggression, paranoia and depression, all of which were to be expected after a brain injury. She had left his bedside knowing that he was safe with people who loved him. His mum and sister had flown over and would be there until he was transferred. Life would never be the same, but that didn't matter. All that mattered was that Nick, her Nick was going to make it. Everything else was a bonus.

It had been hard for his family to accept that Franklin was the man responsible. Nick had admired and looked up to him for so long. Midori herself had struggled. Each time she thought about it a wave of complete inadequacy overwhelmed her. She thrust it to the back of her mind; it was baggage that she couldn't deal with right now. She could try to lose it mid-Atlantic, but she knew pain like that never went away willingly. Thankfully the amazing team of EM3 had been able to answer some of her questions. She still hadn't squared the fact that such a talented medic had been open to murder and bribery. Penny and Harry would not rest until all of the sick piranhas who were involved with Centoria were behind bars. They may have off shore accounts and multiple identities but there really are only so many places to hide. If Penny & Harry's tenacity were anything to go by, the heads of

KLD would be brought to account very soon, especially as they were now the featured faces on Interpol's most wanted list.

'Miss Yates'. The stewardess cut through her thoughts.

'Yes?'

'A gentleman in first class asked me to give you this with his compliments'. She smiled warmly and handed Midori a large manila envelope. She read it slowly. It took her a while to work out what it was.

'Which gentleman? Can you show me please?' Midori followed the immaculately dressed stewardess towards the front of the plane. As she drew closer a smile spread across her face. She'd recognise that salt and pepper hair anywhere. She beamed from ear to ear. It was a feeling she had missed.

'Professor Wallace, I had no idea you were on this flight, and this....' Midori held the envelope high in her right hand.

'I thought you could do with something to keep you busy, once the boy's back on his feet. You guys will need some time together to... you know... to try and get back to normal'. Professor Wallace smiled and touched her hand gently. 'Now before you go getting all humble and righteous on me hear me out..' He stood and beckoned for Midori to sit in the enormous first class seat next to him. She glanced over to the stewardess who nodded in agreement.

'It's no less than you both deserve. Anyway, it's your money really. I've sold my story to those well-known red tops both at home and in Europe, made a pretty packet I don't mind telling you. I know you said you didn't want to sell your story but I've sold mine. For me it was the right thing to do. The world needed to get the real story, well as much of it as I could tell them anyway'.

Seated now in first class splendour she studied the document again.

'But this.... this is... well this is too much, its... it's a coffee plantation in the Dominican Republic for goodness sake, it's... it's too much...'

Wallace chuckled.

'Nonsense, Midori, it is only a small one, 40 acres of organically grown coffee', he said proudly. 'It comes with a house and a pool which I thought would be good for Nick's rehab. There's a farmer who lives in the lodge with his family, he'll tend the plantation year round so you two will be free to come and go as you please'.

'I can't possibly...' He gently placed his hand over hers and shook his head slowly.

'I'm not taking no for an answer. It's yours, I bought it for the both of you...' He held her gaze. His smile was slightly off centre, giving his ripened face a cheeky boyish expression. He had been a good mentor and friend to Nick. It was not so much what he said, more his presence. It said, trust me, I'm a good person coming from a good place. Richard Wallace was a genuinely kind brilliant man. Tears fell gently from her flushed face.

'You're too generous Richard Wallace, this really is... well it's... I don't know what to say except thank you from the bottom of my heart'.

She was overwhelmed. It really had been a hell of a journey. The best neuroscientists in the world (including Professor Wallace) were working to come up with a long term plan to deal with the deficits Nick was starting to display. He was not likely to be the only one. Patients who had been forced to stop taking Centoria were all being monitored closely, including of course her brother. Midori had only glimpsed some of the torture Nick had been exposed to. It had been enough to give her nightmares. Sleep now was a luxury she indulged in very little. She could not shake images of the blank, vacant expression of the man she had witnessed murdered. Of the men killed by Franklin and his cronies. The eyes, dead, and the buried soul would stay with her forever. She knew she had to brace herself, there was worse to come. They had found bodies buried in Monflanquin which had been undisturbed for approximately five years.

She sat staring out at the horizon, the powder blue hue of 35,000 feet instilling a peaceful calm over her humanity. She had struggled to square the two Franklins she knew. She was not sure she would ever know the full truth. The death of Franklin's wife had most certainly been the catalyst but was he really that delusional to think he could experiment on people? Checks made into his personal life revealed a trail of bank accounts and off shore wheelings and dealings that would make the most crooked city bankers proud. Large quantities of cocaine had been found stashed in a variety of his homes and also his hospital offices back in the UK. But was that enough to explain such a cataclysmic character shift? A high functioning addict is what they were calling him. High disturbed addict more like!

Meeting her brother in New York would buoy her spirits. Her mum and dad were already there. Her parents had carried the weight of recent events with their usual calm and dignity. They had sat by her bedside until she had been given the all-clear and had then flown straight to New York. She needed to pick her moment with her mum to talk about what Franklin had said. He seemed to know too much for it all to have been his crazed psychosis. Regular updates from Penny indicated Raiden had made excellent progress. There appeared to be no long term effects from his time on Centoria. That was at least one mercy. Richard Wallace had insisted she stay in first class for the rest of the flight. Knowing he was there she slept soundly and deeply for the first time in months.

16

'Come sit with me'. Katzuko Yates patted the seat beside her. She'd had many weeks to think about the conversation she was about to have. About the right way to say the things she'd carried with her over the years. Was there a right way? Her daughter had been through an awful lot this last year. If she had at any time realised how dangerous... she stopped herself. She knew deep down how dangerous Hugh was. He was the reason she had given up her career, her life in Japan. Her daughter looked tired; the lines on her forehead were new, her eyes, sunken pools of sadness.

'I'm not sure I know where to begin...'

Katzuko's mouth was dry, her voice raspy. She took a sip of the freshly poured tea. Tea never tasted right in the states, never hot enough or strong enough. It was certainly one of the things the Brits got right, she thought. They may be having tea in a nice hotel opposite Central Park but it was not good. Katzuko had chosen the hotel as it was neutral ground. She had considered Raiden's apartment but dismissed it almost immediately. Too risky. No, somewhere reasonably quiet with no association to anyone. Mark had agreed.

'Mum?'

'I had just started my job at Nixian Laboratories, just outside of Tokyo. I was so excited and full of passion. I wanted to change the world and believed I could. My first project was looking at extending the shelf life of vaccines. I loved it'.

Katzuko took another sip of tea. She took hold of Midori's hand.

'Hugh Franklin was my boss...' She squeezed her daughter's hand gently. Franklin had not lied, thought Midori, he did know my mother. She wasn't sure how she felt. She had been so convinced everything he'd said was a lie.

'He was funny and witty and so passionate about the work we were doing. You could easily get swept away with his enthusiasm. Most of us did. We were a team of eight from across the globe. I felt I was right where I was supposed to be. Your father and I talked about him perhaps moving out to Tokyo and trying to get a job out there. Life was good for us'.

'So what changed?'

'Little things. At first I really didn't think anything of it. He always had an explanation, an excuse. He would brush up against me, or follow me in to our small office cupboard. I just thought he was so focused on his work - I suppose I made excuses for him'.

Katzuko fell silent: how could she explain?

'Mum, it's OK, I'm here: nothing you say will make me love you any less...' Midori said gently.

'I had just turned 22 when he first raped me. He had asked me to stay behind with him, to work on an exciting piece of research. That was the start of my work into RBap48...'

Her eyes began to fill. There had been no easy way to deliver the words that had been stored within for so long. Delicate salty tears started to fall. She hurriedly wiped them away. Midori was at a loss. Her mum was always the strong one, the one who never ever fell apart. Yet here she was shattering in front of her. It had taken a lot for her mum to say those words. She needed to be respectful, dignified, behave in a way that her mother would want. She could feel an anger like no other building inside of her. Not only had he defiled her mother, but had she not killed him she had no doubt he would have raped her too. She held her mum tight for what seemed like an eternity. She felt the rise and fall of quiet sobs into her shoulder. She was glad he was dead and she was glad she had been the one to take his life. They had still not found his body, so technically she had killed no one - but he was dead alright.

'I cannot begin to imagine how painful this is for you mum'. Midori's words were soft and tender. Wiping a tear away from her mother's face she continued, 'When you feel able, I want you to tell me everything'. Now she had to be the strong one. Katzuko sighed deeply. It had taken over twenty five years for her to get to this point: she needed to be released, to be free. Hugh's invisible hold over a part of her needed to die.

'Your father only knows in part what happened to me. It would break him to know everything. You must promise me. What I am about to tell you is my story to you. I shall tell both your dad and Raiden when the time is right...' Katzuko eyed her daughter: could she carry such a burden? Midori nodded.

17

'It was Autumn 1991. I had finished my degree in molecular biology and been blessed with the offer of becoming a research assistant for the prestigious Nixian Laboratories back in Japan. I had met and fallen in love with your amazing father during our first year at university. It really was love at first sight and I knew that he was 'the one'. I knew we would be together for all eternity. Luckily for me he felt the same! We decided that my job offer was too good to turn down, and so it was with much excitement and some sadness that I accepted. Mark and I agreed that it would only be for a few years, after which we would decide where we wanted our future to be - England or Japan. Your father was a clever man with so many prospects of his own. We both wanted each other to succeed in our respective fields. At the time it was the right thing for both of us. I remember how happy my family were to have me return to Japan, they were so proud. Their little adventurer had returned!

For the first few months, life was new and exciting. Each day was full of new possibilities and positive challenges. I was like a sponge, absorbing everything. Enjoying everything. Our team consisted of some of the brightest new minds from across the world. I stood in awe of them. Hugh Franklin was our research team's principal, our leader. He was charming and funny. He had a dry sense of humour that was lost on some of the team. Not me - he reminded me of England, of your father, who I missed terribly. I had been there just over three months when your grandfather was taken seriously ill. My mother was beside herself and I was grateful that I was there to help and support them. I had confided in Hugh about how worried I was. He was so supportive and helpful. He even drove me to Shimoda, to the hospital, to visit my father.

It was shortly after that it started. At first I thought I was being too sensitive; an odd comment here, a look there. I began to change my behaviour a little. I wore longer skirts and made sure nothing I said could be misinterpreted. That first night it happened we had been working on isolating a protein that could bind to a specific receptor. We had hypothesised that the protein may have been able to act as a delivery agent for nanoparticles to the hippocampus. We felt we were really close. As we all got ready to leave that night, Hugh asked if I could stay to continue for another hour or so. Of course I said yes, it was an honour to have such an eminent professor asking me to stay to help. We worked well together, made a few jokes. Then things started to turn dark. Before I knew it he had me pinned down...initially I tried to fight him, but he was too strong...'

Katzuko's eyes were downcast. She could not look at her daughter. This was the hardest thing she had ever done but she needed to tell the whole story. She needed Midori to understand what sort of a monster this man was. She felt ashamed. Midori needed to know how sick this man is. That nothing that had happened since was her fault. Katzuko was carrying enough guilt for both of them; her daughter was not going to be one of his victims too. They sat in silence whilst the waitress refreshed their tea. Midori was the first to speak.

'You know it was not your fault mum; you do know that, don't you?'

'I know that now, Midorichan'.

It had been ages since her mum had called her that. It was comforting and reassuring. Katzuko moved closer towards her daughter. Her eyes lifted despite the heavy burden they were carrying. Taking both of Midori's hands, she continued.

'You have to understand, times were different then. I am not making excuses but the world was not mine, it was his. He was the Professor, I was the lowly assistant. At the time I felt I must have done something, behaved in a way that had brought it on. I knew though as soon as I returned to England that was not true...' Katzuko stopped and lifted her cup. OK so it wasn't the best tea but it was hot and much needed.

'My dad was seriously ill, I couldn't tell my parents. I felt such a sense of shame, I didn't know anyone else well enough to trust them. Your father knew something wasn't right, each time he came to visit he knew, but he never pushed me to explain. It is one of the reasons I love him so much.

Hugh became obsessed; I would find him waiting for me outside my apartment, pretending everything was fine. How could it be? I spoke little and ate even less. I became insular, focused only on my work. He would buy me clothes, tell me what to wear. He insisted he drive me to the hospital to visit my father. In fact he insisted on driving me everywhere. I was never far from his sight, except when your father visited. Those were my brightest days. I could pretend I lived a normal existence. I was Hugh Franklin's prisoner, I felt wretched and helpless...

Please Midori, do not judge me. I know what you're thinking. I'm an intelligent woman: how could this happen, why didn't I say anything? For twenty five years I have wondered that...

It was your father who saved me. One day he just turned up in Tokyo. He told me to pack my things and we left on the next plane to Thailand. I was scared but I knew it was my only chance. I found out later your father had been to see Hugh that morning. He told him that if he ever came near me again he would kill him. He knew, without me saying anything, he knew...'

Katsuko smiled. She knew her husband had saved her life that day. What he didn't know was that evening she had planned to take her own.

'We spent a wonderful two months in Thailand before returning to the UK. I had got my life back. I wanted to forget everything that had happened to me. Being locked in an apartment, not allowed out of his sight too often. Your father only found out about the rape after we'd left Japan. What he still doesn't know to this day is that the abuse went on over months. It is something I wanted to forget, to put behind us. I realise this was a mistake; I should have told him everything. It was whilst we were in Thailand that I discovered I was pregnant with your brother. Hugh is Raiden's father'.

The words hung in the air. There had been no easy way of saying it. If they'd been any closer to the edge of the cliff they would have gone crashing into the sea. She searched Midori's eyes for a sign, any indication of how she was feeling. Midori stood up quickly, then sat back down again. She needed to be busy. She stood up again, moving towards the window. The rain on the Manhattan street below had changed the landscape. An abundance of brightly coloured umbrellas moved up and down the sidewalk. Each one held a story, a life, good and bad. All she wanted to do right now was to be amongst them, to weave her way through the crowds and feel the rain on her face. She wanted to be anonymous.

'Does he know?'

'No, only you and your father know. Please Midori, come and sit...I never wanted Hugh to know...I wanted that man to have no part in our lives. He had stolen enough from us. Your father has always been Raiden's father'.

Midori sat opposite her mother and fiddled with the sugar cubes. She had killed Raiden's father - oh my God. The man who had almost raped her, who had... who had... she felt sick.

'I need the loo'.

Her legs would not move fast enough. The bathroom was empty, the sound of soft-piped Kenny G was coming from somewhere but it was doing very little to calm her nerves. Entering the stall she gagged then vomited. The cold water had made an impact. Pulling at the paper towels she carefully dabbed her face. The nausea had subsided, for now anyway. Kenny G had been replaced by Michael Bublé. She stared at herself in the bathroom mirror. How odd her complexion was - sallow, yet her cheeks were pillar-box red. Fire and ice, yep, that summed her up. Her life lay shattered around her feet. She should have thrown it all down the toilet with the rest of the detritus. Before returning to her mum she needed to think. No-one knew about Franklin's death, not yet anyway. She had been economical with the truth, to say the least. She had told the authorities she had stabbed him in self-defence, she had been honest and said his body had disappeared: that bit was true. She had not told them how she sat and watched rigor mortis set in or how she felt nothing seeing the blood drain from his body. She had felt nothing since. No guilt, no emotion, nothing. It was as if it had not happened, as if she had been looking in from the outside at someone else. She was conscious she had done it, she had pushed that blade into him with as much venom and anger as it was possible to feel, but now, oddly, she felt numb, and had done ever since. By whatever power rules the universe it had been the right thing. The anger she had carried around all of her life had some-how been passed down to her genetically from her mother. She had been an angry child and an angry teenager: now she knew why. She had avenged her mother. Was that good or bad? Had the debt been paid?

Whoever removed Franklin's body was not go-ing to come forward and accuse her - she could do that herself! But Franklin was Raiden's father, his blood father. Could she live with that? Get a grip Midori - he was not Raiden's father, he was the man who raped your mother, who would have raped you. Her subconscious was very much alive and kicking. Why had her mother never thought to mention that Nick's boss was a rapist though? And what about all that stuff

Franklin had said, about being 'friends' with her parents? It was messed up, that's what it was.

'Are you OK?' Katzuko looked worried. She had poured more tea.

'Yeah mum, I'm OK, just not what I expected to hear...but I am grateful to you for telling me'.

'I had to, Midori, after everything this family has been through because of that man. I do not want to hold onto it any longer. When I think Rai is strong enough, I will tell him - until then promise me not to say anything?'

Midori nodded.

'What does dad think?'

'We talked it through and we believe this is the best way. He just wishes he had killed him back in Tokyo when he had the chance. He didn't know how trapped I was, how Hugh kept me like a prisoner. He knew I was scared of him. I will talk to him about it soon I promise'.

Midori stared down at her shoes. Her mum had no idea her daughter was a murderer and that was the way it was going to stay.

'Have they found him yet?'

'No'.

'Well wherever he is, I hope he's in pain'. He's in hell, that's where he is, she thought.

'Mum, that's so unlike you...'

'I know, but it's what I'm thinking, it's what I've thought for twenty five years'.

'He told me he was your friend... yours and dad's, I mean. He said you had been to his wife's funeral?'

'I knew his wife. She was also a research assistant. He had moved onto her once I had gone. I felt sorry for her. I only saw her once when we were back in London. She was so unhappy. Yes we did go to her funeral, your father and I. It was out of respect for her. We did not stay, just stood at the back of the church...we did not even speak to him. It made me sad. It could so easily have been me if your father.... Ah, talking of which...'

Katzuko waved over Midori's shoulder. Mark Yates was heading towards them.

'I just left Rai at work. He said he'd join us in a bit, everything alright?'

'I've told her Mark: I've told her everything'.

'Ahh...' Mark sat down next to his daughter. 'We were only trying to protect you and Rai, you do know that, don't you?' Her father looked old. It was the first time she had ever really noticed. Dark semi-circles hung beneath his eyes, his cheeks drawn, almost gaunt – had he lost weight?

'Franklin told her a pack of lies, Mark. He told her we were his friends'.

'Well that's no surprise, the man is a psychopath', he said sharply.

'Why didn't you say something, you know, when you knew I was working for KLD?' asked Midori.

'Last we'd heard he'd gone back to Japan, just after his wife died - good riddance. It was only when Nick mentioned Prof. Franklin did we realise he must be back. No way did we want to mention it, the past was the past, Midori. We didn't want him anywhere near our lives, or Rai's. Last we knew KLD had nothing to do with him'.

Her father's voice was firm and he had directed it towards her.

'OK I get that, I really do but... but how did he know so much about me, about us as a family? How did he know I was your daughter? Or where I went to uni...he got me the job at KLD for goodness sake?'

Mark and Katzuko shot each other a look that said: it's time. It was her parents' turn to comfort her. She was losing it. She could feel the weight of questions crowding into her mind, threatening to consume her. How did he know, why did he know? What was it they weren't telling her?

'While you were recovering in hospital the po-lice asked us to come in and give a statement about what we knew. It turned out we didn't know the half of it. In one of the rooms at his house in Somerset they found....'

Mark Yates found his words catching in his throat. For over twenty five years he had tried to remove Franklin's evil spikes out of his family. That bloody man had been the thorn in his side since Tokyo. He was lucky his family were safe, thankfully. The recent events with Midori and Nick would hopefully be the end of it.

'They found images dating back years', re-vealed Katzuko. 'Of me and your father, of you and Rai. Of visits we all took to Shimoda. He'd been watching us for years. There were files and files.....' Her voice trailed off.

'But why, for what purpose?'

'He was an ill man, Midori, disturbed'.

'And he never knew about Rai?'

'No, your father's name is on the birth certifi-cate. There would be no way he could have known. Only your father and I knew... until now'.

'Are you sure... about.... about Rai being his?'

'He never knew of that I am certain. We got ourselves tested under false names just after Rai was born. Rai is his son. I had Rai in France, just your father and I were present. Rai was thankfully small for his age. That's when we decided to.... I am ashamed to say, lie about his birth date. We registered him two months late, just in case. We wanted no possibility that Hugh would ever find out. It seemed like the best solution'.

Midori sat in stunned silence. For all that had been said they must have truly feared this man. Still the questions came. She felt exhausted but could not rest until she knew everything, until she had pieced together as best she could the fractured pieces of the unknown side of her life.

'Why did he say he had you to thank for Centoria - why would he say that?'

Katzuko let out a large sigh.

'It was my research, my research uncovered RBap48's effect on forbidden colours. It was what I had been working on, what I left behind the day I left...'

'But that was over 25 years ago, mum?'

'Sometimes that's how long it takes. I wish to God I hadn't stumbled across it, I really do. Then none of this – Nick, Raiden, you.... you would all be living your lives in peace'.

Mark Yates held his wife close. Her quiet sobs muffled against his chest.

'It's not your fault love, it's not your fault...'

Midori sat quietly. At that moment she made a decision. What had happened so far would not define her. It had affected her deeply but it would not define her. She would now take up the mantle. She would support her brother as best she could when the time came. She would now be the strong one, the voice of the family.

18

Midori watched as the rain clouds rolled in across the vista. A path of sweat cascaded its way down her back. The rain would provide temporary respite from the humidity. Good for the crops at any rate, she thought. From the porch she could see Nick and Raiden lying by the pool. She watched as they ran for cover under the parasols, and smiled. Finally life seemed to be coming back into balance. It had been a harsh, sharp road this last eight months but now she felt as if things were getting back on track.

Nick had been transferred to Seattle under the watchful eye of Professor Wallace. Months of treatment had seen him improve no end. He had needed to re-learn how to be him again. Gone were the vacant stares and pauses that lasted forever. His memories were coming back slowly, but at least they were coming back. It had taken two months until he had recognised her unprompted. He was becoming more like the man she had fallen in love with two years before. The absences were less and less with each passing day.

Raiden had suffered no ill effects of Centoria. He was one of the success stories. His brush with death had given him a much-needed moment of clarity. He had managed to complete his project with Transcorp in record time. They were now into the prototype phase, which had afforded him a six month sabbatical. He knew nothing about coffee but had agreed to spend his time helping out the plantation. As with everything he had thrown himself in feet first; making local connections, securing funding to buy a much needed roasting facility. His tenacity had paid off and they already had buyers lined up for their first harvest.

Mark and Katzuko Yates had yet to reveal his parentage. They were due to arrive in the Dominican Republic in a few months. He would be devastated, but she would be there to listen to him: it was her turn to be strong. It would change nothing; he was still her brother and she loved him. He would just need to believe it.

Midori rarely thought of those days back in England. She missed her beloved Somerset, but for now here was where they needed to be, here was good. She would occasionally hear from

Harry and Penny. Penny was making another go at things with Professor Wallace; they were due to visit next Spring and had recently become engaged. Midori smiled. Richard's dress sense was akin to Penny's. She hoped Seattle was ready for the two of them.

Harry was still on the investigating team but had very little new information to offer. The investigation was still on going. He had stayed in touch with Laura, who had thankfully made a full recovery. There was little hope of ever knowing the full details. Whatever organisation was behind Centoria had been hidden in the shadows for years. They were well-connected and their influence appeared to be far-reaching. As each layer was slowly unwrapped and dissected, another appeared. Without giving too much away, Harry had intimated more than once that pressure was being brought to bear on closing the investigation. Apparently it didn't 'look good' for any nation to admit that an illegal trial had been conducted under their noses. It would be a long road to justice. Rick Clunie had said nothing. He had faced prosecution but had not uttered a word, his fear greater than any jail sentence. The heads of KLD were still at large. Chances of finding them had dampened, but with Harry and

Penny still on the case all was not yet lost. Franklin's body had not been found.

Nick looked up from underneath the parasol, smiled and blew a kiss towards Midori.

Smiling back, she caught sight of herself in the mirrored wind chime that hung on the veranda.

Her eyes had started to shine once again, maybe things really weren't that bad after all.

Connect with Nicole Fitton

I really appreciate you reading my book! Thank you. If you did enjoy it I would be very grateful if you could write and post a review. It doesn't need to be long and complicated! Just a few words really make a difference and can help new readers discover my book.

What did you think of Forbidden Colours? What are your thoughts on the development of new drugs? I'd love to hear your thoughts. I'm busy working on a collection of short stories, which will be followed by my third novel in 2017. I would love to connect with you on social media:

Facebook:
https://www.facebook.com/nicolefittonauthor/

Twitter: @MisoMiss

My website: www.nicolefittonauthor.com

About The Author

Nicole Fitton is an author and freelance writer who has lived in such glamorous places as London, New York and Croydon. She currently resides in Devon with her family and a very sprightly springer spaniel. Forbidden Colours is her second novel. Her debut 'All Tomorrow's Parties' was released to wide acclaim in 2015. She enjoys writing short stories, some of which feature in a variety of anthologies and have been shortlisted in short story competitions. 2017 will see the release of her own collection of short stories followed by another full length novel.

Printed in Great Britain
by Amazon

16119892R00212